REASONS TO STAY

REASONS PART TWO

LISA J HOBMAN

Lisa J. Hobman
Copyright Lisa J. Hobman 2015

First Published by 5 Prince Publishing 2015
Second Edition Published by Lisa J. Hobman

Front Cover The Graphics Shed

First Edition/First Printing June 2015 Printed U.S.A.
Second Edition/Second Printing February 2018 Lisa J. Hobman, UK

ISBN: 978-0-9956658-5-9

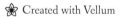 Created with Vellum

For Rich and Gee with all my love

PROLOGUE

Stevie observed Jason as he read, his face a confused mask. The line between his brows deepened. What the hell was in that letter? He peered down at the envelope, pulled out a photo, and stared at it for a long while. From where Stevie was sitting, she leaned forward and could see that it was a photo of Jason with another girl. Judging by his fresh-faced appearance in the picture, it must have been taken just before he disappeared. Handsome eighteen-year-old Jason. The man she had loved so deeply.

She touched his leg. 'Jason? Are you okay?' No reply. 'Jason? Who's that girl in the photo with you?' Still nothing. Panic rose within her and she nudged him. 'Jason!' She raised her voice this time causing him to look up.

'What?' he snapped. His face had paled. Drained of all colour. But in his narrowed eyes she saw anger. And maybe a little fear.

'What's in the letter?'

'Sorry? Oh...it's...' He shook his head and looked back at the letter and the photograph again. His eyes widened. He was clearly horrified at the contents. He opened and closed his mouth as if searching for the right words. Disbelief washed over his features. He stood slowly as if in a trance like state. 'I've...I need...I need some air.' He almost staggered towards the door, clutching the papers and photograph in his grip.

Stevie stood too and followed. Something was very wrong. 'Are you all right? You're worrying me.' She followed him down the stairs and watched as he pulled on his leather jacket, shoved the scrunched up letter and photograph into the inside pocket, and walked out of the front door. 'Jason, for goodness sake, will you *please* tell me what was in the letter? And who was that girl in the photo with you? Please!'

He stopped and turned to face her. 'I...I can't do this now. I need to go. I need some time to think... I can't talk...not now. I need to go... Please let me go.'

'What do you mean you need to go? Go where? What the hell's going on, Jason? Talk to me!' Her chest heaved, and she felt tears needle the back of her eyes.

Whatever was in that letter had changed him. It was like someone had flicked a switch. Loving, sweet, playful Jason had gone. The menacing mask descended once again. Jason from the first days in Scotland was back. He stalked towards her with an angry determination and leaned in until his face was only inches from hers.

His jaw was clenched. 'I. Need. To. Go.' Each word was uttered in a staccato rhythm.

She automatically stepped back. 'B-but you'll be back? I mean...when you say you need to go, you mean for a drive...or for...for some air...don't you? And there's your dad's funeral... and Dillon.'

His nostrils flared, and he stared blankly at her. 'I already said I can't fucking talk about this now. Just leave it, for fuck's sake. Why do you always have to push things?'

Tears welled in her eyes, and she bit back a sob. 'I'm not

pushing things. You're scaring me. Just tell me the truth... Are you running again? After you said you wouldn't to Dillon... and to me for that matter. Is that what's happening here? I know we agreed that you and I were temporary, but I don't want you to leave without explanation. Not again. I don't think that would be very fair of you.'

He snorted. 'Think whatever you like. At this moment in time, I don't really care. The world doesn't fucking revolve around you. All right? It's. Not. All. About. You!' he shouted, pointing at her.

Her eyes overflowed with angry and confused tears, and she watched helplessly as he pulled his helmet on, swung his leg over the bike, started the engine, and sped off up the street and out of sight without looking back once.

'Jason!'

She ran back into the house. A feeling of dread washed over her as she pulled out her phone and dialled Dillon's number with shaking fingers and a racing heart.

'Dillon Reynolds.'

'Dillon, it's Stevie. I need to speak to you urgently. Can you get out of work for ten minutes?'

'I...erm...yeah, okay. What's wrong? Has something happened?' His voice was filled with concern.

'Yes...I mean no...I mean... I can't explain over the phone.' She was aware that her words were a jumbled rush.

'Okay...Okay, calm down. Where shall I meet you?'

'Come to my house. I'll be there in ten.' She hung up, locked the door, and ran to her car. Once inside, she fumbled with the keys in the ignition. 'Come on, Stevie, calm the hell down!'

Exceeding the speed limit wasn't something she usually did, but it felt warranted right then. She pulled up to her house and climbed out of her car. Her legs felt like jelly, and her heart was doing its best to escape its casing as it pounded in her chest. She could hear the blood whooshing in her ears and felt a little nauseated. After several attempts of trying to get the key in the front door, she finally succeeded.

Once inside, she paced the lounge and chewed at her nails, periodically peering out the window until Dillon pulled up in his flashy executive's company car. She watched as he jogged up and was about to knock.

Pulling the door open, she blurted, 'Something's happened. He's gone. I don't know what it said... He looked like he'd seen a ghost and there was the photo—'

Dillon held up his hands. 'Whoa, whoa, Stevie. Calm down.' He gripped her upper arms firmly in his hands and bent to look into her eyes. 'Slow down, okay? Tell me what happened.'

She led him into the lounge and slumped onto the sofa. 'We were clearing out his room and listening to some music. I was...we'd...I was...tidying his bed up.' Dillon raised his eyebrows knowingly, but she ignored him and continued. 'Anyway, I was straightening his pillow and underneath it there was an envelope addressed to him. In it there was a long letter which he said was from your mum.'

Dillon rubbed his hands over his face. 'Shit...*really*?'

'Yes...anyway, he read it and sat there staring. He went pale and shaky. There was a photo of him from before he left, but he was with a girl. She was pretty... I didn't recognise her... Oh, my God.' Shivers travelled down her spine. 'I...I think I've figured it out.' She widened her eyes and covered her mouth with her shaking hands.

'Figured what out? Can you tell me what the *hell* is going on, 'cause I'm lost here.' Confusion etched his features as he ran his hands over his head and stared pleadingly at her.

A sob escaped through her fingers. 'The girl in the photo...

He had an affair, Dillon. That must be it. The photo was of him with a woman...well, a girl of about the same age as we were just before he left. She seemed familiar, but I couldn't quite place... Oh God, I bet she got pregnant. That woman had his bloody child, and now he's finding this out after all this time. Your mum must have found out after he'd gone! It's freaked him out that he has a nine or ten-year-old child out there somewhere and your mum was the only one who knew. It makes sense... He looked horrified, Dillon.'

Tears sprang from her eyes, and she let them fall as she began to gulp for air. Her heart was thumping so hard it was almost painful, and she began to see stars. She leaned over as panic took hold of her. Clenching her hands into fists, she fought for air as her lungs began to sting.

Dillon crouched before her and grasped her by the arms again. 'Hey, hey stop this. We don't know... You can't presume all that, Stevie. You need to calm the fuck down, right now!' He raised his voice and shook her lightly. 'Just stop or I'm ringing for an ambulance, okay? Please...breathe.'

His distress snapped her out of her panic, and she began to take deep breaths, ringing her hands in her lap. 'Sorry... sorry...I'm so sorry.' She sobbed.

Leaning forward and placing his knees on the floor, he pulled her into his arms. 'Come on, it's fine...just breathe... breathe.' He stroked her hair until her heart rate slowed, and she was breathing normally again.

He tilted her face up so that she looked at him. His words were softly spoken. 'I don't mean to be harsh, Stevie, but you don't actually seem to know *what* was in the letter and so jumping to your own conclusions is probably not a good idea, is it?' She shook her head; he had a point. 'Now where did he say he was going?'

Fresh tears escaped. 'That's just it...he *didn't*. He said he had to go and that I could think what I liked. He seemed angry with me. It was as if *I'd* hurt him. I don't get it. But he promised both you and me that he wouldn't run without explanation again. What if he doesn't come back?'

Dillon seemed to calculate his next words carefully. 'I think...if he doesn't come back, you're going to have to move on and get over him. He's pretty messed up about things as it is, and there's no wonder. But I think you maybe need to let him deal with whatever the hell this is in his own way. He was never going to move back here, realistically, and you can't say you really thought he would. Can you?'

She dropped her eyes to the floor. 'I love him, Dillon. I've always loved him. No one else has ever come close to him in my heart. I hoped that would be enough...enough to make him see that he could make a life with me here. I showed him all the places I love and tried to make him see—'

Dillon took her face in his palms. 'Stevie, please. *Think* about it logically. He ran away for a *very* good reason the first time. Being here again was hard for him. If I were Jason, there would be *no way* I'd live here again. And if you're honest with yourself, I think you know...and please don't take this the wrong way as I know how much you think of him, but expecting him to move back here would be...would be selfish.'

His words hit her like a brick wall, knocking the air from her lungs. She pushed him away and leaned forward again, resting her elbows on her knees, her head in her hands. 'You're right.' She rubbed her face. 'I was stupid and selfish. I didn't want to lose him all over again. I *keep* losing him. And now he may have gone again and I have no idea why. I have no clue what was in that letter that would have affected him so badly. Should I chase him? Should I go up to Scotland and see him? What should I do, Dillon?'

He took a deep breath and pulled her to face him once again. 'Stevie...please...for your own sake...just let him go.'

Later, Stevie sat home alone, clutching a photograph of Jason and her when they were aged around seventeen. She had swiped it from his noticeboard before she piled the boxes and bags of his things into her car. She had no clue if this was what he wanted her to do since he had simply gone without explanation, but she figured at least this way he had something of his past if he chose to return.

She stared at the image. Jason's face smiled back at her. Just thinking about what he had been through that made him leave the first time caused her heart to ache, but something equally as painful or hard to bear must have been in that letter, making him bolt again. The pain and anger in his eyes as he had glared at her had both terrified her and made her want to grab him, hug him, and tell him that everything would be okay. But she really didn't know if it would. He had been through enough, *surely*. Whatever it was, she hoped someday he would return and explain, but there was a pretty good chance she would have to get used to life without Jason once again.

CHAPTER ONE

*J*ason sat in the airport awaiting his flight to Maine. His knee bounced up and down, and he chewed his nails, a bad habit from childhood that had resurfaced over the past couple of weeks. But there was no wonder. *What the fuck am I doing? I should turn around and go home. This is just fucking crazy.* He pulled out the letter once again. When they were clearing out his old bedroom after his abusive father's death, Stevie had found the letter from his deceased mother under his pillow. He had read the note over and over trying to force the words to sink in. *Why* wouldn't they sink in?

He glanced up at the illuminated flight schedule on the screen above him. His flight was on time, but he had almost an hour before he was due to board. Focusing his attention on the letter once more, he began to re-read the words that had changed his life, past, present, *and* possibly his future too, beyond all recognition.

Dear Jason,
My darling boy. This isn't the first letter I've written to you

since you left, but I have a feeling it may be the last. I've never had an address to post them to, and so I keep them in a box in my wardrobe. The most recent one I always place under your pillow just in case you ever come home. But of course you never do.

The thing is, now I'm sick, and I'm not getting any better. I'm not sure how many more I can write. It's my heart. I've had lots of treatment and tests, but there isn't much to live for and so I'm giving up. I know that sounds so negative, and I don't want you to be angry with me. I deserve this you see. I'm getting what I should. My just desserts. The things I left unsaid and undone have eaten away at me for all these years, Jason, and now at least it won't be long until I can stop feeling like this.

I sit alone in your untouched room often. I wash and change your bedding in case you return. It's all I have ever wanted, your safe return. To see your beautiful face again.

As I think this may be the last letter I write, there are some things I need to tell you, and they will be painful to hear. But I want you to know that nothing you can think of me will be any worse than what I have thought of myself for the last twenty-six years. I have tortured myself enough for both of us.

I will start at the very beginning. Many years ago before you were born, I met a boy. I fell head over heels in love. He was my everything. We talked of getting married, and we were both so very excited. We talked of nothing else even though we were very young. Anyway, we planned the wedding and had the blessing of both families, which considering our young age was nigh on a miracle. All they asked was that we remain chaste until after the wedding.

The big day arrived, and I dressed in my ivory satin gown and veil, feeling so very excited about seeing my future husband at the altar. It was the most amazing feeling, to know that I would *spend the rest of my life with him. I arrived at the church only to be told that he hadn't arrived. So I waited...and waited. Finally, two hours after the wedding was due to take place, I gave up hope of him turning up and had to admit to myself that I had been jilted. He wasn't coming. My heart shattered.*

A couple of months after the date of the planned wedding, I discovered that I was pregnant. You see, we didn't quite manage to uphold the part of the agreement about remaining chaste. We adored each other, and it felt right to be with him that way. After all, we were to be married, and no one would have been any the wiser. Sadly, this backfired on me when I was left behind. On discovering my situation, my parents sent me away to stay with my aunt where I was to make a decision about the future of the child I carried.

It was whilst I was away that I met someone else. He was a kind-hearted man, a little older than me. But he was a man who would never replace the one I lost. I was honest with him from the start about the child I carried, but he fell for me quickly, and despite my being four months pregnant, he asked me to marry him. He insisted that he would take on my child as his own, and feeling lost and desperate to keep the child I already loved dearly, I accepted. When he proposed, I didn't feel the butterflies or the excitement, but I felt secure and comfortable, which was something I needed desperately at that time. In his own way, he made me feel special and loved.

We were happy and married quickly before the bump became overly obvious. He was desperate to have a family of his own after living in care homes most of his life, and I wanted to give him that. I owed him that much. Sadly, there were many complications at the birth, and I was gravely ill. I almost died. You were that child, my darling Jason. But the saddest part was that we were informed I would be unable to have further children. Michael was devastated. Heartbroken. Children of his own were all he had ever really wanted, and he had always told me that to have them with me was what would make it so special since he adored me so much. I felt so very guilty and told him I would divorce him so that he could go on to have children of his own. He refused. I tried to push him into having an affair to try and make this happen, but whilst it almost tore us apart, we stayed together. He loved me that much. He tried to bond with you, but I feel sure that deep down he blamed you for my infertility and the fact I nearly lost my life.

After a couple of years, we decided to look into adoption. He felt that he could cope with this, seeing as the child would physically be no part of either of us and we would be equally a part of his life. So when you were almost three, baby Dillon came along, and Michael was a changed man. So very proud. It was as if the affinity of being abandoned by their mothers made the bond so much stronger. He was a real dad to what he considered to be his own *baby boy. But at that point, he gave up trying with you. I know he did. He would tell you he loved you whilst I was in the room, but I know he was cruel to you behind my back. He held it over you and blamed you for something you had no part in causing. I was so angry with him for that. Even though we kept up appearances, any amount of love I had felt for him had dissolved.*

I could have left I suppose and taken you away, but I had Dillon to consider, and I loved him so very much too. And I think I resigned myself to never truly having what I wanted. And what I wanted was your real father, Jason. He was a scared teenager when we were first meant to marry, and he had no clue about you, and to this day he knows nothing.

It breaks my heart to know that you felt you had to leave. I wish I knew the real reasons behind it. I know Michael had something to do with pushing you away, but he was good at keeping things from me. I don't know what he said to make you leave.

Maybe he told you about the fact that he wasn't your dad and that he thought you were to blame for him never fathering a child of his own with me, and you couldn't bear to be near me anymore. I wouldn't blame you.

What I find the most difficult to bear is that you were my only connection to someone I loved with all my heart. Seeing you reminded me that I once loved someone so completely that I didn't know where he started and where I ended. But maybe that was also the reason that Mick couldn't love you.

You have your father's eyes. And his looks too. And you certainly have your father's intelligence. He had hopes of being a doctor when we were together. I believe he left the country before I found that I was pregnant with you, and so I was never able to tell him. His family was never informed either. There was no point, seeing as Mick agreed to take you on. All I know is that Oliver went to live in America. That was his name, Oliver Halford. His parents lived in Highfield Lane, Kensington, at one time. They were called Delia and Ronald. As they are your true grandparents, I thought perhaps you might want to know. I can't promise that they still live there, nor can I promise that they are still alive, but if they are I'm sure they would love to meet you.

In the envelope with this letter, I'm putting a photo. It's of your father and me at the Kensington Summer Fair when we were both eighteen. The resemblance between you and your father is uncanny. In the photo, he looks just how you did when you left home. I hope you will treasure it like I did.

To know that I will never hold you in my arms, comfort you when you cry, or meet my daughter-in-law or grandchildren makes my ailing, broken heart ache, son. You were the most precious thing in my life, and any extension of you would have meant the world to me. And no matter what I did, please know that I loved you with all of my heart. I was so very proud of you, and I want you to know that that would never change. A mother's love lives on forever, Jason. And I will take every memory of you with me.

I hope that wherever you went after you left home you were safe and happy. I hope that you found love. Love like you had with Stevie. If you are reading this, you may not know that she got married. But you need to know that she never stopped loving you. And I'm sure you never stopped loving her. You and she were a little like Oliver and me. Two connected souls that just couldn't be together at the time you tried to be. She was heartbroken when you left, and I can sympathise with her deeply. I know what it is to be loved and left. But having said that, I know the situation was completely different, and therefore I'm sure she could forgive you. Perhaps you should pay her a visit?

You should also know that Dillon is unaware of his adoption. Mick would never allow the discussion to take place, even though I desperately wanted him to know the truth. He always insisted that it wasn't necessary for anyone else to be involved in his life. But knowing how much I loved both of you, I'm sure that the woman who gave birth to him will have so many regrets. I think that if you are reading this perhaps it's time for him to know. I have no information about his real parents, but I do know that records are available after eighteen years, and so he will be able to find out what he needs to know. There is another letter especially for him. It's with the solicitor and will only be released when you request it.

Whatever happens in your future, Jason, know that I always did what I thought was best for you and your brother. I never meant to hurt either of you, my darling, precious sons.

Be happy and live your lives to the fullest, and most importantly without regrets.

With much love,

Mum

Reading the letter again brought little comfort. He rubbed his hands over his weary, stinging eyes and drank the remainder of his now cold coffee. As he stared into space for what felt like an age, he realised that what happened from now would change everything. He could be embarking upon the start of a whole new chapter, or simply the closure of a very painful one. Either way, this journey was going to affect him in ways he could simply not predict.

He was flying into the unknown.

A voice came over the sound system announcing that Flight AL542 to Bangor International Airport, Maine, was ready to board. He grabbed his one piece of hand luggage and made his way to the check-in gate.

CHAPTER TWO

*S*itting in the confines of his seat on the plane, beside the window, the scene of the land thousands of feet below held no interest for Jason. He pulled the photograph from the envelope and stared into the eyes of his real father once again. It was like looking in a mirror.

Stevie's words echoed in his mind. '*Who is that with you in the photo, Jason?*'

He hadn't corrected her. He hadn't told her the truth, that it wasn't actually *him*, but the man who was responsible for his very existence. The shock of this discovery had rendered him angry and speechless at the time. But she couldn't be blamed for thinking it was a photo of him.

The man in the picture was around eighteen-years-old, the age Jason had been at the time he had abandoned Stevie a decade ago, when he had taken the drastic step to leave his former life behind and to disappear without a trace, all to escape the man he had once known as his dad but who had never showed him love.

The woman beside his *real* father in the photo was his mum, also aged around eighteen. She was so very pretty and fresh faced, but she was still clearly recognisable to him. Her happiness was evident in her eyes. And that's because twenty-nine years ago she *was* happy.

So in love.

Jason was running away again, just like he'd done ten years ago to escape the abuse he had experienced throughout his childhood. Finding out in a letter from his deceased mother that the man who he'd called Dad whilst growing up *wasn't* his real father had been devastating in one way, but a relief in another. At least Mick's blood didn't flow in his veins after all. But even so, everything he'd ever known had been called into question. He'd lived a lie for twenty-eight years. There were so many conflicting emotions vying for the surface at once that his jaw ached from constant clenching. He needed answers, but staying in the UK wouldn't give him what he needed. In a way, he felt justified in running. He couldn't tell Stevie or Dillon about any of this until the real truth of his existence was straight in his own mind.

At least that's what he kept telling himself.

In the letter, his real father's parents had been mentioned, and he'd gone to the library to check the electoral role to see if they were registered. After an hour of searching, he had found what he was looking for. So on top of all the shock he'd discovered, he had a living grandparent who knew nothing of his existence.

Meeting his birth grandmother, Delia, the week before making the journey to Maine had thrown him completely. He had toyed with the idea of leaving and going back home to Scotland, but curiosity had eventually got the better of him, and so, armed with the letter and the photograph, he had knocked on the door at the home of the elderly stranger.

In a bid to smarten himself up for the visit, he had scraped his hair back from his face, and trimmed his beard. He had even donned the trousers and shirt he had purchased from one of the shops Stevie had taken him to in London. She had encouraged him to spend time there with her after his dad's... *Mick's* death. After locating the pretty house belonging to his paternal grandparents, he'd knocked at the door in the well-maintained suburban street with sweaty palms and a hammering heart. The white haired old lady had opened the door and gasped when she saw him.

She had invited him in as if he *hadn't* been a complete stranger. It was as if she had already known him, but that was ridiculous considering the fact this was the first time she had seen him. Inside the large detached house, she had made him tea and sat patiently listening as he told her what he had discovered only a few days before. She had cried and clutched his hand.

'When I opened the door, I thought for a split second that you were Oliver. My eyesight is admittedly not what it was, but...you look *just* like him.' She had reached into a tall cupboard and retrieved a pile of photograph albums. She spent time pointing out her son and telling Jason stories about him. It was so true. He *was* the image of his birth father. The man and his family lived in Maine in the United States, where he had gone to study medicine after he left Jason's mother at the altar.

Delia expressed how sorry she was for her son's behaviour. 'The silly thing is we knew how much he adored Shirley. We were so shocked when he left her standing in the church waiting for him with her heart breaking. His father— God rest his soul—and I were so angry with him. To do such a terrible thing to such a lovely young woman... I have to admit that I struggled to forgive him. And then out of the blue, he announced he was going to live in *America*...that he had been applying to college's there. He had planned his future out without telling us the whole story, and for some reason known only to him, he couldn't include Shirley in those plans. It was all such a shock, Jason.

'We tried to convince him to go and see her...to explain his reasons and his fears and to see if they could work something out. He refused, saying that seeing her would break his heart even more. He sobbed and kept apologising when we took him to the airport. He said if your mother was ever to get in touch with us that we were to tell her how very sorry he was for everything. She never made contact. And we felt it would be inappropriate for us to visit her under the circumstances. We were so ashamed, and we knew we would be the last people she would want to see back then.'

Delia sighed and made direct eye contact with him. 'We honestly had *no clue* that he and Shirley had even been sleeping together. Oliver had assured us they were waiting until they were married. And now...here *you* are. You poor boy. And your poor mother. How very sad that she passed away before she could tell you. I can't imagine the anger and hatred you must feel towards Oliver over all of this. And I wouldn't blame you.'

Jason shook his head. 'To be honest, I just want answers. I don't feel *anything* about Oliver. I don't know him...I just know *of* him...but only very little at that, and what I *do* know doesn't exactly build a positive picture. Did he...did he marry eventually?'

She nodded. 'You have two brothers, dear. Joshua and Elliot. Josh is just twenty and Elliot is eighteen. Both are fine, handsome young men. Their mother, Hannah, is a chef, and Oliver is a surgeon.'

Jason pulled his lips in as he absorbed her words. It was ironic to think that his real father was a surgeon when his replacement father had been pushing him towards that very career path.

His family was expanding minute by minute, and the fact both unsettled and excited him. 'I think maybe I'd like to meet him. Do you think he'd be angry if I made contact?'

She smiled kindly. 'I think he would be shocked and angry that he didn't know about you. I'm not sure how he will react to seeing you, but I *do* think you need to meet him. In all honesty, I would advise that you go out there as soon as possible. Do things face to face. Hannah is with the boys at her parents for a while and so Oliver is at home alone. It would be the perfect opportunity if you were able to go right now. Obviously, it will depend on your commitments.'

He chewed on his lip and thought for a few moments. 'I can leave my business in capable hands, so I'm not too worried about that. I'm just not sure about going. It's a scary prospect. What if he refuses to have anything to do with me? It's a hell of a long way to go to be rejected.' He sat silently for a few minutes, his brain whirring. 'I don't know what you'll think about this, but I'd like to go without him knowing. Is that okay? I know it's a strange thing to ask, but I'm worried that he'll disappear or refuse to see me.'

'I don't think he'd do that, but I can understand your trepidation. I won't say anything if he calls. But please try to listen before getting angry at him, okay?'

Jason pulled his brow into a frown and contemplated her words. 'Don't worry. I will. I don't think I'm *angry* as such. Disappointed and sad that I missed out on having a good dad, but I'm not sure how I feel apart from that. I'll take things as they come, I guess. Deal with them that way.'

The very next day, Jason had booked flights and made the necessary arrangements for the camp to be covered whilst he was away. He gave no explanation to Dorcas, but simply told her that he had some business to attend to and it would mean he would be gone for a while. She had sounded very concerned but had asked no questions, much to Jason's relief.

The days that followed Jason's *second* sudden disappearance from her life had been very hard for Stevie. He never made contact after he rode off on his bike and left her standing outside his old family home. She had known something wasn't quite right, but he'd given no explanation. She'd seen the photo of him in his hand as he'd been reading the letter. He was with a girl she didn't recognise but who somehow looked very familiar.

The only logical explanation she could come up with for this whole situation was that he had discovered he had an illegitimate child or something. The way he'd reacted to reading the letter told her that whatever the contents had revealed it had been a *massive* shock to him.

She needed to know.

Had he been unfaithful to her when they were eighteen? Could she forgive him if he had even though it was in the past? The immediate answer that sprang to mind was *no*. Absolutely not. She had pretty much offered herself to him back then only to be turned down. Learning he'd slept with someone else would splinter her already fractured heart. To make matters worse, she was unable to get the answers she so desperately needed, as he had checked out of his hotel and literally disappeared.

Again.

She had called Dorcas at the camp a few days after he rode away to check if he was okay.

'I'm sorry, Stevie. He isn't here. He called to say he would be gone a while. We have no idea where he is. He sounded...I don't know...*different* when I spoke to him. He seemed down. I'm worried, Stevie. I've never known him to be like this. He's an arrogant swine some of the time, but mostly he's such a laugh. He didn't seem *himself*. If you hear from him at all, can you let me know please?'

Stevie's heart had sunk. 'Yes, of course and likewise. Thanks, Dorcas.' She had hung up and stared at the phone. Since that call, she had gone through a range of emotions on an hourly basis. Anger at his disappearance, sadness at the whole damned situation, and fear of what he might do in his current state of mind.

Why hadn't he called? Why hadn't he given her the courtesy of a proper goodbye? Especially after disappearing on her before. Did this mean it *wasn't* goodbye? Perhaps he needed some breathing space? What the hell was in that letter? *Had* he discovered an illegitimate child? The questions buzzing around her head like wasps attacking her peace of mind did nothing but cause her more stress and worry her to distraction. Without answers she was adrift in a sea of the unknown.

After speaking with Dorcas, she had invited Dillon around for coffee. Partly to see if he had heard anything and partly to make sure he was okay. He seemed to be as confused as she was about Jason's sudden disappearance.

'I've tried to get hold of him too, but he hasn't returned my calls. It's like he's...I don't know...dropped off the face of the earth,' he told her as they sat at her kitchen table drinking coffee.

'Again.' Stevie stared blankly at the brown liquid in her cup.

Dillon shook his head. 'But this time it's different. Something spooked him. I wish I knew what it was. I can't imagine what was in that letter. I hope he's okay.'

'Me too. I wonder what he'll do about your dad's funeral.'

'I think he'll be there, Stevie. I don't think he'd miss it. Even after everything he told me about the abuse, I...I think he'll be there for me.'

Glancing into the bottom of her mug, she shook her head. 'Really? I'm not so sure. I actually think he's gone for good.'

Dillon frowned at her words. 'Nah, he wouldn't do that again, *would* he?'

She huffed. 'Why are you asking me? You know as much as I do. And I think perhaps we both know a hell of a lot less than we should.'

The chapel at the crematorium was small, and only a few friends had turned up for the service. Sullen people in black filed in slowly, some Stevie recognised and others she had never seen before. She watched the door, fiddling with her fingers in her lap, waiting for Jason's arrival. At the front near the lectern, Dillon was chatting with Reverend Greenough from their village church, and he too kept glancing at the door. Losing his dad had been so hard on him, and learning that Mick had physically abused his older brother, the reason Jason had disappeared ten years ago, had shattered his world. Dillon was coping well on the surface of things, but now that Jason had disappeared *again*, she wondered how long it would be before he fell apart.

She had helped Dillon to contact relatives and old family friends, and she had listened to him talk for hours about his dad and how hard it was to accept that he had treated Jason so differently. Dillon felt so much guilt and had cried on her shoulder on more than one occasion since Jason had left again.

Dana reached out and took her hand. 'Sweetie, you're going to tie yourself in knots if you carry on.'

'I know... I can't help it, Mum. What if Jason doesn't turn up?'

Dana gave a sad smile. 'Honestly, darling, I hate to say this, but I don't think he will. Whatever was in the letter was serious enough to take him away. That and the fact Mick treated him so cruelly. Jason has no real reason to be here. You need to give him time.'

'But what if he doesn't come back? What if I never see him again, Mum?' Panic washed over her again.

'In that case, you will have to let him go. You coped once before and you will cope again, as hard as it will be. Anyway, it's been tearing you apart, all this to-ing and fro-ing that the pair of you have been doing. Neither of you are helping your-selves you know. You'll *never* get over each other if you don't let go, and you told me that's what you *want* and *need* to do.'

Stevie sighed heavily. The main reason for her unwilling-ness to leave London—her mother's illness—remained her own painful secret. Knowing the truth would mean Dana demanding she change her mind, but she just wasn't willing to leave her. And anyway, men left and *this* reason for staying, the one she had verbalised to her mother, was no less true. Stevie took a deep, resigned breath. 'You're right. I know we had no future... It's just...I can't help feeling empty now that he's gone again. It's bringing back so many memories that I would rather forget.'

Dana stroked her cheek. 'I know, sweetie. Believe me I do understand what you're going through. When your father left, I was in such a miserable state for a very long time. I had to accept that Jed wasn't cut out to be a dad. It hurt like hell, and I couldn't understand how he could just leave us. I cried so much and swore off relationships for a very long time, but eventually I realised that living in the past means missing out on the future.'

'I know, Mum. I just…I can't seem to let him go, even though he said he wants us to try a long distance relationship and I said I couldn't do it.'

'You have to do what's right for *you*, sweetie.' Dana patted her thigh with her free hand, and Stevie disappeared into her own mind for a while.

Eventually, Dillon returned to where she sat and took her other hand. 'He isn't coming, Stevie. Reverend Greenough says we can't wait any longer. He has a baptism to get back for. I think maybe Jace said all the goodbyes he needed to say at the hospital. Let's hope he's okay wherever he is.' He squeezed her hand gently.

She clenched her jaw, trying to fend off angry tears. 'No, Dillon, this is crazy. He said he'd forgiven your dad and wanted to move on. He'll regret not being here *so* bloody much. I don't understand him.'

The frail looking old lady seated at the nineteen-seventies, wood-panelled organ began to play 'Amazing Grace'. Her playing skills were beautiful, considering her advanced years. Overcome with emotion yet again, the tears began to cascade down Stevie's face. But the tears were not for the man about to be cremated. They were for the messed up and damaged man whose absence was making her heart ache.

CHAPTER THREE

*J*ason sat in his hire car in the large car park of the St. Honor hospital. It was a huge modern white building rather like a city in its own right and much bigger than any of the hospitals he had been to in the UK. He felt like he was on some kind of stake out as he watched people coming and going completely unaware of his impending journey into the unknown.

He took a deep breath and climbed out of the vehicle. After closing the car door, he stood for a few moments toying with the idea of turning around and driving away. But he hadn't come all this way to chicken out at the last minute. With a firmer resolve than he had thought possible, he made his way to the entrance.

The hospital was buzzing with people. Patients trailing mobile drip stands along with them as they escorted visiting relatives to the exit, a police officer chatting to a nurse, orderlies wheeling patients, people waiting to be seen at the desk. It really was a hive of activity. The familiar smell of disinfectant brought a wave of nausea. He tried to breathe through his mouth, but the longer he had to wait to be seen, the weaker his supposedly strong resolve was becoming.

Eventually, a pleasant looking older lady behind the reception gave him her attention. 'Hello there, sir, can I help you?' Her smile, albeit fake, was wide.

Jason cleared his throat. 'Oh...erm...yes. I...I'm looking for Doctor Oliver Halford. Could you tell me where I might find him?'

'Oh, of course! Are you related to Doctor Halford? I must say you look awfully similar. Are you his younger brother perhaps?' The rambling woman was overly familiar and made Jason feel even more uncomfortable. She fiddled with her hair in a flirty manner, and Jason suddenly felt his throat close up.

'I...I...no...no. I'm not related... Could you tell me where I could find him, please?'

'Gosh really? I must tell him he has a doppelgänger.' She laughed. 'Anyway, he's in surgery right now, I can give you his office number perhaps? You can ask his secretary for an appointment. Or I can leave a message—'

'N-no...that won't be necessary, thank you.' He suddenly felt very warm and a little dizzy. He dashed from the building and walked as fast as he could back to his hire car, dodging numerous people coming and going from the building and gulping the fresh air into his lungs.

Sitting back in the driver's seat, he breathed a huge sigh of relief, turned on the engine and followed the signs for the staff parking lot. He pulled up, parking out of sight of the security guard but ensuring he could see the hospital exit and opened the large bag of chips he had bought from the Walmart on the way to the hospital. The salt began to settle his stomach as he sat patiently waiting for a glimpse of the man who could make or break the next chapter of his life.

Sure enough after around thirty to forty minutes, a tall

familiar looking man with greying hair strode with purpose from the hospital building. He had a huge smile on his face and was being accompanied by a curvy brunette in pink scrubs. Jason was momentarily distracted by how much the woman resembled Stevie and almost forgot his purpose for being there. He snapped his eyes back to the tall man who bore a more than striking resemblance to his own reflection and watched as he made his way over to a black four-wheel drive vehicle.

Seeing the man in the flesh was a huge shock. There was no doubt the man was his father. A cold shiver travelled down his spine as he continued to observe.

As the man climbed into his car, waved goodbye to his colleague, and pulled out of his parking spot, Jason made the rash and ridiculous decision to follow him. Feeling like a rather conspicuous, bizarre stalker-type, he waited until a couple of cars passed before pulling out and following the black car. Around thirty minutes later, they had passed through the towering, glass-covered buildings of the city centre and were in a very pretty residential area of large family homes. It was clearly a well-to-do area, but Jason would have expected nothing less judging by the man's job. Staying as far away as possible without losing sight of the black four-wheel drive vehicle, he observed the man pulling into the driveway of an imposing white, wood framed building. The front door was painted a bright blue, and the lawn looked like a professional gardener had manicured it very recently.

Jason watched as the man, who was now whistling, entered his home and closed the door. *Okay...so this is where my father lives. Okay...time to go to the door and knock. Yep... this is it*. He drummed his fingers on the steering wheel for a few moments trying to figure out what the hell he would say when he turned up to shock the hell out of the completely oblivious man. A thousand different greetings filtered through his mind as he sat there.

'Hi, I'm your long lost son...'

'Hey...do I look familiar to you? I do? Well, here's why...'

'Good afternoon, can I interest you in being my dad?'

Eventually, instead of approaching the house, he growled at himself for his cowardice, turned the car around, and drove away.

Back at the hotel, he set the bedside alarm clock and flopped onto the bed in his modern suite. The soothing palate of chocolate brown and cream went some way to calming the anger bubbling under the surface. *You came all this way and couldn't even knock on his fucking door. You're a coward, just like Mick.* His fists clenched by his sides. All he wanted to do was pick up the phone and call Stevie. Just to hear her voice and tell her all the crazy shit that had happened in the last week, to hear her tell him that everything would be fine. That she forgave him for running again. But he couldn't do it. Not yet. Feeling physically exhausted and emotionally drained, he allowed himself the luxury of drifting into sleep, fully clothed and unwashed.

Several hours later, the alarm woke him from a restless sleep that had been filled with dreams of Stevie, his dead 'father', and the man he would hopefully be meeting later today—his birth father. This time, he would follow Oliver Halford home, and he *would* go to the door. This time, he *wouldn't* chicken out. He showered and dressed in another shirt and cargo pants and ordered room service. When the food arrived, he almost vacuumed it from the plate, feeling quite surprised at the fervour of his appetite. The pancakes, bacon, and maple syrup were delicious, and he almost called down for seconds, but decided he was done procrastinating. He had questions that needed answers, and Dr.

Oliver Halford was the only one equipped to give them to him.

The hospital was just as busy as the day before, and his nerves jangled once again as he made his way to the entrance. Hospitals made him nervous at the best of times. The smell of disinfectant assaulting his nostrils once again as soon as he walked through the automatic doors was enough to floor a rhino at fifty paces. *Breathe through your mouth, Reynolds. Through your mouth.* He repeated the mantra over and over, all the time willing his feet to move as his heart tried to vacate the building through his chest.

Walking over to the reception desk, he noticed that it was a different lady sitting there today, and after yesterday's experience, he was thankful for small mercies. She appeared rather harassed. He approached her carefully as if she held a loaded gun.

She frowned at him suspiciously. 'Can I help you, sir?'

'Oh, sorry, yes. I was hoping to find out where Doctor Oliver Halford might be today.'

The smartly dressed blonde tapped at her keyboard and then glanced up at Jason. 'I'm sorry but he isn't working here today. If you check with his secretary she will—'

Jason held up his hands as he backed away. 'That's fine, don't worry. Thank you.'

He left the hospital quickly, feeling relieved that he could breathe normally again, and went back to his car. After tapping the details into the rental cars built in GPS, he set out for the address near Sebago Lake where had followed Dr. Halford yesterday. Would he even be there? Was he working somewhere else? It was a chance he would have to take. Nervous energy coursed through his veins, and he chewed on the inside of his cheek until the metallic taste of blood stopped him from his actions.

Around thirty minutes later, Jason pulled up in front of the large, white, wooden framed house once again. A sprinkler system was dousing the neatly trimmed grass out front, meaning that someone must be home. The street was wide and all of the houses were individually designed. The space between each house could have fit another two or three homes. It was a very clean, neat, and tidy neighbourhood, and he felt sure that every person who owned property on this street must be lawyers, doctors, or some other profession that attracted a hefty income. Jason stared up at the house for what seemed like an age, trying to pluck up the courage to knock on the door.

Eventually and with no little trepidation, he climbed out of the hire car and made his way to the front door. He pressed the button for the doorbell and felt the immediate urge to turn and run. A few moments later, a man could be seen through the screen door drying his hands on a dishtowel as he walked towards him.

He squinted as he peered at Jason and opened the door. 'Hello there, can I help you?' The man's accent was almost American but with a slight hint of English.

Jason took a deep calming breath. 'Erm...Oliver Halford?'

The man frowned. 'That's me. I'm sorry. Do I know you?'

'Erm...no...but...I think...I think that you're my dad.'

CHAPTER FOUR

*T*he man's eyes widened, and he opened and closed his mouth several times like a dying goldfish. Jason felt very uncomfortable standing on the porch whilst the man was evidently trying to make sense of what he was saying.

Oliver Halford shook his head. 'I'm...I'm sorry but I think you must be mistaken. I...I've never seen you before...I—'

'Shirley Duffy was my mother. You and she were—'

The man closed his eyes at the mention of her name. 'Yes, I know very well who Shirley Duffy is, but she and I never... I mean...we split up. We were together once, but we never married.'

'Please, can I come in? I have something to show you, and I think it best if we don't do this out here on your porch.'

The man eyed him suspiciously for a moment before he nodded his acquiescence and held the door open for Jason. He walked through the hallway and stopped in the living room with Jason following close behind. Oliver threw the dishtowel onto the couch and rested his hands on his hips. 'Okay. Who are you? And what the hell are you doing turning up at my home out of the blue like this?'

He cleared his throat. 'I'm Jason...Jason Reynolds.'

'And what do you want with me, Jason Reynolds?'

'I...I erm...' Adrenaline coursed through his veins and he suddenly felt light headed. He tugged at the neckline of his shirt and scrunched his brow.

Oliver stepped towards him and Jason caught a fleeting glimpse of concern in his expression. 'Can I get you a drink of water?'

Jason swallowed, his throat closing tighter as the moisture seemed to be sucked from his body. 'Water would be good, thank you,' he croaked.

The man nodded stiffly and walked towards the back of the house. He came back through to the lounge a few minutes later with two glasses of iced water and handed one to Jason, who gulped down the much-needed refreshment. His mouth had begun to feel like an arid desert floor thanks to the nerves standing on edge throughout his tensed up body.

Oliver gestured for Jason to sit and took the seat opposite him before placing his drink on the glass coffee table. He leaned forward, resting his elbows on his knees, and steepled his fingers. 'Okay...Jason...I think perhaps you need to explain who you are and what brought you to *my* home, which judging by your accent is far away from your own.'

Jason took out the letter and photograph of the eighteen-year-old Oliver and handed them to him along with a photo of himself, aged eighteen for comparison. 'First of all, I think you need to read this.'

He watched as Oliver read the letter. The colour drained from the man's face, and his eyes became glassy. His lip quivered as he glanced at the photograph and then at Jason, remaining silent the whole time. After blowing out a long shaking breath, Oliver handed the letter and photo back to Jason and rubbed his hands over his face. 'I'm so very sorry... I can't deal with this right now. Please excuse me.' He appeared to be in a daze as he stood and walked out of the room.

Jason frowned as he sat there. Alone. In a stranger's house. Should he leave? Should he stay? Was Oliver coming back? *What the hell?* His knee bobbed up and down as he waited. After five or so minutes, he figured that the coward had fucked off and left him there. He stood and stomped out of the house, slamming the door so hard behind him that the house shook. He stormed towards his rental car. A myriad of emotions fought for priority in his mixed up mind. *I didn't ask to be in this fucking situation! I didn't even fucking want to be here! Fucking coward.*

'Jason! Wait!' The man's voice stopped him in his tracks, and Jason halted with one hand on the door handle of the hire car and the other clutching the letter that brought him here. As his chest heaved, he clenched his jaw and turned his head to the side so that he could see Oliver walking towards him in his peripheral vision.

'What?' he snapped.

'I'm sorry about what happened back there. It was a... You being here... You being *you*... It's a complete shock to me. Please forgive me. I didn't know how to react. I didn't know what to think. I still don't if I'm honest, but I'm sorry. Please come back inside so we can talk.'

Jason turned to face him, a wave of sadness washed over him. 'Don't fucking bother. You don't owe me anything. All you were was a sperm donor, so don't do me any favours.' He couldn't help the hurt and anger evident in his voice.

Oliver stepped tentatively towards him again with his hands held up in surrender. 'Please, come on in. Let's talk...*please*? I would very much like the chance to talk with you about all of this.' He motioned for Jason to follow him. Jason inhaled deeply and followed reluctantly behind. Once inside the living room with its rich cream coloured walls and sumptuous gold hued soft furnishings, Oliver gestured for Jason to sit.

Oliver rubbed his hands over his face again and looked over at Jason. 'You look so much like... I mean you and I look...' He seemed incapable of stringing a coherent sentence together. He stopped and tried again. 'You have to know that I had *no idea* about you, Jason. None at all. If I'd have known—'

Anger rose in Jason's gut once again. 'You'd have done what exactly? Married my mother out of some misplaced sense of *duty*?'

Oliver held his hands up as if to calm Jason down. 'I'm sure you have questions. I know I would in your position, and it's clear that you're angry, but you can't get angry at *me* for something I had no clue about.'

'Why did you leave her waiting at the altar?'

Oliver closed his eyes briefly. He shook his head and looked at Jason. 'I was...too young. We both were. I wanted to be a doctor. At first I thought I could be married and still have that. I loved her so very much, you need to know that, but then I realised it would tear us apart, me studying all the time and being away from her. Long distance relationships are so hard. Eventually, we would have split. I didn't want to put her through that.'

Great, another person who thinks long distance is a mistake. 'So you didn't show? You left an eighteen-year-old girl who loved you...no, *adored* you, so you could go off and pursue your own life without her?' Jason suddenly clamped his mouth shut. The realisation that he had done *exactly that* to Stevie ten years ago hit him like a runaway train. He dropped his head forward, feeling physically sick.

'J-Jason, are you all right?' Oliver reached out and touched his arm.

Jason flinched and lifted his head. He glanced at Oliver and was met with a compassionate gaze. 'Why didn't you come back to her and explain why you were going to leave? You slept with her knowing full well that you wouldn't be staying around to deal with the consequences. Why would you *do* that to her?' *At least I hadn't done that to Stevie. At least sex wasn't involved when I left.*

Oliver's nostrils flared. 'You want the truth? Well, here you go...I did it because I *loved* her, Jason. I always have. I couldn't get enough of her. Leaving your mother was the hardest thing I ever did. It broke my heart, and I have *never* truly recovered. But I left for *her*. I left to save her from a life of misery with me. Sleeping with her was a one-time thing that went too far. It wasn't meant to happen. But I never regretted it. I loved her so much. You have to believe that, Jason. In all honesty I can tell you that I have *never* loved like that again. Don't get me wrong. Of course I love my wife, but the intensity with which I loved your mother... I...I can't put it into words.'

Jason snorted. 'You left her to save her from a life of misery, but that's what she ended up with anyway.' He could completely understand the notion. Oliver's reasons for leaving were totally different to his own, but nevertheless, *he* had made the same decision, to leave the woman he loved more than anything in order to try and achieve a better life. *So damned selfish.*

Jason went on to explain in detail the life he'd had with Mick and Shirley, the struggles, the beatings, his love for Stevie, and how he couldn't tell her what was going on but that, instead, he too had left home at eighteen to get away. Oliver's lip trembled, and he slid along the couch to be next to Jason. He put an arm around his shoulders and pulled him into his chest. Oliver's body shuddered as he sobbed. It felt weird having a complete stranger hug him and pour out grief for him, for what he had gone through in the absence of his real father. He didn't quite know what to do. How to react.

After a few moments, Jason reciprocated the embrace as overwhelming grief took hold. He clung to his father, giving an outlet to his own feelings of sadness and regret at the time that he had been denied with this man. Although a complete stranger, Oliver seemed to be a decent, caring person. The anger he had felt and the questions as to why he had abandoned his mother just melted away. The man holding him *would* have been a good father. He *would* have loved him. This much was clear. He seemed such a warm and kindly man. Misguided when he was younger, but he couldn't criticise him for that. How could Jason stay angry with a man who knew nothing of his existence? Especially when he had done pretty much the same thing to Stevie when he left. Oliver had wronged Jason's mother, but Jason too had done that when he left without saying goodbye. He had more things in common with the man than he liked to admit, and so far they all seemed to be negative things.

Oliver spoke in a strangled sob. 'If only I'd have known, Jason. You would *never* have suffered like that. I'm so very, very sorry.'

Jason wiped his eyes and cleared his throat. 'No, it's a shame that you didn't know about me. I hate the fact that I missed out on knowing you or even knowing *of* you until now.'

Oliver clasped his shoulder. 'We can start afresh now. I...I need some time. I must go and speak to Hannah...my wife... this will be a *major* shock to her...and you should know...you have two brothers.'

Jason smiled. 'Delia told me about them. She's very proud.'

Oliver beamed. 'Oh, you met my mom?'

'Yeah, I went to see her after reading the letter. She was so sweet.'

Oliver's smile diminished. 'She's a good mother. I hurt her badly when I left the UK.'

'Much the same as I hurt my mother when I left. We all make mistakes.'

'Some of us more than others, son.'

Jason stood to leave. 'I should go. I'm sure you have things to do. Calls to make and such. So...where do we go from here?'

Oliver rose to his feet. 'You're right. As I said, I need to speak with Hannah. That's my priority right now. I was travelling down there in a few days anyway. She's in Boston with her parents and the boys. I'll explain everything to them in person. It's better that way. When I come back, I'd like to meet with you again...if you'd like to.'

Jason nodded enthusiastically. 'Yes, I *would* like that. I wasn't sure how long I'd be staying, so I paid for an open ended return flight. I'll stay for as long as it takes for us both to get the answers we need. I think...I think I've ruined things for Stevie and me now...not that things would have gone anywhere anyway. We live over five hundred miles apart at opposite ends of the UK and—'

'Jason, don't do what I did. Don't lose her over your own pride and stupidity. Make things work with her or at least try, okay?'

Jason felt awash with sadness again. A feeling he was becoming startlingly accustomed to, albeit reluctantly. 'I think it may be too late. I haven't told her any of this. I up and left...*again*. She doesn't know where I am or why I left. And my little brother doesn't know he's adopted. I need to think about how I'm going to tell him that. He'll be devastated.'

Oliver pulled his lips in for a moment before speaking. 'You have a lot to think about, Jason. And it's not going to be easy riding. But I'll help or advise you in any way I can, if you want me to.'

'Thanks, but I need to figure this whole thing with Stevie and Dillon out for myself. I have no clue how at the moment.'

Oliver and Jason agreed to meet again when Oliver returned from Hannah's parents in Boston. In the meantime, Jason went back to his hotel and decided to do a little research whilst he waited for news. Dillon hadn't known about his adoption, and another few weeks would make no difference. He could go to the Internet café and do some web searches on how to find one's birth parents. At least that way, when he arrived home, he would be armed with something other than bad news. On returning to his hotel, he dialled Delia's home number.

'Hello?'

Jason felt the butterflies take flight in his stomach. 'Delia, it's Jason...your...your...'

'Grandson,' she answered.

He could tell she was smiling, and a warm feeling spread through his chest as he went on to tell his Grandmother about his first encounter with his real father.

CHAPTER FIVE

Several days later, Jason was sitting by a sparkling lake when he received a call from Oliver.

'Hi, Jason. How've you been?'

'Hi...erm...Oliver...not bad thanks. Although I think I've walked about a thousand miles in the last couple of days.' He chuckled. 'Nerves about this whole situation kind of got the better of me. How are things with you?'

'Things are...really good actually. I'm calling to invite you to meet with me at the country club near my home. I thought perhaps we could catch up a little and talk some more.'

Jason cringed. 'Country club? Aren't those places a little dressed up and snobby?'

'They can be, but the place I go is real nice. And you're my son, so people will take you as they find you.' He laughed. 'Long hair and all.'

'Gee thanks,' Jason replied. 'That fills me with such confidence.'

'Come on, I was kidding. It isn't what you think. The guys are great. They'll all be happy to meet you. Although there may not be anyone there at this time of day. Let's meet, and see how it goes. If you feel uncomfortable, we'll leave and go somewhere else.'

'Okay. I'm sure it'll be fine. I'm struggling with this whole thing, that's all. I wish I could talk to Stevie, you know?'

'If that's what you need to do, then you should give her a call.' Oliver advised.

'I can't...I want to but...I can't yet. I need to get this whole thing straight in my head before I go involving others. And she'd want to tell Dillon everything. I need to speak to them both face to face.'

'Okay, that's your call.'

After agreeing to meet Oliver and jotting down the address of the country club, Jason said goodbye. The one thing he'd forgotten to do was to ask about the dress code. He hadn't brought anything overly smart with him. He considered calling Oliver back, but after mulling it over, decided it wasn't something he would bother him with. They would have to take him as they found him.

At two o'clock the next day, Jason walked into the country club feeling a little out of place in his black cargo pants and white long sleeved T-shirt. Oliver wore black slacks, a yellow polo shirt, and a grey sweater. Jason's dark hair hung loose, falling to his shoulders and very shaggy, whereas Oliver's was perfectly styled to the side and gelled in place. Jason held his hand out to shake Oliver's when they greeted each other, but his father pulled him into a bear hug embrace, patting him on the back. Jason was taken aback at the outpouring of affection from this virtual stranger but his heart warmed a little too and he reciprocated the gesture.

They were shown to a table by the window, which looked out onto a patio area and small boating lake. It was a very pretty location, and Jason found it surprising that he could almost forget they were on the edge of a city.

Once the pleasantries were out of the way, Jason cleared his throat when his curiosity got the better of him. 'So...did you talk things through with Hannah?'

'I did. She was shocked to say the least, and she was angry too...at first. She cried and it broke my heart. I felt like I'd betrayed her somehow. I think the fact that the children I have with her weren't my first hit her hard. But I explained that I hadn't known about you, and that it didn't change how much I love my boys. There was a whole lot of shouting. But when she calmed down and we talked things through, she was quite accepting. She's a very levelheaded woman, thankfully, and the fact that this happened long before I met her was the main factor in her acceptance. I told her about things with you and...and Mick. I hope that's okay. She needed to understand the full picture, you know?'

Jason nodded as guilt washed over him. 'Yes, of course. I feel bad for disrupting your lives like this, but I had to know for my own peace of mind who you are, and I guess, who *I* am too.'

'Absolutely. I showed her the photo of you as a teenager, and we looked back at some of my old snaps. She was amazed at how similar we look. She said there was no doubt about you being a Halford.' His brown eyes lifted as he smiled warmly with his whole face. The crow's feet at his eye corners crinkled as he did so, making Jason smile. *At least judging by his full head of hair, I know I won't go bald.*

After a thoughtful pause, Jason spoke. 'I want you to know that I don't want *anything* from you...just a little of your time...and...perhaps to know you better...that's all. I'm not after money...nothing like that. I'm independent financially and in every other way.'

Oliver listened intently and then smiled. 'Jason, it's clear to me that you are your own man. I need no reassurances on that score.'

Jason smiled back and nodded with relief at his words. 'So...how about your sons? What did Joshua and Elliot say when you told them?'

'I think they were a little disappointed at me for not keeping it in my pants like I keep lecturing them to do until they're in serious relationships, or even better...married. The number of times I've talked to them about the dangers of unprotected sex and the possibility of knocking up some poor girl.' He laughed humourlessly. 'And now I seem like the biggest damned hypocrite and jack ass that ever walked the earth.'

Jason cringed. 'Hmmm, I bet that went down pretty bad, eh?'

'Oh yeah. They ripped me a new one, pretty much.' He laughed heartily this time.

'Are they pissed off about me then?'

'Are you *kidding* me? Not at all. They were pretty damned happy once they knew their mom was okay. They... ah...they all want to meet you. In fact, we're having a cookout tomorrow...just the family. Hannah and the boys want me to ask you along.'

Jason's spirits lifted. 'Really? I have *no clue* what a cookout is, but I'll be there!' He nodded enthusiastically.

Oliver threw his head back and laughed louder. 'You have no clue what a cookout is, huh?'

'Not a bloody clue.' Jason joined in with the mirth.

'I believe you Limey's call it a barbeque.'

'Ahhh! I get it now! Cooking outdoors. A *cookout*.' Jason slapped himself in the forehead. 'Good grief, you must think I'm as thick as pudding.'

'Ha ha! Your accent takes me back, son. I can hardly call

you a Limey, can I, when I was born in the same area as you?' The pair laughed again.

Oliver called the waitress over and ordered coffee. The men sat without speaking for a few minutes, but Jason felt comfortable with the silence. He didn't get the urge to talk drivel to fill the space in conversation.

As Oliver stirred creamer into his coffee, he glanced over at Jason once again. 'So...tell me more about Stevie.'

'Pfff, where do I even start? We met at school. I adored her from afar for a long time. Pretty much from the moment I discovered girls, I was in love with her. She was such a *lovely* girl. Popular but shy and really didn't get how gorgeous she was back then. Still doesn't even now. We became closer as we got older. She was...so beautiful...still is.' He stared at his coffee cup aware that he was repeating himself. 'She had the most beautiful hair...long and dark with a hint of red and a slight wave. Her eyes are the colour of the sky on a clear sunny day...you know, the kind of bright blue that almost looks like she must be wearing coloured contacts.' He smiled and shook his head as images of Stevie danced through his mind. 'And her laugh... You can't help joining in when she's in full guffaw.' He laughed at the memory. When he glanced up, he could see that Oliver was anticipating more.

Nervously he continued. 'She and I were so...*in love*. We spent so much time together that neither of us had proper friends outside of us. There were a couple, but we preferred each other's company. As time went on, things were getting worse at home. Mick was losing his temper with me more and more, but I was getting to the point where I feared what *I'd* do to *him* each time he hit me with a belt or his hands and fists. I couldn't take it any longer. I couldn't take the next step with her even though I desperately wanted to.'

Oliver frowned. 'Next step?'

Jason felt his cheeks heat. 'Sex. I wanted to be her first and for her to be mine, but I couldn't undress in front of her because of the bruises and scars. She couldn't understand why I was so reticent, and I couldn't explain. Things were getting beyond difficult. Then it was prom, and...well...she had expectations. But I couldn't go through with it, and Mick went ape shit on me for something ridiculous, and so I walked. I'd been planning it all. The army...the train tickets. Things came to a head, and I had to go.'

Jason was surprised that it didn't feel at all strange to be talking so frankly with Oliver. He was a good listener and clearly wasn't judging. *How strange to feel so at ease talking about such personal issues with a man I've only just met.*

'Why didn't you tell her what was going on?'

'Because...she was so sweet...innocent... I didn't want to hurt her with it all...you know? I didn't want to taint her. And I know her so well. She'd have reported the abuse. I couldn't have that. I couldn't do that to Dillon. I knew Mick hadn't hurt him, and I didn't want to shatter Dillon's world.'

Oliver nodded. 'I understand your reasoning. I can't say I agree with how you handled it, but I do get it. How have things been since you two connected again?'

'Great for the most part. When she turned up at my camp, I was...well, shocked doesn't even come into it. But seeing her again re-ignited all the feelings I thought I'd gotten over. That made me angry, and I treated her like shit. I'm ashamed of some of the stuff I said to her. She didn't deserve my malice.' He ran a hand over his head, still struggling with how he felt about his behaviour.

'She's still beautiful. Not skinny anymore, but I like her curves. In fact, I *love* her curves. She's feminine and sexy, but she still doesn't realise that. I wanted to make a go of things. See where it all went. But she won't move to Scotland, and I won't move back to London. I can't live there again. She says long distance relationships don't work.'

He paused feeling that he should explain the reason for this. 'Her dad left when she was a baby and he tried the long distance thing with her mum, but eventually he abandoned them. Stevie won't even try and...and no matter how much I've tried to convince her that I could be trusted...that I'm not like her dad...it hasn't changed anything, and now I've run again...and so we're at an impasse. Or we were. I think the impasse is probably a distant memory now. At least at a fork in the road there are two routes possible. I think I'm at a dead end of my own making.' He glanced at Oliver and exhaled loudly. 'Sorry. I'm rambling now.'

Oliver looked thoughtful. 'No, you're not rambling. But it is a tough one. I wish I could talk to her. Help you both. In all honesty, it sounds to me like you two are meant to be together. You have such a strong connection that's clearly soul-deep. You can only *try* and get her to see how you feel. You'll find a way. Let her know that this time you didn't run. You needed space. You didn't turn your back on her as such. You've been through a lot, and I'm sure she'll understand. Just don't let her slip through your fingers. Don't let history repeat itself.'

Jason felt the weight of the world resting on his shoulders. He needed to brighten the mood. 'Anyway...back to this cook-out. I thought Hannah and the guys were on holiday in Boston? How can you be having a cookout tomorrow?'

'They decided meeting you was of paramount importance, and so they came home right away with me. They're very keen to meet you.'

Suddenly feeling a little overwhelmed and more than a little nervous, Jason rubbed his temples to eradicate the onslaught of the threatening headache. 'Wow...that's so nice.

I'm looking forward to meeting them too...scared to death, but excited at the same time.'

Oliver patted Jason's shoulder. 'No need to be scared Jason, honestly.'

'No? That's good to know...'

'But?'

Jason huffed out a long breath. 'But...this...this can't be happening. It's all a bit too...too *easy*.'

'I think perhaps it's about time you had an easier ride, son. Don't you?'

'You got that right. It would be nice, but I feel...*odd*. And guilty.'

'Well don't. You're more than welcome to come to dinner. And as you'll be returning to the UK soon, I think it's only right that you and I get to know each other a little better before you leave.'

'Yeah...yeah that would be good. The past few months have been...' Again Jason struggled to find the right words. 'Finding out my mum was gone was such a wrench...then Mick dying...and now I have a dad, brothers, and a grandmother. It's going to take some getting used to. Having a family.'

'We'll get there, son. We'll all get there.'

CHAPTER SIX

*J*ason lay in his huge bed. Alone. Being so far away from home was starting to get on his nerves. Not being able to talk to Stevie about all the shit going on in his life was weighing him down. He glanced at the clock beside his bed. *Two a.m. Great.* He wondered what she was doing and if she missed him or if she was too pissed off at him to even care anymore.

Closing his eyes gave little comfort because as soon as he did her body sprang to mind to torture him. The curve of her hip and the way she wrapped her legs around him. He groaned and ran his hands roughly over his face. Grabbing his iPod, he stuck in his ear buds and decided to listen to something soothing that would help him get off to sleep. He eventually drifted off to the sound of *Same Mistake* by James Blunt.

The breeze tickled at his naked chest as her hair trailed over his chest and she kissed her way down to his abs. The grass swayed as if dancing, and he inhaled her tantalising scent deep into his lungs as she teased him. Pleasure radiated through his body like a warm glow. He caressed her breasts, loving the way they fit his large hands so perfectly. Hearing her moan, he looked up into bright blue eyes filled with what looked like love and tucked her auburn hair behind her ears. Reaching up to cup her face, he whispered, 'I love you so much,' and waited for her to say it back. Instead she stood and began to run through the long grass. He leapt to his feet. 'Stevie! Wait!' he shouted after her. 'Please...come back...I can explain...don't leave me!'

Feeling panicked, his eyes jerked open. His arms and legs were tangled in the sheets. The same damn dream had come again. Fear that he had lost her washed over him and oozed out of every pore along with the sweat that covered his body. Sitting up, he inhaled and exhaled slowly and deeply, trying to calm his erratic breathing. The urge to pick up the phone and call her was almost all consuming. But he fought it with all his might. He had to do this face to face. Explain everything to her when she could see his eyes and know that he hadn't *meant to* run from her, that he wasn't running from *her*. But would she understand?

After a day of Internet research into adoption in the UK and the ins and outs of finding birth families, he showered and prepared for his visit to Oliver's home. He arrived at the white house near Sebago Lake at five as requested. He had stopped off on his way there to purchase flowers, wine, and chocolates, and he had dressed fairly smartly in dark indigo jeans and a pale blue button down shirt. His hair was scraped back into a low ponytail again.

With jangling nerves, he pressed the doorbell. A minute later, a tall, stunning blonde woman, whom Jason surmised must be in her late forties, came to the door. She had the most beautiful green eyes.

'You must be Jason,' she said with a warm welcoming smile.

Jason returned her smile. 'I am...and you're Hannah?'

'That's right. Come on in.' She held the door open, and once Jason stepped inside, she enveloped him in her arms, pulling him down and holding him tight. 'It's so good to meet you. Oliver has told us all about you. I want you to know that we're all very happy to have you here. Welcome to our family, Jason.'

Her words made him very emotional. A lump seemed to lodge itself in his throat and his eyes began to sting. He cleared his throat and tried to swallow past the lump. 'Thank you, Hannah. That means such a lot.' His voice broke as the words fell from his lips.

She hugged him again. 'Oh, Jason. I can only imagine what this whole situation must be doing to you.' Her voice wavered too, and when she released him, he saw his emotion mirrored in her verdant eyes. She held him at arms-length. 'I hope you don't mind but I asked Oliver if I could greet you at the door alone. I wanted to see you by myself for a moment first. I have to say that I'm quite taken aback by this whole situation too. I was upset at first. But I realise that you aren't a threat. You simply want to know the man who is partly responsible for your existence, and I get that. I think initially I was terrified that things would change dramatically for us, but from what Olly has said, I can tell that you are going to *add* to our family...not take anything away. And wow, I'm so shocked by how much you look like your father.' She squeezed his arms.

'He's a good man, Jason, warm, giving, and so *very* kind. He's a wonderful father to Elliot and Josh, and he will be to you, if you give him a chance. I know he made bad decisions in his past, and I know what he did to your mother is almost unforgiveable. But he's so very sorry for that.'

She paused as if wondering whether to say what was on her mind. Jason stayed silent by way of encouragement for her honesty. 'But I *can't* be sorry, and I feel so bad for saying that. The thing is...you see, if he'd acted differently, I wouldn't have him *or* my beautiful boys. I...I hope you understand. And I hope you know that you are as much a part of our family now as Elliot and Josh. They can't wait to meet you. You all have the same eyes, your father's.' Her smile was wide and warm.

He understood what she had said about Oliver's treatment of his mother, and even though it hurt, he did his best to brush it aside. 'My mum said I had his eyes, and I didn't quite believe it until I looked into them myself. It's strange to be so much like someone physically. I never noticed how unlike my dad...erm, *Mick,* I was until I met Oliver.'

'It must all be very strange for you... But I hope we can all work through this together...as a family. Come on...come through and meet your brothers, hmm?'

Brothers...plural...wow. Knowing he had three of them now made butterflies set about dancing in his stomach. He followed her down the long hallway into the large family dining kitchen. The space was bright, traditional, and very homey. It led straight out onto the patio where a pool covered a third of the huge yard. There was a large dining table and a patio heater. He spotted two younger men, both with dark hair, throwing a football around on the grass. When they saw their mother and Jason, they stopped and made their way towards them.

'Boys this is Jason...your older brother.' Hannah said with a smile, and her arm linked through the crook of Jason's.

The two young men had wide smiles. 'Good to meet you,

man. I'm Joshua...most people call me Josh.' The older of the two gripped Jason's hand firmly.

'Hey dude, I'm Elliot...most people call me...erm...Elliot,' the younger one said with a grin and a chuckle as he shook Jason's hand. Jason grinned in return. It was like looking at himself through a mirror to the past. There was that striking family resemblance again. Elliot was more like his mother Hannah, but Josh was very much like his dad *and* Jason.

'It's good to meet you both. Wow...spot the brothers, eh?' Jason said as he gestured between them. The three men looked at each other and laughed.

'Aw, come on big bro, gimme a hug.' Josh grabbed Jason and pulled him almost right off his feet. Elliot joined the hug. Jason glanced over at Hannah, who had now been joined by Oliver, and they both looked on smiling. Hannah's eyes were misty, and Oliver looked like he was trying to rein himself and his own fragile emotions in.

Once the introductions were out of the way, the whole family sat at the round table under an umbrella that shielded them from the early evening sun's glare. 'Wow, this all looks delicious,' Jason said as he glanced over the delectable spread before him. 'Compliments to the chef...literally.' He laughed, remembering that Hannah was *actually* a chef.

Hannah held up her hands. 'Ahhh, on this occasion, it's Oliver you should be thanking. Cookouts are *his* domain. Something to do with men and fire, I think,' she teased as she smirked at her husband.

'Me man...me make fire.' Elliot said in a ridiculously gruff voice as he beat his chest. They all shared a laugh.

Oliver reached into the cooler by his feet and handed Jason a beer.

Jason held his hand up. 'Oh, I shouldn't. I'm driving.'

'Go on, you're fine. Hannah made up the guest room for

LISA J HOBMAN

you. We wondered if perhaps you might like to stay with us until you have to leave for the UK?' Oliver asked tentatively.

As the others chatted and filled their plates with chicken, salad, and coleslaw, Jason leaned over to Oliver so that no one else could hear. 'I just want to say that I appreciate all of this, but I still feel a little strange about it all. I mean...don't you want to...I dunno...check me out...you know, like DNA tests or something like they do on TV. I mean I could be *anybody*.'

Oliver laughed and placed a firm grip on his shoulder. 'If you have doubts I'd be happy to oblige, son, but I only have to look at you to know that I'm your father.'

He shook his head. 'I just...I can't believe how accepting you're all being,' he whispered.

Oliver shrugged. 'The dates all add up. I knew your mom very well...she was not *easy*, if you know what I mean, and I can assure you she wouldn't lie to you about this. And you can't deny the family resemblance.' He took a deep breath and looked directly into Jason's eyes. 'I *want* you to be mine, and that's half the battle. The way I treated your mother was... Well, let's just say I'm not proud of it...and hearing how that... that...*man*, if you can call him that, treated you...I figure this is me being given a second chance, a chance to do what's *right*. To do right by you *and* your mom, God rest her soul. Do you understand what I'm rambling on about here?'

Jason placed his fork down. 'Yeah...I do...I know...it's just...I'm not used to...' He couldn't figure out how to end the sentence.

'You're neither used to being wanted by anyone other than Shirley, nor are you used to being part of a *proper* family. I get that. Things between your mom and Mick were clearly strained after the birth complications. And that's plain awful. I feel so bad that she suffered. I suffered too, believe me. Although I know what I went through was nothing compared

54

to the life you and your mom had. And so I can understand why you feel strange about all of this, but you'll get used to it. We all will. And, Jason, *not* all things that seem too good to be true actually *are*.'

'Thanks, Oliver. This means such a lot to me. I feel like I've been given a second chance here...to know a real father. Finding out I have brothers... Wow...that knocked me sideways.'

'Well, that's no surprise, son. And listen, maybe one day... when you're ready...in your own time and if you want to...you can call me Dad, huh? No pressure. And if it never happens, that's fine too. This is all new to each of us. Just think about it.'

'Okay, I will.' Jason wasn't sure what to think about that. He didn't feel he knew him well enough to start calling him *Dad*. But deep down he *wanted* to feel able. Just seeing this man with his family made him envious of what Josh and Elliot had had growing up. How wonderful to actually be loved and wanted, to not feel like a failure in everything.

'And you know, I think when you get back to the UK and when you've spent time with your brother and helped him deal with his new reality, you need to have a long think about that girl of yours. I think you and she maybe could work things out. I understand your desire to leave London again, but perhaps if you talk to her some more, she might be willing to come north with you or to *try* the long distance thing. You never know. Being away from her will have given her time to miss you.'

But Jason *did* know. He had tried to talk to her before. He had almost begged. But he knew that she would never leave London. She had desperately tried to make him see the good things about the place. She clearly wanted nothing more than for them to make a life together in the big city. But no matter how much he loved her, Jason couldn't do it. The place had nothing to offer him. He was a different person than the one who had grown up there. And Stevie had made it clear that a long distance relationship was not going to happen. Not after what she had experienced as a child.

But rather than going into all of that again he smiled and nodded at Oliver.

After a long evening of chatting and passing the football around, everyone was exhausted. Jason yawned and stretched.

'Come on, I'll show you to your room. You can borrow something of Olly's to sleep in if you like?' Hannah offered.

'Oh…thanks…just some pyjama bottoms will be fine.' He followed Hannah up to where he would be sleeping.

She showed him into a large room. 'Bathroom is through there. I took the liberty of putting some toiletries out for you, toothbrush, toothpaste, what have you. You should have whatever you need, but just ask if I missed anything. I'll be back in a sec with your PJs.'

Jason glanced around the room. It was nicely decorated and neither too feminine nor masculine. The walls were pale blue, and the bedding was a deeper blue with stripes. The furniture was a mahogany colour and fairly modern. The sleigh bed with its curved kickboard looked comfy and oh-so inviting, and the carpet was the kind that you could sink your feet into, letting the pile come up around your toes.

Hannah brought him the pyjama bottoms. 'Here you go, Jason. Sleep well.' She kissed his cheek, patted his arm, and left him to it, closing the door as she left.

After taking a soothing, hot shower, he climbed into bed. Reaching for his phone, he played the new voicemail back.

'*Hi Jason…it's me, Dorcas. That woman Stevie called. She*

sounded worried about you. And to be honest so am I. You are coming back, aren't you? It's just that...well...we...we miss you... I miss you and that Stevie apparently does too. I hope you're okay. Drop me a text if you don't feel like talking...and... take care, okay? Bye.'

Feeling a stab of guilt, he typed a text...

Hey Dee. All is fine. I'm still alive. Things are a little crazy, and I'm out of the country. Will be home in a few days, but have things I need to sort out, so may be away a little while longer. Will explain when I can. Thanks for doing such a great job. I owe you all, big time. See you soon

J x

He drifted off to sleep quickly and was soon in the midst of another dream about Stevie...

She stood before him on the riverbank beside his cabin. She wore a loose white cotton dress, and the hazy sunshine shone through it, causing her naked body underneath to be clearly visible. Her nipples protruded through the fabric, and he instantly wanted her. Suddenly, she was running away from him in slow motion, and her musical laughter filled the air as she ran. Her auburn hair floated behind her and fluttered across her face each time she looked over her shoulder towards him. It was reminiscent of one of the photos on his old pin board. He was trying to run faster to catch her, but he too was running in slow motion like a clip from a romantic movie.

A sense of panic took over him and he reached out, grabbed her arm, pulled her into his bare chest and immediately devoured her mouth with his own. They tumbled to the soft, mossy ground, and she wrapped her legs around him as the neckline of her dress slipped to reveal the creamy coloured flesh of a perfect breast. He took her nipple into his mouth and savoured it, loving how she arched and moaned beneath him. He fumbled to free his arousal so that he could sink inside of her, but suddenly she was free from his grasp and running again. This time she was crying as she ran. He tried to shout after her but no sound would come. He tried to climb to his feet, but he felt paralysed, rooted to the spot by his knees. Why was she crying? He reached out to her, but she had travelled too far. He could hear her calling his name. She was looking for him. 'I'm right here!' He wanted to shout. 'Come back!' But again the words wouldn't form in his mouth.

'Jason! Jason, no! Don't leave me!' she called.

He awoke with a start covered in sweat and breathing erratically. His heart pounded in his chest, and his mouth was dry. He sat up and reached over to a jug beside the bed. Removing the small glass resting over the top he filled it to the brim with water and downed it in one gulp. Slightly different from the dream he usually had where she was leaving him, this time she was searching for him. Why was it different this time? *What the hell does it all mean?*

CHAPTER SEVEN

Stevie clutched the phone to her ear, listening intently.

'And he said he's out of the country but has things to sort out.' Dorcas sounded as confused as Stevie felt at hearing this news.

'What did he mean he's out of the country? Out of the country *where*? Where the hell *is* he? And *why*?' *Unless that's where his illegitimate child and it's mother are living. Bitch.*

Dorcas sighed. 'Search me. Is he on holiday? Is he visiting friends? Who knows? I sure as hell don't.'

'Did...did he mention me at all?' Stevie asked hopefully.

Dorcas paused before replying. 'I'm so sorry, Stevie, but even though I mentioned you in my voicemail, he didn't mention you in his text.'

Her heart sank. 'Oh...right...I see. And he hinted that he'd be back with you soon?'

'Yes.'

'Okay, thanks. I think I'm getting the message loud and clear...for the *second* time. Thanks, Dorcas.'

'Hey, I'll let you know if I hear anything else.'

'No, it's okay. I need to move on now. You don't need to give me any more updates. I think he's made things quite clear, don't you?' Stevie's voice wavered and her heart ached.

Dorcas didn't reply straight away. 'Okay. If you're sure. I mean, I don't know...I mean...I have no idea what's going on or what he's thinking. But I'll leave you to it. If you want to know anything, just call. If I have news, I'll share it. B-bye then.'

'Thanks, Dorcas. Bye.'

Stevie hung up the call as the tears began to flow. She cried for a solid twenty minutes until she felt that she must have no tears left. Once she had calmed down, she called Dillon and told him that she still had no news. He had also heard nothing.

'Shall I come round? I could bring some beers...or...or wine maybe? You sound like you could use the company.' Dillon sounded hopeful.

'Sure, why not. Although I'm not sure I'll be very good company.'

'It's okay. We don't need to talk. It's sometimes good to just...*be* with someone.'

'Very true, Dillon. Very true.'

Thirty minutes later, Stevie opened her front door to Dillon. He stood there in his fitted black T-shirt and low-slung jeans. His mousey brown hair styled in its trendy crop. He was a handsome man, tanned and well toned with the same dark chocolate brown eyes as Jason.

He held out a small bouquet of roses. 'Hi...I got you these... Thought you might need cheering up.'

Feeling the sting of tears again, she cleared her throat. 'Oh, you're so sweet. Come on in.'

Once inside, the two friends chatted and made small talk whilst drinking the wine that Dillon had brought. Once that bottle was polished off, Stevie opened a second.

The wine was starting to have the desired numbing effect. 'I don't get it, Dillon. Why would he just disappear *again*? He promised there would be no more running.'

'I know. I know. I'm guessing he had good reason. Judging by the last time it happened, it seems that he does this over major stuff.'

'I can't keep going through it, though. My heart won't take it.' She rubbed at her sore eyes.

He sat beside her and slipped his arm around her shoulders. 'Hey...hey come on.'

She glanced up at his understanding expression. 'I can't keep letting him in only to be let down. I've lost him, and I need to deal with it and move on. Don't you think?'

Leaning forward, he kissed her forehead lightly. 'I think it may be best. I hate to see you like this.' His words slurred a little as he rested his forehead on hers. Spending time with him felt familiar and comfortable. Her head spun a little as she looked into his eyes. He rubbed his nose along hers, and his hand slid from her shoulder up into her hair. 'You should be happy. You deserve to be happy. You should be with someone who loves you and *stays* regardless of the shit they're going through.' His jaw clenched as his eyes remained fixed on hers. 'I could be that person, Stevie. If you'd let me.'

Confusion and alcohol fogged Stevie's mind, and she thought perhaps she'd misheard. 'I'm sorry. What?'

He pulled away and looked at her mouth longingly. Before she could protest, he pressed his mouth against hers. His lips were soft, but unfamiliar and wrong. He flicked his tongue out trying to coax her to open for him. She froze. *Shiiit!*

Suddenly she felt *very* sober.

He stopped and stood quickly, opening and closing his mouth as if searching for the right words to save the crazy situation he had placed them in. Pacing around the room, he glared at her with panic in his eyes. 'Oh fuck...I'm an idiot...a fucking idiot. How to misread signals in one easy step.' He laughed derisively at himself, ran his hands through his hair, and then covered his face. 'Stevie, please forgive me. That was stupid. So, so stupid.'

She stood to grab his arm and stop him. 'Hey, will you please *stop* for a second?'

He did as she requested and finally made eye contact. His face was flushed and his breathing ragged.

'Dillon...I *do* love you but only as a brother. I'm so sorry. I'm not looking for a Jason replacement. All I want is... I want to stop hurting. Please don't be upset.'

'No, no I'm sorry. It was a stupid thing to do. I can't believe I did it. Can we...can we put it down to the alcohol?'

She smiled. 'Of course. Wine will do strange things to a person.'

He snorted. 'Yeah but that was *way* beyond strange.'

She held up her hands. 'It's forgotten.'

'Thank you. God, if Jason knew, he'd *kill* me.'

'He won't find out, and he's not my keeper. He has no claim over me. But I don't see you that way.'

'No, I know. If I'm honest, and I may as well be, I've had a crush on you for years.' He flushed again as he made the admission. 'I always dreamed that one day you'd realise you were in love with *me* instead of my idiot of a brother, but I know it's stupid. And fuck, I did *not* need to tell you that.' He shook his head as his cheeks coloured an even brighter red.

She touched his cheek. 'I think it's sweet. And I don't want you to feel awkward around me.'

'No...no... But I think I need to go. Maybe I need to look after my bruised ego for a few days. Don't be upset if you don't hear from me, okay?'

Stevie's heart ached at his words. 'Dillon, please, it's fine.'

He grabbed his coat and walked to the door. 'Take care, okay? I'll call if I hear anything. Please do the same.'

'I will, but I'm not holding my breath.' She hugged him, but he stiffened as she did, and so with a little sadness, she released him and smiled. 'We're okay, aren't we, Dillon?' But he smiled weakly and stepped out of the front door. She watched as he walked off up the road without looking back.

Jason had been staying with his new family for almost a month, a lot longer than he had originally intended. His employees were being so understanding and were doing a great job of handling the corporate events during the latter part of the school summer holidays. He had texted Dorcas every so often but never mentioned where he was or why he had run. He hadn't contacted Dillon or Stevie, and the longer he left it, the harder it became to contemplate them forgiving him for his actions again.

Josh had taken him for a walk, and they had ended up on the shore of the nearby lake drinking soda and bonding.

'So how are you coping with all of this...with me?' Jason asked as he looked out over the water, watching the sunlight dance on the surface.

'It's kind of strange...having a big brother. I've always been the big brother, you know?'

'Yeah, I'm sorry, Josh. I guess I've mucked your life up in a pretty big way, eh?'

'No, Jason. No you haven't. I didn't mean that at all. Please don't feel that way. I think it's cool actually. Now I have someone to look up to.'

He laughed. 'You have your dad for that, don't you?'

'Yeah, and he's great and all, but he's an *old* guy. You're... you know, more my age. I think it'll be cool to talk things through with you...if I need to. You know about girls and shit.'

'Girls and shit, eh? So is there a girl in your life?'

'Yeah, there is.' Josh blushed.

Jason nudged him. 'Yeah? Come on then, little bro. Spill.'

'Weeeell. She's called Cassie. She's beautiful. Long dark hair and bright blue eyes. She's in a few of my classes in college. We spend every possible minute together when we're not in school. I think...I think she's the one.'

Jason smirked, thinking how Josh sounded like he had when he'd been with Stevie as a teenager. Josh was twenty and seemed like a really switched-on guy. 'So when you said you'd want to talk things through about girls and shit, you meant *one* girl, eh?'

Josh smirked and nodded. 'Yeah, pretty much.'

'I'll make you a deal. You call me before you make any major decisions, okay? And I'll do the big brother thing and share my words of wisdom.'

Josh nodded enthusiastically. 'Deal.' They shook hands.

It was the day before he was due to fly home. Jason finished off the last of the homemade pancakes whilst Hannah sat opposite him drinking coffee. The boys had gone fishing with friends, and Oliver had been called into the hospital to help with an emergency. It felt good to chat to Hannah. She was an excellent listener, and he desperately wanted a female perspective on the whole ridiculous situation he found himself in.

Once he had stopped telling his side of the story, he waited whilst she pondered his words for a few moments.

Eventually she looked him in the eye. 'Dillon may struggle to come to terms with what you have to tell him, but he'll need you so much. If he knows that you're still there for him, to support him, then he *will* get through it. You'll have to be patient. I can imagine he'll be very angry, and you must be prepared for some backlash. Partly because he's about to discover he's been living a lie his whole life, and partly...and please don't take this the wrong way...but he may be angry with you for leaving before you told him.'

She took a deep breath, and Jason's heart sank when he realised she was correct. There was going to be blame flying around again. 'And as for Stevie, if you love her, you need to try one last time to make things work. But if things are beyond that and you truly believe that they are, then you have to decide what's right for *you*. You can't base your most important life's decisions on what someone *else* wants if it will make *you* unhappy.'

He shook his head. 'I really do think it's over this time. There's no way she'll forgive me for running again.'

'But you haven't given her a chance. You haven't even spoken to her about these recent events. It may completely change things. You can't possibly know what her reaction will be. You can *guess* but where's the good in that?'

'I know. I don't have a clue what to say to her though.'

She patted his arm. 'Start with 'I'm sorry for running away, Stevie' and then tell her why you did it.'

'Yeah, I should, shouldn't I?' He nodded his head, feeling firmly resolved to at least *try* to make amends. 'I think that when I land tomorrow I need to go straight around to her house. I think I'm hoping for too much but...you never know.'

The day Jason had been dreading arrived too quickly. They headed for the airport and sat in contemplative silence. Once they arrived, they walked through the terminal, and Jason checked in for his flight. So many thoughts were going through his mind. Fear of going back, excitement at the same thing, sadness at leaving, plus what felt like a million other emotions all vying for the surface. The anticipation of what awaited him back in the UK filled him with dread, whilst leaving his new family made his heart ache.

The goodbyes at the airport were emotional. Oliver clung to his newfound son, and Jason clung back just as fiercely. Regardless of the short amount of time they had been aware of each other, the bond was made and it was getting stronger.

'You call me as soon as you land, son. And make sure to come back soon, okay?' The older man seemed to be struggling to keep his voice on a level.

Jason nodded, unable to do much else. Next he stepped before Hannah. 'Thank you, Hannah. And I mean for *everything*. You've made me feel like I actually belong with you all. I can't tell you how wonderful that feels.'

She touched his cheek affectionately. 'That's because you *do*.' She hugged him, and he kissed her cheek.

Next Josh and Elliot pulled him into a group hug. 'Make you sure you email plenty, okay?' Josh insisted.

Jason managed a smile. 'I will. And make sure you take care of yourselves and each other. I haven't known you for long, but we're brothers, so if you need anything you pick up the phone or email or whatever, okay?'

Elliot slapped him on the back. 'Yeah, and someday soon we're gonna come over and stay at your camp, man. It sounds awesome. In fact, I've been saying to Mom and Dad that I think I'd like to spend a year in Scotland when I'm done with college.'

'You'd be more than welcome, buddy. You could come and work for me.' Jason liked that idea but wondered if maybe it was too soon to suggest such a massive step.

'Whoa, that'd be cool, bro.' Elliot's face lit up with a wide grin. Clearly, he had no misgivings about the prospect.

Once Jason had hugged his brothers tightly again, he slowly walked towards the gate as the final call for his flight to Heathrow came over the loudspeaker. Oliver put his arms around his remaining family, pulling them close.

Suddenly, with a heart beating like a locomotive engine, Jason stopped and turned around. 'Ol...Oliver...' he called.

Oliver stepped away from his family and jogged towards him with a frown. 'Yes, Jason? What is it, son?'

'I wanted to say...it's been so good meeting you. You've been so understanding and kind. You *all* have. I'm very much aware that things could've gone a lot differently for me here and you made this all so easy. I still can't quite get my head around how easy this has all been. I'm so grateful. I can't really express what I want to say...except to say...thanks...*Dad*.'

Oliver's lip trembled as he pulled Jason into another hug and shuddered in his arms as he sobbed into his shoulder. 'You've made my day, Jason. Thank you.' He held his face in his hands, tilted his head forward, and planted a kiss on his forehead. 'Thank you, son.'

Jason's eyes clouded over and his throat tightened, rendering further words completely impossible. He smiled, turned, and walked through the gate.

Stevie sat in the pub opposite David, drinking Jack Daniels and wondering what the hell she was doing there. She wore her best jeans and a plain black, scoop-necked T-shirt. Her intention was *not* to be noticed.

David, her work colleague, had talked pretty much none stop since they arrived, and Stevie was feeling comfortably numb as she listened to him waffle on about whatever. Well, she wasn't *really* listening.

'I must admit, Stevie, I was surprised when you called. I'm glad you did though. And I know I've said it about twenty times tonight, but you really do look gorgeous.'

Stevie glanced down at her plain attire and forced a smile. 'Thanks, David. But I'm not intending to lead you on in any way. This,' she said as she gestured between them, 'is purely platonic. I needed some company, and I had to get out of the house. And typically everyone seems to be on holiday with the love of their lives.' Her thoughts skipped to Mollie and her latest man.

David frowned. 'I know...I know. A guy can hope though, eh?' He leaned across the table to make himself heard now that the pub was getting busier. 'So you're telling me he up and left again?'

Stevie took a large gulp of the amber liquid in her glass. 'Yep, not a word from him for a month. I'm done. No more.' She shook her head and made a swiping motion with her hands, spilling a little of her drink as she did so.

To his credit, David did actually look pissed off on her behalf. 'Shit. Why would he *do* that again? I don't get it. What is the guy's problem?'

'Not a clue. At first I guessed something major like...I don't know...an illegitimate child just based on the reaction he had to the letter I found, but the more I think about it, the more I think he wouldn't have cheated on me back then. We *adored* each other. And we spent so much time together, plus he's a crap liar and I would've known something was up, so your guess is as good as mine.'

He shook his head. 'So what are you going to do if he comes back?'

Sadness washed over her as she stared into the bottom of her glass. 'I'll be his friend, but I'm done with the rest. I can't do it anymore. I can't stand thinking that he'll run every time there's a problem. And to be honest, it was going nowhere anyway. He'll be going back to Scotland eventually, and I'll be staying here. Long distance relationships don't work. It doesn't matter how much you love someone, resentment always rears its ugly head, followed by suspicion and jealousy, or worse than that, boredom. That's not how I want to live my life.'

David placed his hand on hers. 'If ever you need a friend or if ever you feel like dating again, I'm here.' He smiled and squeezed gently.

She smiled back but pulled her hand away, knowing that it wasn't going to happen between them. She liked him, despite his arrogance and the fact that he acted older than his years. But it wasn't a romantic connection. Never would be. She refused to lead him on.

A while later, Stevie arrived home by cab, escorted by David. He had insisted on taking her home even though it was quite out of his way. It was around midnight. Through her blurred Jack Daniels induced alco-vision, she thought she could see a figure sitting on her doorstep. She rubbed her eyes and looked again, but the figure appeared to still be there.

David leaned forward. 'Shit. Is that who I think it is?' he asked as he paid the cab driver.

'Depends who you think it is,' Stevie slurred with a giggle.

He squinted his eyes in the darkness. 'I think... I think it's Jason Reynolds.'

She stopped in her tracks as the realisation hit and his words sank in. 'Then you would appear to be right,' she said almost disbelieving it her herself.

David huffed. 'Awww, crap. I suppose I'll be going home then?'

Without taking her eyes off Jason, she replied, 'I think perhaps it's best. Sorry, David.'

Despite the amount of alcohol she had imbibed, and it had been a lot, Stevie suddenly felt *very* sober.

'If he gives you trouble, you just call me!' David shouted loud enough for the whole street to hear before he closed the cab door, mumbling to himself about stupid exes turning up unannounced. The cab pulled away down the street and disappeared into the night as she slowly concentrated on putting one foot in front of the other and shakily walked towards Jason.

He stood, looking sheepish as she approached. 'Hi...I...I have some explaining to do. Can I come in?'

She sighed heavily. 'You can come in for ten minutes, and then that's it. I'll be your friend, but other than that, it's best if we... I'm not going there with you again. I'm sure you can understand.'

Jason dropped his gaze to his boots. 'Yeah, I understand.'

She unlocked her front door with remarkable ease considering an attack of nervous energy and the level of alcohol in her bloodstream. Jason followed her inside.

Throwing her bag onto the sofa, she turned to him, suddenly feeling incensed. 'You leave for over a month, you don't contact me *at all* during that time, I receive *no* explanation, and then you turn up here? I should kick you out, Jason. I should tell you to fuck off out of my life!' Tears stung at her eyes, and her chest heaved as she pointed to the door.

He held up his hands as he walked towards her. 'Please, let me explain to you now... Things have been crazy... I didn't know what the hell to do.'

'So you thought, 'I know, I'll fuck off and leave everyone wondering...AGAIN!' Is that it?'

He stepped towards her again. 'No, that's not it at all. I swear, Stevie.'

She jabbed her finger at him aggressively. 'Don't come any fucking closer, Jason. I don't want you anymore. I'm not forgiving you again. Please *leave*. I can't do this now. Please just go.' Tears of anger over spilled from her eyes as she stared at him, hating him for making her swear.

Jason took the final step to close the remaining gap between them and gripped her arms. 'You don't mean that.' His brow was furrowed, as he fixed his penetrating gaze on her. The pain she saw there was mirrored in the soul deep ache inside of her.

She turned away, feeling far too vulnerable under his scrutiny. 'Yes...yes I do. Please just go and leave me alone. I'm not some toy you can pick up and put down whenever the fuck you please.' When his grip on her tightened, she turned back to glare at him. 'I said GO!' Still he didn't release her, and so she pounded at his chest with her fists. 'You can't keep doing this! You can't keep leaving and then expecting me to just be fine when you choose to come back! It's not fair! It's cruel!'

He backed her up against the wall and pressed into her so that she could no longer hit him. 'I can explain if you'll stop swearing, shouting, and hitting me, and just for once listen!' His chest heaved and brushed hers as his hot breath made her face tingle. She suddenly became hyper aware of every inch of his hard body pressed up against hers. He wanted her. Still.

'Jason...please...just leave.' Her voice was calmer this time, but her eyes focussed on his mouth. As if taking the look as an invitation, he crushed his lips into hers. At first she resisted his aggressive kiss, pushing at his chest with her own and bracing against his grip, but after only a few seconds, she opened her mouth to allow access to his tongue. His hands that were pinning her arms to the wall, relaxed, and he slid one around to cup her bottom as the other fisted in her hair. She kissed him back with anger and ferocity. The anger aimed at herself for her weakness where he was concerned. She could taste the salt water of her own tears in the kiss.

Her hands grasped at his jacket, pulling him closer until he lifted her legs so that she could wrap them around him. The hard ridge of his arousal pressed at her sensitive place and she was ready to rip at the clothing that caused a barrier between them, but instead she pulled her mouth away. 'Jason, stop. I can't keep doing this. I keep letting you into my heart and I can't do that anymore. You're breaking me. I need to defend myself and my heart against you.' More hot tears trailed slowly down her already damp face.

His brow creased, and he closed his eyes for a second as he clenched his jaw. When he opened his eyes again he shook his head and the sadness evident in his eyes was almost palpable. Lifting a shaking hand he stroked his thumb across the apple of her cheek. 'Stevie, I belong in your heart and you know it. Just like you belong in mine. Don't keep me out...*please*.'

'But we keep going round and round in circles. This is a lose-lose situation. Nothing ever changes. No conclusions are ever reached.' She turned her face away.

'There's only *one* conclusion *to* reach. We belong

together. That's it. I love you and I know I messed up, but we *do* belong together. We *need* each other. *I* need *you*, Stevie. I belong in here.' He covered her heart with his palm as he spoke through gritted teeth. His desperate words brought her attention back to his eyes. His desperation was evident there too.

She came to her senses. 'No...no...I need to breathe. I need some space. It's too much. Please...please leave. I can't do this right now. I've been drinking and my head is messed up.'

He placed her down and cupped her cheek, rubbing his thumb to catch a stray tear. Then, appearing resigned, he turned and walked towards the door. 'I'm staying in the same place as last time. When you're ready to listen to me, please come over. So much has happened, Stevie. I need to tell you about it all, and I *am* sorry for how badly I handled all of this... again. I guess I need to learn how to deal with my emotions better. I...I hope you'll help me.' He opened the door and left.

Stevie collapsed to the floor with an aching heart, placed her head in her hands, and began to sob.

CHAPTER EIGHT

*W*hen Stevie awoke the next morning her head pounded as if her brain was trying to escape her skull by the use of a pickaxe. She staggered to the bathroom as a wave of nausea washed over her. After retching over the toilet a few times, she sat on the side of the bath, reached to turn on the shower, and tried to gather herself. The room filled with steam as she stripped out of her underwear and eased herself inside. Hot water battered her aching muscles, and she finally began to relax. As the tension ebbed away, so too did her headache. Once she was washed and feeling a little more human again, she dried her skin and dressed in a long red and white summer skirt and white tank top.

Coffee...coffee is what I need.

She tramped down to the kitchen and set a pot of the magic elixir brewing whilst she ate a plain, dry croissant in the hope it would settle her stomach. She knew that she had to see Jason today, and the thought of that made her stomach lurch yet again. She gulped down her coffee and grabbed her car keys. *Best just to get it out of the way. Rip off that Band-Aid, Stevie.*

She drove across town, taking the short cuts that would help her avoid the busiest areas of London and pulled up outside the Sure Stay hotel at ten o'clock. Making her way through a large group of tourists, she finally reached the harassed looking receptionist. 'Excuse me, could you tell me which room a Mr. Jason Reynolds is staying in, please?'

'Certainly. I'll need to ring and announce that you're here. What name shall I say is visiting, please?'

Stevie's nostrils flared and she breathed in a deep, annoyed breath. This hadn't been the case last time she had come to see him here. Gritting her teeth, she said, 'Tell him it's Stevie.'

The heavily made up woman frowned at her. 'S*tevie*?' The word was spoken as if it tasted bad, and she had to bite back a nasty retort.

Instead she rolled her eyes and sighed heavily. 'That's what I said, yes.'

The receptionist dialled Jason's room and announced her arrival. She cleared her throat and addressed Stevie again. 'He asked would you prefer that he meet you down in the bar or would you like to go up?'

'Tell him I'll go up.' After the receptionist relayed the message and Stevie acquired the room number, she made her way to the elevator and pressed the button for the fifth floor. Once the doors opened, she walked down the long corridor and with every step wondered what awaited her once she arrived at Jason's room. Her deep breath did little to calm her jangling nerves as she plucked up the courage to finally knock.

As if Jason had been waiting and watching her through the spy hole, the door opened immediately, and he pulled her into his arms before she could protest. Being pressed against his hard chest didn't help her resolve at all, and she struggled to break free. He held her at arms-length, his lips in a hard line.

Closing her eyes, she whispered, 'Please let go of me, Jason.' He stepped back and freed her from his grip. He appeared to be tired but so, so handsome. His long, shaggy hair was loose around his shoulders, and his tight white T-shirt showcased the sculpted body beneath. She swallowed hard wishing that she didn't desire him quite so much. Things would be far less complicated if she didn't.

He walked over to the bed and sat, leaning his elbows on his knees and his head in his hands. 'You're not going to believe what's happened, Stevie.' His voice was croaky as he spoke. He looked up to where she stood frozen near the door-way. 'Come and sit down, please?'

Recovering the use of her legs, she reluctantly walked over to a chair in front of the desk in the corner. Avoiding being near him was the best idea, but he clearly didn't like it as he came and crouched before her.

He rested one arm on her thigh and tilted her chin so that they made eye contact. 'You're avoiding touching me. You can't even seem to look at me.'

She snorted. 'What do you expect? Just tell me what you have to say, and then I can go.'

His eyes saddened. 'Yesterday, you said you'd be my friend. Today, you don't seem to even want that.'

'I'm still hurting, Jason. To be abandoned once is bad enough. But for it to happen again... I don't know what you expect me to do or how you expect me to react.'

'The letter you found at my mum's house...it contained some...pretty life changing information.'

Before she could think she blurted, 'You have a child with someone else, don't you?'

Jason's face scrunched in disgust and he stood. 'What? No! How the hell did you come to *that* conclusion?'

'That photo with the letter I found at your mum and dad's…I saw it. It was of you with another woman. She seemed familiar, but I haven't quite figured out where I knew her from. She wasn't at our school. But you clearly had an affair, and your mum was telling you the girl had your child, wasn't she?' Her fists clenched along with her jaw, and her stomach roiled as the words fell from her lips.

A smile spread across Jason's face. 'Oh, I get it. I get why you're so touchy.' He crouched before her again. 'The man in the photo wasn't me. And the woman seemed familiar because it was my mum.'

Stevie was finding it hard to get her head around what he was saying. 'So who was the man? He looked like you did when you left ten years ago.'

'I know. Uncanny resemblance, isn't it? The man in the photo was my dad.'

She folded her arms over her chest in a defensive gesture as anger surfaced again. 'Erm…no, Jason. I *know* your dad, and that man was nothing like him. Even *I'm* not that gullible.'

'Stevie, he was my *real* dad. My *birth* dad. My mum was pregnant with the child of her first love when she met my… when she met Mick. He knew she was pregnant but asked her to marry him and said he would look after both Mum and me. But things didn't go smoothly for them.'

Her stomach plummeted. 'What? I don't understand.'

'There were terrible complications at the birth which rendered my mum infertile. She almost died too.'

With a spinning mind, she tried to understand what he was telling her. 'Hang on…hang on. You're making this up.

This is just lies, Jason. It doesn't make sense. It's too...too dramatic and unrealistic.' She scrunched her brow and shook her head. 'How the hell do you expect me to believe your mum was infertile after you when she had Dillon?'

'Listen, Stevie, that's what I'm getting to. Mick had wanted children of his own, but thanks to me being born and my mum ending up infertile, he couldn't have that. They adopted Dillon a couple of years later, but he blamed *me* for the fact that he was left unable to father his own children with Mum.'

Her jaw dropped, and she struggled to find the right words. 'Oh my God. Dillon is adopted? And Mick wanted... and that's why—'

'Yes, that's why he resented me so much. Everything fell into place once I knew. But as you can imagine my brain went into complete meltdown. I couldn't get my head around any of it. I know I handled things badly, but please try to understand what reading all of that did to me.'

She nodded, still reeling from the news. She couldn't speak for a few minutes as the new information whirred around her head. After a silence, she asked, 'So what happened after you left the house? Where did you go?'

He exhaled noisily. 'I went to try to clear my head and re-read my letter. And then I went to see someone mentioned in the letter, a lady named Delia. Stevie, she's my grandmother. I have a *living* grandmother.' His eyes were glassy as he spoke, and her heart clenched in her chest.

Her voice dropped to just above a whisper. 'Did she tell you where your father is?'

'She went one better than that. She gave me his address. I put Dorcas in charge for a while longer up at *Wild Front Here* and jumped on the next available flight to America. He actually lives in a little place called Sebago, in Maine, in the USA. I met him.'

She gasped as tears formed in her eyes. 'Was he aware of you all these years?'

'No. He had no idea I even existed, so you can imagine the shock when I turned up literally on his doorstep. But we talked, and I showed him the letter and photos. He was brilliant. I look just like him, and I have two more brothers, Josh and Elliot.' His enthusiasm and excitement were almost palpable. Yet again, she felt her heart melt once she heard his reasoning.

'Wow...you have a whole new family, Jason... that's...wonderful.'

'It really is. They just accepted me. I couldn't believe it. Any of it. I stayed with them for a few weeks and just needed to get my head straight on everything else.'

His apparent disregard for Dillon's place in the situation suddenly affronted her. 'And what about *Dillon* in all of this? He has a right to know, yet you didn't think for a minute that speaking to him would be a good idea?' She frowned. 'You jumped on a plane to sort your *own* life out? And you never thought that a simple text to me would be a good idea? I'm happy for you, Jason. I really am, but poor Dillon. What this will do to him...and to not tell *me*...after everything else.'

He seemed annoyed. His brow scrunched again, forming a line between them. 'I'm telling you *now*.'

'But why could you not tell me before you left? After everything we've been through since we reconnected... We were so close. You should've spoken to Dillon first, and then *I* should've been the next person you wanted to tell. It goes to show that you and I are not meant to be. As I said I'm happy for you, but I can't keep playing this guessing game. And as we both know, eventually we'll both have to get back to our respective lives. I think it's best that we keep things platonic from now. It's the right thing for both of us. I'm sure of that.'

Jason closed his eyes, and his head dropped back, opening them again to stare at the ceiling. 'I knew I'd ruined things. I knew it and I was told to do things differently but of course I didn't listen.'

Her voice dropped to a whisper, and she shook her head sadly. 'Jason, it would make no difference, would it? We're going to end up hurt even more if we continue as we are.'

He lowered his gaze and locked eyes with her. 'I think if I'd have known that making love to you in my old room was the last time, I would've held you close for longer.' With deep sadness in his eyes, he touched her cheek again tenderly. 'I would've made the most of it. To know that I won't get to do that again...' His voice was a mere whisper as he spoke. He shook his head and didn't finish.

A shiver travelled the length of her spine, but she stood to create the distance she desperately needed. 'It's not all about sex, Jason. It's about *trust* too. And having a relationship based on trust is very important to me.'

He frowned at her words and stood to face her. His eyes darkened, and his expression told her she had angered him with her accusative words. 'I know it's not *all* about sex, Stevie. I happen to *love* you, and sex is a way of expressing the feelings that I have. I'm...I'm not great with words...but...but I can *show* you how I feel.'

She shook her head. 'It's too late for that. We can't keep going round in circles like this. I'm dizzy from the ride. It's time to stop.' She inhaled deeply as if doing so would give her the courage she needed to leave. 'I'm going to leave now. We'll meet for coffee next week if you like.' She attempted a bright voice. 'And...please...contact Dillon. He's been worried sick, and you have a world of pain to help him through from now on.' She leaned to kiss his cheek and hesitated there longer than she should have, inhaling his scent and committing it to memory. Thankfully, he didn't move to kiss her lips. If he had, she would've given in, and they'd be right back to square one. Instead she left the hotel with a heavy heart, and tears relentlessly streaming down her face.

CHAPTER NINE

*W*atching her leave and letting it happen were hard things to endure. He fought with the urge to grab her and throw her on to the bed, to show her how much he loved her and how he regretted his actions. But once again, she had stated her case clearly. What good would it do to try to force the issue?

Picking up his phone, he dialled Dillon's number. The call was answered after two rings. 'Jason? Where the hell have you been?'

'Hi, Dill. I'm...I'm so sorry for disappearing like that. I know I've messed up again.'

'I'm guessing you had good reason. But I want to know what that reason is, Jason. You've messed with Stevie's head again. She's been in such a state.'

'I know...I know. She was here at the hotel with me—'

'Awww shit, Jace, you didn't?'

'Not that it's any of your business, but no. I didn't fuck her, okay?'

'Is there any reason to be so blunt and crude about it, mate? She fucking loves you, you idiot.'

'Yeah? I don't necessarily agree with you there. Anyway, I didn't call to talk about her. I called to say I need to see you as soon as possible. I have things to tell you. Difficult things.'

'Oh fuck. The last time you said that I didn't like what I heard.'

'Yeah, I know. And I'm afraid it won't be much better this time, mate.'

Dillon clutched the letter that had been mentioned in the one addressed to Jason from their mother. They had gone together and collected it from the solicitor. He stared at the floor as silent tears left glistening trails in their wake. Jason sat opposite him in the armchair by the window that looked out over the rooftops of the nearby houses. Dillon's top floor flat was spacious and very pleasant. It was part of a conversion of a large Victorian town house and he had told Jason how he had been very lucky to buy it when prices were reasonably low for London. He had lived there since starting his training as a Financial Advisor with the well-known and highly respected bank that he still worked for.

Jason's news had understandably floored Dillon. The letter from his mum had explained and filled in the gaps that Jason couldn't. But Dillon appeared to be stunned. His pallid features were a blank mask.

After a while, Jason cleared his throat. 'Are you all right, little bro?'

'What?' He wiped his eyes as if realising Jason was there. 'Oh...sorry...yeah, yeah just...you can't call me that anymore, can you?'

Jason pulled his brows into a deep frown. 'Eh? What do you mean?'

Dillon snorted. 'I've been replaced in my position of *little bro* thanks to...what's-his-name and the other one. Both younger than you...both now your *little bros*.'

'Elliot and Josh? Nah, *you'll* always be my little bro. Look mate, you were there first, I grew up with you. It's—'

'For a few years, you did. Then you left, and I didn't see you for *ten years*. I probably know as much about you as *they* do. And who the fuck *am* I anyway? I know as much about *me* as I do about your new family.' He laughed without humour.

'Dillon, *nothing* has changed. I still consider you as my brother.'

Dillon grunted and curled his lip. 'That's big of you. Couldn't be arsed to set me straight before you went swanning off to meet *Daddy* though, eh?'

Jason closed his eyes as the words stabbed him. On opening them again, he was greeted by Dillon's pained expression. 'I had information overload. I'm truly sorry, but I had absolutely *no clue* where to even begin on this with you.'

Dillon stood and threw the letter at the floor. His voice came out in a strangled, angry growl. 'You don't have to be here *now* do you? We don't even share blood, so you can fuck off back to America or...or Scotland, and get on with your *new* life. At least *you've* got family. At least *you* know who the fuck you are!'

Jason stood too. 'I can assure you there is no favouritism here. I want you to meet them. They're my family, which makes them yours too.'

Dillon shook his head and smiled sadly. 'No, it doesn't. It in *no way* makes them *anything* to me. Just like *I'm* nothing to anybody else'

He appeared devastated, and Jason couldn't blame him. Guilt weighed heavy on his shoulders yet again. It was becoming his mantle, one he very much wished he could shrug off.

'Like I said, this changes *nothing*. You and I are *brothers*. End of.'

Dillon stooped, picked up the bottle from table, and took a long pull of his beer. He walked over to the other window.

Without looking at Jason, he said, 'It changes *everything*. You've now got a dad who actually cares about you. *And* he's still alive. You have brothers that actually *look* like you and want to get to know you. I don't fit in anywhere. I've *literally* got no one. I don't even know who I fucking am, Jason!' he shouted, turning and slamming his beer bottle down on the table.

Jason rubbed his eyes. 'I know it's a hell of a lot to take in, mate, but please don't be so down about it. We can look into who your parents are...if you want to. I can help you.'

He swung his head up to meet Jason's eyes. 'And how do you propose to do that? Are we going to chat about it over the Internet? Will we meet virtually in some fucking chat room?'

Jason walked over to his brother. 'Hey, we'll do whatever it takes, Dillon. Whatever. It. Takes.'

Dillon stared into space for a while. 'I get why you didn't come to dad's funeral. I honestly do. He was nothing to you. *And* he hurt you. But you say you care about me, and I would've liked you to have been there...for *me*.' He turned, and Jason saw the distinct sign of tears in his eyes. 'But now I know why you couldn't even do that. I mean it, Jace. I have *no one* now. You'll go back to Scotland and I'll be here. Mum's gone thanks to the guilt she felt her whole fucking life, and dad...well, *he* wasn't the person I thought he was anyway, and now to find out that I didn't belong to *either* of them...'

He ran his hands through his short mousy hair. 'I thought there was some...I don't know...legislation, or that at least they had a moral obligation or something saying that adoptive parents *had* to keep their kids informed these days. But instead I've lived in the midst of a fucking ginormous lie my whole life. And now that lie has blown up in my face, and the one fucking person I hated through it all...the one person I *could* blame...he's got a new life. A new family. And what have I got? Big fat fucking zero.'

His voice cracked with the weight of emotion it expressed. 'And to make matters so much worse, I want to still hate him, but I *don't*...and he doesn't deserve my hate. He actually deserves happiness and the good things that are happening to him now. And I have to be honest, I'm so fucking jealous right now that I want to jump of a sodding bridge.' Dillon crumpled to his knees as a sob broke free from the depths of his soul.

Jason moved beside him, cradling him in his arms in a split second, with mixed emotions knotting his insides. Anger, sorrow, regret, and the big one...*guilt.*

Speaking through his tightened throat, he said, 'Hey now, Dill, for what it's worth you've still got me...and you've got Stevie. I know I live a long way from here, but I'll see you whenever I can, and we can talk on the phone. Please, come on, I hate to see you like this.'

Dillon sniffed and wiped his eyes. 'Stevie? Yeah, I fucked that up good and proper.'

Jason pulled away. 'What do you mean?'

'Seeing as we're sharing, I may as well tell you...I kissed her. While you were away. I misread something she said, and I fucking *kissed* her.' He covered his face with his hands.

Jason felt winded. He blinked and shook his head to try and dislodge the mental image of his brother and Stevie locked in a passionate embrace. 'And...and what did *she* do?'

The distraught younger man shook his head. 'Don't worry. She didn't kiss me back. She said she sees me as a brother or something equally as bad. I've had a crush on her for years. The whole time you were missing I tried my best to get her to see me...I mean *really* see me...to see who I was and why I'd be good for her. I never actually told her how I felt. I hoped things would just happen. I thought with you gone she'd see me differently. And I don't feel fucking guilty for you. You fucked off *twice*. But I did come out of it feeling like a prize prick, and I haven't spoken to her since.'

Jason puffed his cheeks out and ran his hands over his head, unsure how to handle this latest piece of information.

Dillon glanced up. 'Are you going to punch me? I deserve it, don't I? I tried to steal your girl. And if she'd have been interested...I'll be honest...I wouldn't have hesitated.'

Jason pulled his lips into his mouth and closed his eyes. After a brief pause to gather his wits, he spoke. 'No, I'm not going to punch you, and she's *not* my girl.' He sat back on his haunches.

'What are you talking about? Of course, she's your fucking girl, you moron. She's never going to belong to anyone else as long as you're still breathing. I don't care how many hundred miles there are between you.' He sat on the floor. 'Jumping off that bridge is sounding pretty bloody appealing right now.'

Jason snapped. 'Stop it, okay? So you kissed her. I can't say I'm happy that you did it. And I can't say I'm comfortable knowing how you feel about her, but like I said, we're not a couple. She doesn't want me, and she's made that more than clear. So we're both prize pricks on that score. And no more talk of jumping off bridges, okay?'

'Argh...ignore me. I'm being stupid. I'll be fine. I'm sorry. It's a lot to take in admittedly, but I'll be okay. I'm sorry for shouting at you, and I'm sorry for kissing Stevie.'

Jason gripped his brother's face in his hands. 'Stop. Saying. Sorry. It's me who's sorry...for so much. For running...*twice*. For not telling you everything from the start. I've made so many stupid mistakes. I've got so much making up to do. And I will...if you'll let me, little brother.'

He smiled. 'Oy, I'm not that little anymore.'

Dillon drank a few more beers whilst Jason turned to coffee and regaled his younger brother with the details of the Halford family, their home, and the information about locating birth families for adopted children. Eventually, when Jason realised it was gone midnight and his brother had work the following morning, he called for a cab and bid his brother goodnight.

CHAPTER TEN

S tevie could hear a phone ringing, but it took a few moments before she realised it wasn't in her dream. She scrambled to her feet and fumbled for her cell phone. Glancing at the screen, she was surprised at what she saw. *Dillon?* He hadn't been in touch since the kiss incident, and she had left him to sort his head out, not wanting to force the issue. *But it's four in the morning. Why is he calling me so early?* Fear descended at the automatic assumption that something had happened to Jason.

She pressed to answer the call. 'Dillon?'

'Ish me...ish me...Dillon. I'm shorry I kished you, Stevie. I'm such a fucking prick. I ruined it all.'

She sighed. 'Dillon, are you drunk?'

'I am...I am a bit drunk. Jason was here...he told me... everything...that I'm not his brother...that I'm nobody.'

She gasped and clutched her chest. 'What? He said that?' Anger and bile rose in equal amounts.

'Not exactly...no...but...it's all the fucking same.' His words slurred together.

'No, Dillon. It's not like that, sweetie. Please, listen to me. Jason loves you. You're still his brother.'

A sob came over the airwaves. 'No...no...you're wrong. I'm nobody and I *have* nobody. My whole life has been a...a lie. What's the point of going on with it all, eh?' He seemed to be struggling to separate his words out and Stevie was trying to understand hard what he was saying.

Panic washed over her. 'Now, Dillon, you mustn't say things like that. Jason loves you. *I* love you. What happened with you and me was a misunderstanding. It's forgotten. We're fine. And Jason loves you to pieces. You must know that.'

He laughed dryly. 'Yeah? Why did he fuck off and leave me twice? Why did he leave *you* twice? You've got your mum, but I've got nobody. I can't stand it. I'm alone. I hate being so alone.'

'You are *not* alone. Listen to me. We *will* get through this. *You* will get through this. I'll help you. I will do whatever it takes, Dillon.'

He sobbed again, and her heart broke for him. 'I should've done something. It's my fault. I think I knew...I should've said something. It's all my fault Stevie...all mine. He would've stayed if it wasn't for me. I shouldn't be here anymore.'

Her heart began to race at his anguished words. 'What are you talking about, Dillon? You're scaring me.'

'No...no I won't say anymore. I'm shorry to scare you...and it's too late anyway.'

Dread weighed heavy in the pit of her stomach. 'What do you mean it's too late, Dillon? Why is it too late?'

Silence.

'Dillon! Why is it too late?'

She heard a thud. 'I'm tired...really tired. They're kicking in now...got to go.'

'Wait! What are kicking in? Talk to me, Dillon, please!' She could hear the desperation in her own voice. 'Dillon!'

He sighed heavily. 'I took some pills. I need to sleep now.'

'Oh God! How many pills did you take, Dillon?' She scrambled for her landline and dialled emergency services.

'A bottle...a bo...bottle of pillsss...so tired... Don't want to be alone anymore. Don't have anyone anymore.' His words were becoming quieter and more slurred. 'I can't be alone...so tired...got no one.'

There was a crash and the call ended.

'Emergency services, which service do you require?' A disembodied voice at the other end of the line dragged Stevie's attention away from her mobile phone.

She snapped back to reality. 'Oh God...ambulance... ambulance please. My friend...he's taken an overdose!'

The emergency services operator suggested that she should go to the house, try to gain access without risking injury, and sit with the casualty, and that the ambulance would be there as soon as possible.

Stevie pulled on her coat over her pyjamas, and even though Dillon lived within walking distance, she grabbed her car keys. Fumbling to get the key in the lock, she managed to start the engine and drive around to Dillon's home. The outside door was locked. She buzzed one of Dillon's neighbours who knew her and thankfully let her in. Taking the stairs two at a time, she reached his floor feeling ready to drop.

Trying the handle, she was relieved to find the door wasn't locked. She burst through, and much to her horror, Dillon was sprawled on the floor by his coffee table. Blood oozing from a cut to his head where he must have caught the table as he collapsed.

A sob escaped her as she went to him and dropped to her knees. 'Dillon...Dillon can you hear me?' Not daring to move him, she checked his airway, and seeing that it was clear, she checked him further for signs of life. It was very faint, but he was still breathing and his pulse was weak. 'Dillon, it's Stevie. The ambulance is on its way. Please hold on. Don't you dare leave me...don't you dare. She stroked his hair and patted his hand, rocking herself back and forth as warm tears trailed down her face.

'Jason will be so bloody pissed off at you for this stunt. How could you think you were alone? Eh? How could you blame yourself for any of this? *None* of this is your fault. None of it, Dillon...Dillon, sweetie, it's me, Stevie. Can you hear me?'

The buzzer sounded alerting her to the arrival of the paramedics. 'Come on up! Top floor. Please hurry!' A minute later, she heard the pounding of footsteps, and she pulled the door open to let them in.

'Please help him...please.' She sobbed as her hands covered her mouth. The paramedics quickly took over Dillon's care, working efficiently to ensure his safety.

Her heart broke as she watched them trying to revive him.

Jason was woken by the ringing of his phone. He rubbed his eyes and glanced over to read the display. It was almost six o'clock in the morning, and he was filled with hope when he saw that Stevie was calling.

'Hey Stevie. To what do I owe—'

'Jason, oh thank God. Are you still in London?'

He frowned at her urgent manner. 'Yes, of course. I wouldn't go without saying goodbye.' He cringed as the words fell from his lips.

'Really? *That's* what you're going to say?' Her tone was terse, and he couldn't blame her. 'We haven't got time for this.'

Concern rose within him at the sound of her voice. She was clearly upset and anxious. Her voice was wavering. Something wasn't right.

He sat up and swung his feet to the floor. 'Is everything all right, Stevie?'

'No...no, it isn't. Dillon's in hospital.'

Jason gasped and stood as his heart began to hammer at his ribcage. He began to grab the items of clothing he had discarded on the chair in the corner of the room the night before. 'What? Why? What happened?'

'*You* happened, Jason. I got a call from him a few hours ago. He sounded very drunk. He kept saying sorry. He said that you disappearing was entirely *his* fault and that if he'd have done something about it all that you would've still been here. He said he had nobody and he was alone. He said he'd taken a bottle of pills, and so I called an ambulance and went straight round.' Her voice broke with emotion. 'He was just lying there...on the floor unconscious... He'd taken an overdose.'

His heart plummeted in his chest. 'Oh God! Where is he? I'll be right there.'

She gave him the necessary details, and he scrambled to get his clothes on, falling in the process and banging his head on the opened bathroom cabinet door. Blood from the cut above his eye trickled down his face, but he grabbed some toilet paper and dabbed it, neither caring nor feeling the pain.

Climbing onto his bike, he rode at break-neck speed, desperate to get to the hospital, the same hospital that he had visited not so long ago when Mick had been dying. Random thoughts darted through his mind, but he did his best to concentrate on the road, trying to eradicate them. He abandoned his bike in the parking lot and ran through the entrance up to the intensive care unit.

Stevie greeted him in the hallway. 'Oh, Jason.' She clung to him, shaking.

'H-how is he?' Jason held her at arms-length, feeling his legs weaken as the adrenalin coursing through his veins began to subside and fear set in.

'He's stable. They won't let me back in at the moment. They're running tests. There was this beside the empty pill bottle. You'd...you'd better sit down before you read it.'

She handed him a scrunched up wad of paper. 'Awww, Dill.' Jason felt physical pain in his chest as he staggered over to a row of chairs and slumped down to read the tear stained writing scrawled, just legibly, across the torn page.

Jason and Stevie,

I'm so very sorry, but all of this is too much for me to handle. I can't cope with losing everything that I loved in one fell swoop. My mum is gone, and she was so sad for the last ten years. Dad is just some bastard who I obviously didn't know. And it turns out that I wasn't even their son. To find this out after all these years of living a lie is more than I can take. And now, Jason, you have this amazing new family.

I saw the bruises, Jason. I saw them a couple of times, and I did nothing. I was in some kind of childish denial. I think deep down I knew that he did it. I think I knew what he was doing, but I did nothing and so you left. If only I'd told someone. If only I'd reported it at school or something. Or even if I'd confronted you about it. Then you would have stayed, and you'd still be my brother. Instead you left and broke Stevie's heart and mum's. But it wasn't your fault. It was mine. So really it was me that broke their hearts. And I'm so sorry. More sorry than I can express.

And then I fucked up again and kissed Stevie. What an idiot! Another ruined relationship under my belt there.

Stevie, I should never have said those things to you about my feelings. It was stupid and pointless. And I think I hurt you too. Everything is so messed up, and I feel so alone. I need to get out. I can't cope with all of the mess that I made myself. All my doing.

I don't want to be alone. I felt lost before, but at least I had my memories. But now I know it was all a lie. My whole life. And I don't want to carry this guilt. So I'm sorry for doing this. I know they say it's the coward's way, but what choice do I have?

We used to be so happy as kids. We'd play footy in the garden or go to the park and sit on the swings for hours. You taught me to ride my bike. You were the best big brother back then. Then you left and I hated you. I hated me too. But please know, Jason, that even though I know now that we have no real connection by blood, I love you. I was angry with you for a time, but I've always loved you.

Dillon

Jason's silent tears dripped from the end of his chin and splattered onto his leathers. He pinched the bridge of his nose as if it would abate the falling moisture. Stevie squeezed his arm as she sat beside him.

His voice was weak, yet angry and wavering. 'It's not his fault, Stevie. How can he even think that? *I* did this...*all* of it. It should be *me* laying in this hospital not him.'

She gripped his arm harder, the pain made him flinch. 'Hey, you can stop that right now,' she growled through her gritted teeth. 'I won't listen to either of you saying things like that. This is all just a cry for help. Suicide attempts can be just that. He needs you to be there for him. So pack in feeling guilty and step up, Jason. No more running.' Her words stung even though she meant no harm.

A nurse came towards them. 'Ms. Norton?'

Stevie stood and gestured towards her companion. 'Yes, and this is Jason Reynolds, Dillon's older brother.'

'Hello, Mr. Reynolds. You may go and see him now. He's been treated for his overdose, so he's feeling very groggy. He's drifting in and out of consciousness. Please bear with him, but *do* talk to him...reassure him. He may be angry and upset when he realises that his attempt to end his life wasn't successful. And we'll need to have him assessed by a psychiatrist. Obviously, we can't have him leave here if he's still a danger to himself.'

Jason held his hand out and grasped the nurse's. 'Th-thank you so much for looking after him... If anything had happened—' His voice cracked, and he gulped past the lump in his throat.

Stevie touched his arm gentler this time. 'Hey, we're not going there, remember? He's going to be fine. Let's go and see him.' The nurse pointed them in the right direction, and they rushed down the long corridor towards Dillon's room.

CHAPTER ELEVEN

*D*illon was laid out on the bed, wearing a pale blue hospital gown. His lips had a strange blue/black tinge, and his eyes appeared sunken and dark. Jason walked over to the bed and gripped his brother's hand.

'Hey, little bro, gave us quite a scare, you did.' He tried to keep his voice light. 'You'll do anything to get out of work, you will.' He laughed but didn't quite feel the humour.

Dillon's eyes fluttered open. 'J...Jason? Am I...am I dead?' His voice was croaky and dry.

'No, mate. You're still with us. Can't get rid of us that easily.' He squeezed his brother's hand.

Dillon raised his hand to his eyes and pinched the bridge of his nose as tears escaped along with a guttural sob. 'Can't even fucking *die* properly.'

Jason bent towards his brother, put his arm around his head, and leaned into his ear. 'Hey, hey now. Come on. I for one am bloody *glad* you didn't manage it, thank you. I happen to fucking love you, all right? What would I have done, eh? How would I go on knowing you did this out of guilt for me?

You *daft sod*. None of this is your fault. Do you hear me? *None* of it. You were a kid when all that shit was going on, and I don't blame you one little bit. Do you hear what I'm saying? Not. One. Bit. Now I want you to get better and get out of this place, and then I'm going to kick your arse for scaring the shit out of me.'

He ruffled Dillon's hair. Dillon smiled a little and Jason's heart ached. He kissed his brother's pale forehead. 'When you *do* get out, me and you are going to sort Mick's will out, and then you're going to decide what you want to do. You'll have a decent inheritance, and I think that you could do whatever you like, whether that's searching for your birth parents or doing something you've always wanted. You could fulfil a fucking dream and make it all worthwhile. All that shit. Do it for me, eh? That one thing I will ask of you. I want you to be happy. Forget all the bull that's passed. Think about it, eh?'

Dillon nodded.

Stevie wiped her eyes and stepped forward. 'Hey, you. Thank you for calling me. I'm so glad you did. We both love you so very much and would've been so heartbroken if...well... thank you.' She leaned in and kissed his cheek.

Dillon smiled up at her. 'Stevie...I'm so—'

'No more apologies. They stop right now, okay?'

He nodded his acquiescence. 'Can I have a hug first and then some water please?' he croaked. She bent to hug him and more tears escaped his eyes as he clung to her.

Jason poured a cup of water and lifted his brother's head so that he could sip it.

'I'm so sorry for scaring you both. I felt like...I didn't know what else to do. I felt like I'd lost everything.'

'You haven't and you know that now. Onward and upward Dillon. You and me against the world, little bro.' He glanced over at Stevie. 'And Stevie can tag along in case we need a girl's opinion.' She stuck her tongue out at him, drawing a small laugh from the brothers.

Later that evening, Jason sat on Stevie's couch, nursing a glass of wine that she had thrust upon him in a bid to calm his evidently still ragged nerves. She had asked him to come back with her so that they could formulate a plan for Dillon's recovery. Having him near again was proving difficult. She wanted to comfort him as she always did when he was hurt. But she knew that she had to keep her distance. She sat on a chair at the opposite side of the room.

'What do you think we should do? I don't know if he'll cope if you go back to Scotland and he's left here by himself. What if it happens again?'

She rubbed her temples as unwelcome images of Dillon lying unconscious on the floor played in her mind like a horror movie. Seeing the pill container and the empty vodka bottle beside it had sent shivers down her spine. If she hadn't made the decision to go to him, he would be dead.

She shuddered.

'Hey, come here. You're shivering. Come on.' Jason patted the couch beside him.

Overwhelmed with myriad emotions, her resolve weakened. She gave in and went to him.

He pulled her into his side and nudged her head to rest on his shoulder. 'You did the right thing, and I'm so grateful, Stevie. Thank you. Going forward, we'll deal with whatever crops up together. I'm...I'm thinking of asking him to move to Scotland with me for a while.'

She sat bolt upright. 'What?'

'It makes sense. I think he needs me. Maybe he'll settle there. And he's good at what he does, so I could even help him set up in business for himself, if he wants that. He could get a wee place in Aviemore. He'd have new friends and a fresh start. I think it'd be good for him.'

She pulled away. 'But what about his job...and his friends here?'

'He doesn't have many. He worked such long hours that he used to socialise with the people from work. He told me that his last relationship ended sourly just before Mick died, and I think he'd be happier up there.'

She slammed her hand onto the seat beside her. 'Bloody hell, Jason! Scotland isn't a sodding cure all, you know. You can't expect *everyone* to bloody move up there because of you!' She felt her anger rise.

He frowned. 'Hey, why are you being so hostile about this? I'm trying to do what's right by my brother, seeing as I fucked up so monumentally in the past. You can't get pissy with me over that!' His scowl deepened.

She threw her hands up in exasperation. 'It seems to me that you think Scotland is some...magical bloody panacea that will resolve every issue, and you're wrong! Sometimes people have to face what's in front of them and bloody deal with it. Running away solves *nothing*.'

He moved to the edge of his seat. 'Maybe I should go. I'm not in the mood to argue tonight, okay? My brother is lying in hospital thanks to me, and I want to do the right thing by him for once. I thought you would understand that. But I don't want to argue with you.' Silence ensued for several minutes.

She sighed and closed her eyes. 'You don't have to go. I'm sorry. I just...I think it's been a hard day. Maybe we both need some sleep, eh?' She climbed off the sofa.

He reached for her hand, his hardened features softening a little. 'Thank you again for today. I owe you...so much.'

She stroked a finger down his cheek, regretting it immediately as the gesture was far too intimate. 'You owe me *nothing*, Jason. I'm just glad I was there.'

He kissed her hand and her skin tingled as he brushed his thumb over hers tenderly. He gazed up at her with such longing that her breath caught in her throat. He didn't need to say a word, and all she wanted to do was to take him to her bed and make love to him. Take his pain away in the only way she could think of right then.

But she couldn't.

Instead she smiled and walked away.

Jason followed her upstairs a few minutes later, went into the guest room, and closed the door. He stripped out of his clothes and lay down on the bed, gazing up at the ceiling. What he wouldn't give to be able to go back in time. Not just for this latest situation but for the last ten years to be re-lived. He would do so many things differently.

Stevie clearly hated the thought of him taking Dillon to Scotland, but deep down he knew it was the best thing. His brother would need to be watched. He'd need counselling and after care. There was no way he could risk this happening again. If it did, he knew that he would follow close behind, eaten up by the guilt of everything he'd done.

As he lay there, he realised he was in the same situation he had been in before. Stevie was so close by but not close enough. He sat up and stared at the door when he heard the floorboards outside his room creak. As quietly as he could, he stood and walked to the door, opening it a tiny crack and peeping out. She stood there in one of his old T-shirts that just about covered her modesty. Her fists were clenched and her eyes too. She was toying with the idea of coming to him. He could just tell. And God did she look sexy. Her hair was shaggy and hanging down her back. Her nipples were peaked under the T-shirt. He immediately felt aroused as he watched her.

As he pulled the door open wider, he remembered that he was butt naked, but realised it too late when she opened her eyes and raked them down his body. Her gaze filled with hunger. She licked her lips and began to walk towards him. He closed his eyes and bit down on the inside of his cheek to make sure this wasn't another of his cruel erotic dreams. But feeling her hands smoothing the skin over his chest and tracing the tattoos there with her fingertips, he opened his eyes again as she bent to kiss him over his heart.

'I thought…I thought you didn't want this…that you didn't want me anymore.'

'Jason, I've had a shitty day. I don't want to think. I don't want to play the consequences of my actions over and over in my head right now. I just want to feel. If you don't want this, then I can turn around and go back to my room.'

'You can turn around and go back to your room,' he said as he stared down at her. Her cheeks coloured, and she dropped her gaze. 'But I'm coming with you.'

Her eyes sprang up to meet his, and she opened and closed her mouth. 'Oh…I…erm.' She pursed her lips. 'You're such a shit sometimes.'

One side of his mouth quirked. 'I love it when you talk dirty,' he purred as she turned and he followed her to her room.

Once inside, she stripped her T-shirt over her head and

stood there naked before him. He suddenly felt a pang of conscience. 'Are you sure about this? Won't it complicate things? I mean what happens tomorrow?'

'I want sex. And I want it with you. So please shut the fuck up and take me before I think this through.'

Needing no further encouragement, he encircled her in his arms, his erection pressing into her hip. He pushed her down on to the bed and sunk himself deep inside her warm, yielding body.

Several days later, Dillon was released from the hospital, and Jason temporarily moved into his flat with him. Stevie brought Chinese food and alcohol free beer on account of the anti-depressant medication Dillon had been prescribed.

Things between Stevie and Jason had been strained the following morning after their slip up. The sex had been intense and wordless, desperate and needy. But they had slept separately afterward. Jason's mixed up feelings had been scrambled further, but Stevie had been trying to act like everything was fine.

Dillon's release had been conditional on the fact that he was to undergo an intensive run of therapy sessions and grief counselling, which he was not in the least bit happy about.

'I don't see what talking about my feelings is going to do to help,' he moaned as they sat munching on spring rolls and prawn toast.

Jason rolled his eyes. 'They clearly think it'll help. Just go with it, eh? It's not going to be for long.'

'Absolutely, Dillon. What have you got to lose?' Stevie interjected.

'Durrr, only the last tiny shred of sanity I have left.' Dillon shook his head as if it was obvious.

Jason laughed. 'I think you'll find that these people are supposed to *stop* you from going crazy, mate. Give them a chance.'

Just before midnight, Stevie announced that she was ready to go home. Jason walked her to the door.

'Are we...are we okay, Stevie? I mean after the other night.'

She frowned. 'The other night? Course we are. Why wouldn't we be?'

'Because we weren't going to do that anymore.'

She rolled her eyes and smiled. 'Jason, it was great sex. Stop being such a girl again, will you? Nothing's changed. I think we needed a distraction from all the shit. It seems to me that we're good at distracting each other.'

Jason's brain raced with so many responses. He wanted to ask how she could use sex with him like that when there were feelings running underneath. How could she treat him like a fuck buddy? *What the hell?* But after her comment about him being a girl, he instead nodded and inhaled a deep breath.

'Okay then. As long as we're okay.'

'We're fine. Good night, Jace.'

'Goodnight.' He closed the door and ran his hands over his hair. He couldn't get inside her head, and it drove him mad. She was a walking contradiction. Shaking his head, he walked back through to the lounge.

The brothers sat drinking the mock beer, and Dillon scrunched his nose up. 'Argh, this stuff doesn't give you the same buzz as the real deal.'

'Yep, that's the point, you muppet. I want to talk to you about something.'

Dillon cringed. 'Awww no, that sounds serious. Whenever you want to talk to me, I end up in a mess. I'm not going to like this, am I?'

'I dunno. That's why I'm going to go ahead and come right out with it.' He took a deep breath. 'I want you to come to Scotland and stay with me for a while...maybe permanently if you like it. What do you think?'

Dillon nodded. 'Okay.'

Shocked, Jason clamped his jaw closed for a few moments. Eventually, he recovered the use of his mouth. 'Maybe you should think about it for a bit, eh?'

'What's the point? Mum's dead, Dad's dead, Sarah dumped me, I was fucking adopted, and I hate my stupid job, so a break from it all will do me good.'

Jason raised his eyebrows. 'You *hate* your job?'

'Yup, always have. It pays well and I get to meet people, but I'm bored rigid being indoors all day long. I wish I could do something else. Something fun that I get a real buzz out of. But other than what I do, I have no skills.'

'All right then. You'll come and stay with me and think things through, yeah? I mean we're seeing the solicitor again tomorrow, so we'll know a bit more about what we're dealing with. Once it's all sorted, I really do need to go back up north. I've been away so long that there may be a mutiny up there. We can sort the counselling up there if we get a letter of referral. You can follow me up in your car when I go...or you can wait a while and—'

'Sounds like a plan...following you up, I mean. Like I said, no thinking needed.' Dillon stood and took the plates into the kitchen. 'Look, bro, I want to thank you. And tell you again how sorry I am for what I did. It was...selfish.'

'Hey, I don't want to hear another apology, okay? You were desperate and lost and...we're going to get through it, you know. No matter what's happened and what happens in the future, you *are* my brother.'

'Thanks, Jace. I...I'm not good with the sloppy stuff you know, but...I love you.' His cheeks coloured.

Jason swallowed the lump in his throat. 'And I love you too, Dillon. Don't ever forget that.'

CHAPTER TWELVE

*J*ason and Dillon sat in the waiting area at the solicitors. Mr. Jackson's secretary eventually told them that he was ready to see them, and so they made their way into the austere office in the Victorian building in central London.

'Ahhh, Misters Reynolds and Reynolds. Good to see you both. Please have a seat.'

The brothers sat and nervously awaited the news. 'Now, contrary to what you see in the movies, I'm not at liberty to sit here and read the last will and testament of your father *to* you. Rather what will happen is that you will sign for it. Mr. Dillon Reynolds, as executor you will be legally obliged to handle the last wishes therein. I trust that you'll find all that you need. However, if you should require assistance at all, please don't hesitate to make an appointment, and I'll be happy to advise you. Obviously, there were certain fees to settle from the estate, and I have already handled these as requested by the deceased Mr. Reynolds. Any monies, property, and personal effects are therefore yours to deal with as per the will.'

Feeling a little shell-shocked, Jason placed his hand on Dillon's shoulder on seeing the same feelings etched in his expression. The two brothers left the office with the large envelope in their possession. They went back to the flat and began the arduous task of reading through the documentation.

'God, Jace, I'm so sorry. This is terrible. I can't believe that apart from mum's necklace it's all been left to me, and the necklace isn't even for you. It's just wrong.'

Jason huffed. 'It isn't wrong, mate. He knew I wasn't his son. And he had no clue where I was. Of course, he would leave it all to you. And I'm glad Stevie gets Mum's necklace. She'll be touched. It all stands to reason.' Jason felt no malice or bitterness to his younger brother. It simply had been the outcome he had expected.

'I want you to have half...half of it all. It's my decision to do with it what I see fit. Mr. Jackson said so. And that's what I want.'

Jason smiled at his brother's kindness. 'I don't need nor want it, bro. I'd like some of the family photos of when we were kids. And I'd maybe like some of Mum's things, but other than that, I want you to use it to your advantage. Especially the cash. Sell the house...or rent it and make an income. Just make sure something good comes of all this *for you*. Right?'

Jason took Dillon's car and dropped his brother off at the hospital for his initial counselling assessment. He decided to take the time to call around and see Stevie.

When she opened the door, he was greeted with a frown. 'Hey, what are you doing here?' Her reaction to his visit made his heart sink.

'I thought I'd come and chat to you about some...stuff. But if you're busy, I can come back.' He pointed over his shoulder.

'No, come in. I'll put the kettle on.'

Jason followed her into the house, feeling nervous at the news he had to share. His palms were sweaty, and his heart was doing a great impression of a jackhammer in his chest. *Come on man...pull yourself together.* He discreetly wiped his palms down his jeans and sat on the sofa.

She brought the fresh coffee through to the lounge and placed it on the table. She sat on the floor beside the sofa, clearly keeping her distance again. 'So what stuff did you need to tell me? And where's Dillon?' She handed him a cup of the fresh brew.

'Oh, he's fine. Don't worry. He's at the hospital. I just...we got the will. Everything was left to Dillon, which is exactly what I expected. There was something for you though.'

'What? Me? Why?' Her hand touched her throat. Jason found it quite an ironic gesture.

'He left you Mum's heart shaped locket. You always loved it when we were younger, and I think it's actually very sweet that you've got something of hers. She adored you. I'm not sure why she didn't give it to you herself, but...well...here you go.' He handed the locket to Stevie, and she clutched it as a tear escaped the corner of her eye.

'Thank you,' she whispered. 'That's so lovely.'

'And I need to tell you that I spoke to Dillon at length about things. He's coming to stay with me for a while. He's taking a compassionate leave of absence from work, and he's going to take the time to think about what to do with the inheritance and...the rest of his life.'

Her eyes dropped to the floor. 'Oh...I see.' More tears drifted down her face.

He leaned forward and caught a tear as it made a glistening, damp trail down her cheek. 'I know you're not happy about this, but I think he needs to take some time away. He's been through a lot, and I wasn't there for him. I need to make up for that.'

'Yes, I understand...it's just...' She swallowed hard and wouldn't make eye contact.

'Stevie? Just what?'

She shrugged and swiped the tears from her cheeks. 'It sounds ridiculous, but having Dillon nearby when you were gone was kind of comforting. And now that he's going too, I won't even have that. I know it's selfish, but I'll miss him.' She glanced up at him through red-rimmed eyes. 'I'll miss you too.'

He dropped to the floor in front of her and took her face in his hands. 'We've been through this before. I don't *want* to hurt you. I want you to come too, but I understand your reasons for staying. Your job is important to you.' He caught more tears as they made their escape. 'Stevie, please don't cry.' He rested his forehead on hers. 'Have you...changed your mind?' he asked, feeling a tiny flutter of hope deep inside.

Stevie shook her head. 'No...sorry. I'm up for promotion at the beginning of the school year...and long distance relationships—'

He closed his eyes briefly. 'Don't work...I know...you've said. I still don't understand. If two people love each other, why *can't* it work?'

She frowned. 'Love? Who says love is involved?' She sniffed.

Jason clenched his jaw. 'Well...it *is* for me. It's always been you. I've never even been *close* to love with anyone else. You've always been the one, Stevie. Probably always will be.' He tilted her head up so that his lips could brush lightly over hers. 'Having said that, I do understand. But you can't blame me for wishing things were different. I can't stay here. I'm needed back at the camp. The business is only going to do well for so long without me. I *am* the owner after all. And it's my true home.'

She chewed on her lip as if fending off more emotions vying for release. 'When are you going?'

'The day after tomorrow. We need to find Dillon somewhere to be seen for his counselling, and the sooner we do so the better for him. I'm not saying that he'll move there permanently. He may use it to convalesce, but I'm leaving that up to him.'

She nodded her understanding slowly. 'Will you come and say goodbye?'

'If you want, we could come by tomorrow night.'

'Yes...I...I want to say goodbye this time. I need some...I need closure, Jason.'

He nodded and kissed her forehead. 'I'd better be going. Dillon should be finished shortly.'

'But you haven't drunk your coffee.'

Jason cringed. 'I know...I'm sorry.'

'No...it's fine. Give Dillon a hug from me.' She pulled him into her and squeezed him tight. 'I'll see you tomorrow.'

'You will.' Jason stood and left the house without looking back. He couldn't bear to see her cry over this. Not when there was a clear solution right under her nose. But he knew that the solution was only of benefit to him. He was being selfish. *But love will do that to you.*

Once Jason had gone, Stevie examined the locket more closely. She opened it up and more tears sprang forth as she looked into the smiling dark eyes of the young man who broke her heart ten years ago. It was a beautiful photo of her first love just as she remembered him at the time he left. There was no doubt in her mind that Shirley had meant this for her. She had always known how much Stevie loved her son. She even referred to her as the daughter she never had and was devastated when he broke her heart.

And the terrible thing was, through no real fault of his own, he was about to do it all over again.

CHAPTER THIRTEEN

*J*ason stared at his reflection in the mirror. He wondered what the hell he was going to do when he got home to Scotland and Stevie was hundreds of miles away, over *five hundred* miles away. He had admittedly managed before she came back into his life. He could pretend that it didn't affect him. But this time was different. This time was permanent.

In the back of his mind, there had always been the possibility of seeing her again when he knew nothing of what had become of her, when he had left without a trace ten years ago. He could conjure up a million different scenarios where they ended up together. But now he knew her true feelings, he could no longer do that. He gritted his teeth and closed his eyes, leaning on the sink unit for support.

When he opened his eyes and turned, Dillon appeared in the doorway. 'You okay, Jace?' he asked with a look of concern.

The corner of Jason's mouth quirked in a half-hearted smile. 'Yeah...I'll be fine. I'm a bit nervous about tonight.

Saying goodbye this time means it's really over. I knew it was anyway, but this...us leaving...just confirms it, I guess.

'I can't even begin to imagine how it feels. And I wish it could be different. Maybe things will change, eh? Once you've gone, maybe she'll realise, and she'll—'

'No, this is it. I need to get used to it.'

'But is tonight a good idea? Really? Don't you think this will make things worse?'

Jason dropped his gaze to the sink. 'Things couldn't get much worse. I think not going would be harder. I need to say goodbye. I owe her that much. I've left her twice without saying it, and I can't do it again. I was never really meant to see her again when she left Scotland after her trip there with her school, but this visit here has been...so *fucking hard*. Every time we've parted since reconnecting, my heart's broken a little bit more. It's funny...I didn't even realise I could actually *feel* anymore. Turns out I can...and I do.'

Dillon gripped his shoulder firmly. 'Have a good night, okay? Don't worry about me. It doesn't matter what time you get back. I'll be fine. I'm all packed. Just got the car to load up.'

'Okay, I have no idea how it'll go, and so I'll see you when I see you.'

Jason climbed out of the cab and paid the driver. He'd decided to leave the bike at Dillon's for this evening in favour of having a glass of the wine he had picked up to take with him. He needed a drink. Stevie had texted to say that she was cooking and that he and Dillon should arrive by seven. He didn't bother to text back to say that Dillon would be staying home.

After walking nervously up the path, he knocked on the

door, and she opened it with a wide smile. She looked over his shoulder. 'Where's Dillon?'

'He...he...decided to stay home tonight. I hope that's okay. He thought maybe we needed to be...he thought we might...' He shook his head. 'He decided to stay home.' He was aware that he was rambling.

Colour blossomed from Stevie's chest up her slender neck to her cheeks. 'Oh, right. You'd better come in. I've made a beef casserole. We can eat whenever you're ready.'

Even though the food smelled wonderful, he didn't want to admit he had lost his appetite on the way over, and so he simply nodded as he entered the house. He handed her the bottle of wine and she smiled.

'Gosh, that's spooky. I have the exact same wine open ready in the kitchen. I got some fruit juice too for Dillon, but...would you like a glass?'

He scrunched his face. 'Of fruit juice? I'll pass and go straight to the hard stuff please.'

She cocked her head to one side and rolled her eyes at him. 'I meant wine, silly.'

'The food smells great.' He smiled.

As if reading his mind, she narrowed her eyes. 'You're not hungry, are you?'

He dropped his gaze to the floor and cringed. 'I'm so sorry. My stomach has been in knots all day. Can we skip dinner and talk? Maybe warm it up later if we feel like it? Unless you're particularly hungry, in which case—'

She gave a small laugh and suddenly looked relieved. 'No, to be honest I'm feeling the same.' She made her way through to the kitchen. 'I'll turn the oven off. It'll reheat.'

Jason slumped onto the couch, and Stevie brought two full wine glasses back through. She looked stunning. Her long auburn hair fell around her shoulders in soft waves begging for his touch. Her eyes were surrounded by smoky shadow, and her lips glistened invitingly. She wore a knee length, pale blue summer skirt and a fitted white, V-neck T-shirt that clung to the curve of her full, rounded breasts. He shook his head to remove the wayward thoughts that had invaded his mind and took a glass, taking a large gulp.

'Whoa, steady on cowboy, or I'll be scraping you off the floor.' She giggled, sat down beside him, and turned to look at his face. 'Just let me know when you're ready to eat, and I'll go and heat the food up.'

He stared into her vivid blue eyes and said nothing for a few minutes. His mind raced through so many things he could say to her but none of them seemed just right. Eventually, he placed his glass down and took hers, putting it next to his.

He took her hand. 'Stevie, this can't be it. It can't be over,' he said, fighting down the emotion that was desperately trying to break free. She had such an effect on him, turning him from a tough, arrogant arse to a pile of lovesick mush.

She sighed. 'Maybe we should make the most of tonight, and then move on as best we can, eh?' She seemed resigned to their fate, but he still refused to let go.

He couldn't.

Not just yet.

He pulled himself towards her on the couch. 'When two people have this kind of connection, it can't be easily broken, Stevie. We're a part of each other. Always have been, and I'm sure we always will be. I can't see either of us moving on. Can you? Honestly?'

Her expression was pained as she spoke. 'We don't have any choice. I want you to be happy, and that means you going back to Scotland. And *I* need to be happy, which means me staying here. I would hope you wanted my happiness too.'

'Of course I do. But we could visit each other and try to

make things work. Won't you reconsider? Won't you even try it?'

She cupped his cheek. 'No. I can't. I won't. I know how it'll end if I do. I've seen for myself how these long distance relationships go, and it's never good. There's no reason that we would be the exception to the rule. I've lost you before, and I can't keep going through that.'

'But why? I know you feel something for me. It's there in your eyes. I know it. We're not your mum and dad, Stevie. We're different people. And it's not like it was back then. There are so many ways to keep in touch—'

'You can't hold someone over the Internet. I can't sleep in your arms over the phone. I can't kiss you by text message.'

His frustration was rising, and he gripped her hand harder. 'But you're putting obstacles in our path before you even try. I honestly believe this was meant to happen. We were meant to find each other again.'

'Maybe we were. But maybe not for the reasons you think.'

'What do you mean?'

She sighed. 'Maybe we were meant to meet so we could figure out how to let each other go. We both had so many unanswered questions. Maybe this was fate's way of giving us the answers so that we could move on with our lives.'

His stomach knotted. 'You believe that?'

She nodded slowly with sadness in her eyes. 'I really do.'

He swallowed the ball of emotion that had lodged itself in his constricted throat once again. 'So you're telling me all we have is tonight?'

Looking straight into his eyes, she nodded. 'Yes.'

He closed his eyes and tried to calm his jackhammer of a heart again. 'Can I ask something of you?'

'What is it?'

'Can I make love to you one last time? I know it sounds corny, but I want to remember this night with a smile and I...' His voice cracked as he tried to rein in his emotions again. 'I want to memorise every detail of being with you. Your every curve and sound...every feeling...every touch...everything... I know it's a lot to ask, and I know it's maybe not the best—'

Stevie stopped his words with her mouth as she took his in a passionate kiss. She slipped her tongue in between his parted lips and a groan escaped her. He grasped at her hair, cradling the back of her head to deepen the already fervent exchange. She clambered into his lap, never breaking her lips from his own. Jason was breathless from her onslaught but hardened as she straddled him, her skirt riding up her thighs. He cupped her behind, squeezing and kneading as she rocked back and forth grinding herself into him.

She pulled the T-shirt she was wearing over her head and threw it to the floor. His breathing was a series of ragged inhales and exhales. 'Let's go upstairs, Stevie. I want to do this properly.'

She climbed off him and without a word pulled him towards the door that led to the stairs. They slowly ascended to her room, and once inside she began to unfasten the buttons of his shirt. She smoothed her hands up over his chest, drawing a hiss through his clenched teeth as she caught one of his nipples and it peaked under her caress.

Reaching back she unfastened her skirt and allowed it to fall, pooling at her feet, so that she could step out of it and kick it aside. He held her at arms-length and dropped to sit on the bed, so that he could take her image into his mind and fix it there permanently. The ache in his chest was growing as he remembered that this was their last time.

She wore a pale cream lace bra that pushed her breasts up into the most beautiful soft mounds of flesh. Her matching panties skimmed under her belly button and over her rounded hips. He pulled her to him and rested his head on her tummy. He felt the sting of tears behind his eyes and did his best to fight them away. Placing soft kisses across her stomach and up to the curve of her breasts, he savoured the taste of her skin as she ran her hands roughly through his hair.

He reached up and unhooked her bra, letting it slip down her arms and to the floor to join the rest of her relinquished clothing. Sliding his hands up her stomach, he eventually took her breasts in his hands and kissed both reverently, taking her nipples into his mouth one after the other and back again as her head rolled back and a moan vibrated up through her chest and out of her parted lips.

Desperate to savour every second, he looked up to watch her reactions as he touched her. She gazed down into his eyes as hers filled with so many unreadable emotions. Standing once again, he removed his pants and boxers in one sweep of his hands and dropped to his knees before her. As he nuzzled her mound and inhaled her scent deeply, she gripped his shoulders and gasped.

Eventually, her panties were discarded, and he pulled her back onto the bed with him, covering her mouth with his. Her lips were soft and yielding to the demands of his mouth. He skimmed his hand down to her breast and ran his thumb over her nipple eliciting a whimper from her throat. Sliding his hand down further, he reached the junction of her thighs and caressed her over and over until her breathing rate increased, and with her head thrown back, she cried out his name. Once she had calmed, she urged him on, pulling him atop her where her curves melded to his hard, lean body. Looking deep into her eyes, he sunk himself deep and rested his forehead on hers, never breaking eye contact.

'Don't say it's over, Stevie. Please...don't say it's the end of us.' He could hear the desperation in his own voice.

Hearing his heart felt words, Stevie reared up to tug on his bottom lip, anything to stop the heartbreak his words were causing. The thought of telling him about her mother's illness crossed her mind. Dana had insisted that Myasthenia wasn't going to rule her life and had made Stevie swear to keep the diagnosis private. Betraying her mother's trust wasn't something she could bring herself to do and she knew that if Dana was aware of the way she felt she would make her go. Stevie couldn't risk leaving her mother all alone and so she shook her head to dislodge the thoughts as she slipped her hands down Jason's smooth back, relishing the feeling of his taut muscles as they moved. Being so connected to him was an amazing feeling, and she was sure he could feel her heart hammering against her ribcage, but she didn't care. She wanted to memorise every tiny detail of holding him inside her.

But it was becoming too much.

He kissed and bit at her neck as his movements became more urgent. He thrust inside her like he couldn't get close enough, the expression on his face a combination of desire and heart wrenching pain. He moulded her breast and circled her nipple, sending the most delicious sparks of pleasure throughout her body. His mouth replaced his fingers as he pulled each nipple into his heat. She could hardly stand it. His fingers moved down between their slick, writhing bodies, and he found her sensitive nub, circling her as he thrust himself deeper still.

She was heading towards ecstasy once again, and the emotions within her were raw and raging, searching for release. His damp, hard body slipped and slid over her own. His breath was hot on her skin as he kissed every available inch. He muttered loving words that she couldn't quite make out as she began to soar. She cried out once more and let her head fall back as he followed her over the edge into sweet oblivion for the last time. She shuddered as the tears fell. He lay still with his face in the crook of her neck. She couldn't tell whether the moisture on her shoulders was from her own tears or those of her lover, and she didn't much care.

He silently moved his body so that he lay beside her and pulled her back into his chest, possessively enfolding her in his strong, muscular embrace. He kissed her hair and caressed her stomach until his breathing evened out and she could tell he was asleep.

She covered his hand with hers and stroked his knuckles in soft circles as she whispered, 'Goodbye, Jason. Be happy. Please don't ever forget me.'

The next morning, the light streaming through the curtains alerted Stevie to the start of a brand new day. For a split second, she stretched lazily, enjoying the feeling of her tender muscles protesting at the languid movement.

But all too soon she reached behind her to find that Jason had gone.

CHAPTER FOURTEEN

*T*he brothers loaded up the car and set off at the break of the dawning day. Dillon followed Jason's bike as they drove the journey north. After several hours of being on the road, they pulled into the service station at Annandale just as they had arranged. This was only the second stop they had made in the ten-hour journey. It was two o'clock in the afternoon, and he should be hungry, Jason's stomach disagreed vehemently. The large knot that had formed since he left Stevie's bed seemed hell bent on staying put, rendering him unable to stand the thought of food.

Thinking back to the previous night put the lid on his non-existent appetite. She had looked so beautiful laying there, sleeping peacefully. He had slipped his arm from under her carefully, deciding it was better to leave than to suffer the painful goodbye he would have to endure. Goodbye was what she needed, but he was incapable of saying the word. So he sat there watching her sleep for a few moments taking everything in. Her exquisite naked body before him, soft and curvaceous. Her smooth skin bathed in the early morning rays that were just beginning to peep through the curtains. Her long auburn waves fanned across the pillow, framing her gorgeous face as she dreamed. A serene smile playing on her lips. What was she dreaming about? He had no idea, but he *did* know that he had never seen a more beautiful sight.

He had dressed as quickly and quietly as he could and took one last look. Bending down, he kissed her forehead gently and inhaled the smell of her hair. His jaw clenched and his heart cracked. This was wrong. He felt the urge to wake her and tell her so, demand that she reconsider. But instead he had left the house, dropping the dead bolt behind him, and walked away without looking back.

Now he sat opposite Dillon in the service station restaurant, feeling numb whilst his brother was eating anything that stood still long enough. Dillon ate his way through a large plate of steak pie and chips and then sat eyeing Jason's untouched plate.

Seeing the hunger in his brother's eyes, Jason pushed the plate towards him. 'Here, bro. Just take it. I can't eat.' He huffed out a long breath.

Dillon pulled his lips into a thin line. 'You *should* eat you know. You only had coffee this morning. This won't do you any good. I know you're hurting but—'

'Just leave it, Dill, eh? I can't think about food. I honestly thought there was a chance she'd choose me. I guess I was wrong.' He swallowed past the ever-present chunk of emotion in his throat.

'Look, Jason...and I mean this with love...she never lied to you. She said all along that she *wouldn't* be coming with you. Maybe you should've let her go when she tried to step back. Last night was unnecessary, man. All you've done is create a whole heap of heartache for both of you.'

Jason's jaw tensed. 'Don't you think I know that? But do you know what? If I had the chance, I'd do things *exactly* the same. I wouldn't change a single second of last night...maybe apart from the moment where I pretty much *begged* her to change her mind...that was pointless.'

Dillon shook his head. 'Awww, Jace. I'm so sorry. I really am.'

Jason pushed up from the table. 'I'm going to stretch my legs and get some air. Eat up quick, okay? I want to get home now.'

The men pulled into the campsite at around eight o'clock in the evening. Jason led the way to his cabin. Dorcas had been living on site whilst Jason had been away, and the light was on, meaning she was in. He wouldn't barge right in just in case Dorcas was in a state of undress or with someone. So feeling it a bit strange, Jason knocked on the door of the building he considered home and waited. Dillon joined him a few seconds later and stood behind him.

The door opened and there stood Dorcas. Her blonde hair in pigtails, spectacles perched on her nose covering her bright green eyes. 'Jason! You're back!' She launched her petite frame at him and clung on tight. He hugged her back, smiling at her enthusiastic greeting.

'Dorcas, you're choking me,' he spluttered in a cross between a laugh and a cough.

'Ooh sorry. Got a bit carried away, I think.' Her lilting Scottish accent was music to Jason's ears. He turned to Dillon, who stood there staring at her. He half expected the music to 'Dream Weaver' by Gary Wright to begin playing around them. He smirked and shook his head.

'Who's your friend, Jason?' Her cheeks blushed crimson.

'This hunk of man is my little brother. Dillon, the woman you are very rudely staring at is Dorcas.'

Dillon snapped his head to Jason. 'I'm sorry, what?'

'Dillon, Dorcas...Dorcas, Dillon.' He tried again, gesturing between them.

Dillon held out his hand, took hers, and smiled. 'H-hi... Dorcas...what a nitty prame...*shit*...pretty name...what a pretty name.' Dillon's cheeks coloured to match Dorcas', and Jason chuckled to himself.

What a bloody pair.

'I'm off to get a shower. I'll leave you two to get to know one another better, eh?' He raised his eyebrows, not that either of them noticed.

Sidestepping his brother and assistant, he went straight to his bedroom. Dorcas had apparently not been sleeping in his room, as his bed was as tidy as he had left it. There was a pillow and blanket folded neatly on a chair. He collapsed backwards onto his bed and rested his arm over his eyes. He was exhausted and needed sleep desperately. But as he was dozing off, there was a knock at his bedroom door.

'Yes?' he called, feeling more than a little irritated.

Dillon poked his head around the door. 'Sorry to disturb you, but Dorcas is talking about going for pizza and a few beers. Are you up for it?'

'No mate. You go though. Get her to drop you back here, and you can sleep on the couch. It's comfy enough. Take that blanket and pillow that Dorcas has been using. Then you can smell her perfume and dream of her.' He grinned.

Dillon kicked Jason's boots as they dangled off the end of the bed. 'Funny. Seriously though,' he lowered his voice, 'why have you never...you know...asked her out yourself?'

Jason raised his head up to glare at his brother. 'Because

she's my employee, that's why...and because she's not...she's not my type.'

'You were going to say because she's not Stevie, weren't you?'

Jason rolled his eyes. 'Maybe I was. Can you sod off now, please? I'm knackered and I need some sleep. Goodness only knows where you put it all. You ate two lots of food at two o'clock.'

'Growing lad.' Dillon sniggered as he patted his belly and left Jason in peace.

Jason clambered to his feet and stripped out of his leathers, piling them on the now empty chair. He walked to the bathroom and switched on the shower, letting it run until the steam billowing into the room fogged up the mirror where he was examining the dark circles under his eyes.

The hot water soothed and relaxed him, making him feel even sleepier. After towel drying his hair, he slipped on a pair of lounge pants and climbed into bed. Checking his phone, he was disappointed at the lack of messages. He toyed with the idea of letting Stevie know that he had arrived back safely but decided against it. It was time to move on. Not by his choice. But the decision had been made.

Jason awoke at ten the next morning to the smell of something burning. He rubbed his eyes and clambered out of bed in a panic, making his way hurriedly to the kitchen just as the smoke alarm kicked in and blurted out its piercing, high pitched squeal. The kitchen was filled with thick smoke, and Dillon was waving a dishtowel around in the air. All the windows and the door were open.

'What the fuck are you trying to do? Burn my house down?' Jason shouted over the noise.

'I was trying to make you breakfast *actually*, but Dorcas and me got chatting and I forgot about the bacon under the grill. Sorry, mate.'

The brothers managed to stop the smoke alarm from screeching by a series of wafts and waves. Once the kitchen resembled a place to cook in again, Jason and Dillon sat outside drinking coffee and eating toast. The bacon was now feeding the garbage bin.

'So...you two are getting on well?' Jason asked his brother.

The smile that spread across Dillon's face said all he needed to know. 'Yeah, she's great. I mean *really* great. I'm thinking of asking her on an official...you know...date. Is that okay?'

Jason frowned. 'Course it's okay. Go for it. She's very sweet.'

'Yeah, she's great.'

Jason rolled his eyes and slapped his brother on the shoulder. 'I think you've got it bad, mate. You already said that...twice.'

Stevie sipped on her coffee as Mollie stared open mouthed. The start of the new term had come around rather too quickly, and Stevie hadn't done half of the things she had intended to do. Her friend and colleague was still nursing a healing ankle. Although the cast had been removed, she was still having difficulty getting about following her surgery. The two friends hadn't seen each other until the start of school thanks to the ankle issue, and so Stevie had a whole lot to tell her friend.

'Good grief, Stevie. No wonder I haven't seen you over the summer. I can't believe all that has happened.'

'You know me. I attract drama.'

'So how do you feel about Jason *now*? I can't believe he was at the camp. Just think, if I'd never broken my ankle, you'd never have seen him.'

Stevie picked at her lunch. 'I think that scenario would have been less painful for me.'

'Oh, Stevie. I'm so sad for you. I think you should've given the long distance thing a try. From the photo you showed me, he looks absolutely dreamy. I don't usually go for men with longer hair, but he's...well, he could be a male model.'

Stevie smiled, but felt more than a little sad. 'Yes, he is gorgeous. Inside and out.' The familiar and unwelcomed stinging feeling at the back of her eyes occurred yet again.

Mollie reached out. 'Hey, I'm sorry Stevie. I didn't mean to pour salt in your wound.'

Stevie shook her head as if doing so would eradicate the threatening tears. 'No, it's fine...really. I'm fine. I think being back at work is probably a good thing.'

'Probably...and the interviews for Head of Science will be taking place soon. Have you heard anything yet?'

Stevie had submitted her application on the first day of term.

'Nothing yet, but it's early days, I suppose. I'm not holding my breath.'

'Are you kidding? I reckon the job's yours. And then you'll be so busy it'll be 'Jason who?' before long. You mark my words.'

She wasn't in the least bit convinced. 'Hmm. We'll see, shall we?' She had always wanted the Head of Science position. It was the next step. And Mollie was right. The job was such a busy one that she would have no time to feel melancholy. She could hope.

The bell for afternoon lessons sounded, and the staff room began to clear. David from P.E. approached the table where the two women were reluctantly rising to leave. He was dressed in long shorts and the school's bottle green polo shirt and fleece.

He cleared his throat. 'Hi...ahem...hi, Stevie. I was wondering if you'd maybe like to go out for a...um...drink again on Friday evening?' His cheeks coloured.

Mollie smirked and walked towards the door. Stevie scowled at her, hoping to communicate the phrase *I'll get you for this Mollie!* with her eyes. She glanced back at David. 'Oh...I'm not sure what I'm doing Friday yet, David.'

His eyes dropped, and he looked a little like a chastised puppy dog. 'Oh...right. Not to worry. I did wonder with Jason turning up on your doorstep like that. Never mind. See you later.' He turned to leave.

Stevie felt overwhelmed with guilt. David was a good-looking guy and very sweet. *Plus, I need to move on.* 'David, wait...a drink would be nice, thank you.'

His face lit up and a handsome smile emerged. Anyone would think he had just won the lottery. 'Fantastic! I'll pick you up at seven.'

She felt her heat rise in her cheeks. 'Great...lovely. I'll see you before then, obviously.'

He beamed at her. 'Oh yeah...sure...it's only Wednesday, after all.'

Stevie made her way down the long corridor to her lab where a line of twelve-year-olds awaited her arrival. Some of them were being sensible, but the usual handful were wrestling each other, causing her to break out her death stare.

'Are we doing an experiment today, Mrs. Norton? We

haven't done one for ages,' one of the more challenging members of the class asked as she unlocked the door.

'There's a good reason for that, Jonathan. Perhaps next time we try something as exciting as burning magnesium, you will refrain from dropping the hot tongs onto someone's sweater. Melanie could have been seriously hurt. And *you* were lucky not to be expelled.'

The boy dropped his gaze and went as red as a beetroot. The other class members laughed and jeered at him as they filed into the room. Stevie shook her head and waited for the class to take their seats and settle down.

'Okay, you lovely lot. Today we're going to look at the reactions of metals with acids, and so this *does* mean we're doing practical work.' A cheer erupted around the laboratory. 'But you will need to be *sensible*. The first sign of anyone messing around, and you will *all* suffer my wrath!'

'You're the best, Mrs. Norton!' Jonathan shouted from the back of the room. Stevie turned to write on the board and made a mental note to look into getting her name changed.

CHAPTER FIFTEEN

*F*riday night rolled around, and Stevie was beginning to regret agreeing to a date with David. Was it a date at all? Was she worrying over nothing? Whilst she was getting ready, her landline rang. *Mum.*

'Hello?'

'Hi, sweetie. I was ringing to check how you are. See if you're nervous.'

'No, Mum...not nervous. I don't think I want to do this. It's not wise mixing work and home life as it is, and although David is lovely, he's not... He's not Jason.'

Her mum sighed. 'Oh, sweetheart, I know. After I pushed you into dating Miles, I'm not going to tell you what to do here. All I will say is be happy. If David isn't the one, don't waste your time on him. But if you go out with him and he gives you a fire in your belly, then you have my support.'

Stevie smiled. 'Thanks, Mum. And will you stop worrying over the Miles issue. It wasn't your fault, okay?'

'Hmm. I pushed you into dating him, and now you have a divorce under your belt. Anyway...I'll speak to you tomorrow. Love you.'

'Love you too, Mum.'

The calls with her Mum these days were brief but frequent. Dana knew how much heartache Stevie had been through over Jason and was evidently still worried. She let Stevie know she loved her and was there for her at every given opportunity.

The Queen's Head was a traditional real ale pub on the outskirts of Wilmersden. It was a place that Stevie usually went to with the people from the Science Department and so she felt comfortable there. No airs and graces. Just real pub grub and good beer. Except Stevie still drank wine.

She sat next to David as they chatted about school. Despite her initial trepidation, being with David had been easy this time, and Jason had never been mentioned. Of course when she realised this, he was immediately lodged at the forefront of her mind and her mood plummeted. The past month since he went back to Scotland had been filled with tears and heart to heart sessions with her mum where she tried in vain to cheer Stevie up. There had even been talk of a blind date with Mollie's older, recently divorced brother, Marcus. Stevie wasn't too keen, but Mollie seemed to think he would be just what she needed. She had seen a photo, and he was very handsome. Tall and dark...just like Jason. *Oh Jason.*

'So...have you heard from him?' David asked as if stepping into her mind.

She feigned ignorance. 'Who?'

He frowned. 'Come on, you know very well who I mean, Stevie. It's my guess that he's just popped into your mind. Your face suddenly dropped.'

Good grief, how perceptive is he? 'I'm sorry, you're right. And no...not a word.'

'I'm sorry things didn't work out for you.' He seemed genuine. 'I was hoping that perhaps you'd give me a chance. I wouldn't hurt you like that. I know I'm no hunky, panties melting, male model type like he is, but...I really do like you. And I don't mean as a friend... Obviously, I *do* like you as a friend...you're a great girl. But what I mean is...good grief I'm rambling... What I mean is that I find you very attractive. Stop me anytime you want to... I know I'm making a complete pillock of myself here.' He smiled.

'No, you're very sweet, David.' She leaned in to kiss his cheek, but he turned his head and met her lips with his own. His lips were firm where Jason's were soft. His skin was smooth where Jason's stubble rasped deliciously at her skin, making her senses spring to life. His kiss was gentle where Jason's was lust-filled and passionate. She returned the kiss for a moment, and he cupped her head tenderly.

When she stopped kissing him back, he pulled away and stroked her cheek looking into her glassy eyes. 'Thank you.'

She was confused by his choice of words. 'W-why are you thanking me, David?'

He tucked a stray strand of hair behind her ear. 'Because I've wanted to do that for a very long time. And now I know that it *does* feel wonderful to kiss you, just like I imagined. And even though I know it'll never happen again, you gave me a chance to try with you.'

His tender words made salt water escape from her eyes. 'I'm so sorry,' she whispered.

'Hey...no need to be sorry. Come on, I'll take you home.'

Jason sat on his bed, book in hand. He had tried several times to get past his current page but couldn't quite manage it. The words weren't registering in his brain at all. It was nine at night, and he was feeling agitated and distracted. It had been just over a month since he had left London...and Stevie. There had been no contact on either side, and he had decided it was probably time to let go and move on.

For the past couple of mornings, he had awoken to find blankets still neatly folded on the chair in the lounge. Things between Dillon and Dorcas were getting fairly serious very quickly, and being around the two of them was becoming increasingly unbearable. They couldn't keep their hands off each other and seemed to touch at every given opportunity. From simple strokes of a hand down an arm to full on passionate embraces. *Urgh!* Whilst Jason was aware he would be the same if Stevie were here, his tolerance levels were falling rapidly.

That morning after the staff briefing for the next arrivals to the camp, he had caught the cringe-worthy couple kissing through the trees on the riverbank, the same place where he and Stevie had kissed. It made his stomach knot tightly when he remembered the taste of her kiss and the feel of her body melded to his.

He hadn't realised he was staring until Dillon spotted him and shouted, 'Oy! Are you perving at my sexy girlfriend?' The couple had sniggered, and Dorcas had pulled Dillon behind a large, thick tree trunk where they could continue sucking face to their hearts' content, out of the view of prying eyes. Jason had shaken his head and walked away.

Back in the present, he heaved out a heavy breath and threw his book aside. Running his hands through his shaggy damp hair, he made a rash decision. Grabbing his phone, he rifled through the contacts and hit dial.

'Hello, stranger,' came the sultry voice at the other end. 'Long-time no-speak.'

'Yeah...hi, Jenna. Are you busy?'

'Well, I *am* busy painting my toenails...*naked*...but for you I can be free any time,' she purred.

'Great. I'll be up in a little while.'

'Hmm...need to de-stress a little, do we?'

'Something like that.'

'Okay, bring a nice bottle of Pinot. I'll be waiting.'

Jason pulled on his bike leathers and helmet, grabbed his keys, and went out to his bike. The moonlight glinted off the shiny, black metal, and he threw his leg over, inserting the key into the ignition and starting the engine. He paused for a moment. *What the fuck am I doing?* He switched off the engine, dropped his head, and sat for a few moments. *Awww fuck it. She's probably dating by now. And I need to release some tension. Just sex. No strings attached, sweaty sex. That's what I need right now.* He started the engine and set off before the two sides of his brain could argue further.

Twenty minutes later, after calling for some wine, he arrived at the flat in Aviemore that he had become familiar with in the past few years. Meeting Jenna a couple of years earlier had been a happy accident. She was over from Aus taking a year out from work and had been employed in the Australian bar he frequented. After spilling a drink on him and apologising profusely, they had hit it off, talked for hours, and he had gone home with her that first night. After falling in love with Scotland, Jenna had made the decision to stay and make a life for herself. They had been friends with benefits for over a year, but Jason had stopped the hook ups when it began to feel a little too much like a rela-tionship.

Jenna opened the door, and Jason looked her up and

down. 'I thought you said you were painting your toenails *naked*?' He pouted.

'I thought you'd maybe like this little ensemble instead.' Her husky voice was enough to drive a man insane with lust.

There she stood, her black, poker straight hair just reaching her shoulders. Her very slim frame and minimal curves covered in black lace undies complete with stockings and stilettos.

She looked out from under her bangs and crooked her finger at him. 'Come on in, hunk.' She backed into the hallway of her flat and he followed. Once inside the door, Jason kicked the door closed with his heavy boot and made a grab for her. He slipped his tongue into her mouth and pressed her against the wall until she lifted her legs and wrapped them around his middle. 'Hmmm, there are no prizes for guessing what you need tonight,' she whispered in his ear, sending shivers down his spine and spiking at his groin.

'Yeah, don't expect me to be gentle.' He growled in between the determined thrusts of his tongue.

'Oh I never do and I don't care. Come on, let's take this somewhere a little more comfortable.' He let her place her feet back on the floor, and she pulled him further into the flat. 'Do you want a drink?' she asked, looking over her shoulder.

'I think you know what I want, Jenna. I'm not in the mood for small talk, drinking, or anything else for that matter. I have one thing on my mind right now and that's to forget. You can help me do that.'

Jenna led him into her bedroom. The girly, pink cocoon was a little too cloying for his taste, but he would have to look past it to achieve his goal. And his goal was to nail another woman. Forget Stevie. *Shit...Stevie.* He glanced back at the black haired beauty that now lay provocatively sprawled across her cerise faux fur throw, patiently waiting. He clenched his jaw and stripped down to nothing as quickly as he could, making sure to grab the condoms he had brought.

He paused, looking down at the semi-naked woman. She looked *nothing* like Stevie. Stevie's hair would fan out on the pillow around her, making her look like she was suspended in water. Jenna's hair was so neatly styled it was too perfect and quite severe. Jenna was very slim with small breasts. Her stomach concaved when she laid back and her hip bones protruded. Stevie was soft and comforting and felt so good beneath him. Jenna looked up in anticipation, her eyes burning with lust. Stevie would have had more than that behind her eyes. There would have been *love* too.

Stevie, Stevie, S*tevie.*

She overtook his every waking thought. And it was driving him mad.

With ice poured on his libido at the thought of cheating on the woman he *couldn't* have, he clearly wasn't going to be able to go through with sleeping with the one he *could* have. He slumped down on the bed with his back to his scantily clad companion.

After running his hands through his hair, he rested his elbows on his knees. 'I'm sorry, Jenna, you'll think I'm crazy, but I don't think I want this after all. I'm really sorry. I'm getting over someone. Well, I'm *trying* to get over someone. I thought that if I just had no-strings-attached sex with someone else that it'd help me get her out of my system, but I'm kidding myself if I think it'd work. I'd end up regretting it and feeling like shit.'

Jenna sat behind him and put her arms around his shoulders. 'You're in love? Oh Jason, I wish you'd have said. I would've refused to see you. Even *I* know that rebound sex isn't the way to deal with heartbreak. You always think it is until you've done it and you end up feeling cheap. I should know. I've been there.'

Jason turned his head slightly and glanced at her. 'You have? I thought you didn't do relationships.'

'I didn't. But I met this guy with a weird accent a couple of years ago. Long hair...scruffy looking...runs an Outward Bounds camp...you may know him.'

He turned to fully face her. 'What?'

'Yup, it's the truth, hunk. I fell for you way back then. And I fell hard. I knew it was just fun for you, and that was enough for a while. Any attention from you was still attention, and so I told myself it'd eventually turn into more. But you suddenly stopped calling and you hardly ever came into the bar. One night, a little while ago, Matt from the Rothiemurchus Rough Trax came in. He said he'd seen you with one of the school groups. He said you were upbeat, laughing with the kids, and that you seemed really happy. That you'd warned him off this teacher who was with the group, saying she was off limits when he'd expressed an interest in her.

'I laughed when he told me. I didn't believe him. He said she was a hottie and that he was trying to ask her out but that you were cock-blocking him at every possible avenue. I couldn't believe it. You were always so serious all the time. Never really bothered about female company. But Matt said he'd never seen you smile as much. Said the way you looked at her was possessive like you thought she *belonged* to you. Anyway, one of my friends who knows Dorcas told me there was a woman staying with you and that you two were crazy about each other. I figured that was the end of any chances I had. I grabbed the first interested guy and shagged him, thinking it'd get my mind off you. It didn't. But then you called tonight, and I figured it had all been a mistake...that they'd got it wrong.'

Jason rubbed his hands over his face. 'Oh hell, Jenna. I had no idea. I'm so sorry.'

She shrugged. 'No biggy. I'll get over it, eventually. But believe me, if she cares for you half as much as I do, she'll find you impossible to get over too. My guess is that she's sitting at home as fucking miserable as sin...just like you. I knew there was something when I opened the door. Your eyes...you looked...empty.'

He stood and pulled on his clothing. 'I feel like such a shit. I called what I have with you no strings sex. What an arse. I'm so very sorry. You must think I'm—'

'Hey, I think you're a great guy with a body that melts undies and you happen to be crazy about a woman who must also be fucking crazy cause she clearly let you go. Now, once you see sense and realise that this is what you want,' she gestured at her body with a grin, 'then I'll be here, but I won't wait for long. There are a gazillion guys out there who want me, you know.' She winked. Why was she being so great?

'They'd be the crazy ones.' He sat back down and pulled her into his arms. 'Don't let anyone use you again, Jen. You deserve so much more. I can't believe I was such a heartless bastard.' He kissed the side of her head. 'Hang on a minute. You think *I've* got a weird accent?'

'Ahhh, you've only just cottoned onto what I said, eh?' She nodded, giggling. 'Well come on, at least I have an Aussie accent, mate. What's yours? Are you Scottish...are you a cockney? Who the fuck knows? I know. We'll call you a Scottney! That about covers it, I reckon!' She fell back laughing, and he couldn't help laughing along with her.

Jason stood. 'You are one fruit loop, do you know that?'

'Yeah, I know that.' She stopped laughing. 'Now fuck off

home will you. I need to load my Internet dating profile up!'
She threw a pink fluffy cushion, hitting him on the head.

Smiling, he shook his head and left. Once outside the door, he ran his hands over his head before putting his helmet back on. *Fucking idiot, Reynolds. Total fucking idiot.*

CHAPTER SIXTEEN

*M*ollie had been trying to convince Stevie for ages to agree to a blind date with her brother, Marcus. The story was that his divorce had only recently been finalised, and he was ready to get back in the dating game. He was a lawyer and quite shy from what Mollie had told her. He had apparently returned home from working late one day and found his wife in bed with their male nanny. The divorce had been rather fast, thanks to his connections, and he had felt it was important to put it all behind him and move on.

Mollie had already made it abundantly clear she would love nothing more than for Marcus and Stevie to end up together living their happily ever after in his flashy London town house. Of course he already had a four-year-old son and was paying his wife child support and an allowance to enable her to live rent free in a lovely apartment in Kensington. The whole thing rang alarm bells for Stevie. But Mollie was a good friend, and Stevie figured Mollie wouldn't steer her wrong.

So after more cajoling from Mollie, it was set. Marcus Sumner would take Stevie to dinner at *Little Italy*, the best

Italian restaurant in the area. He would pick her up at seven on Friday evening. *Great.*

So another Friday evening rolled around rather too speedily. Rowdy was safely ensconced in the home of her neighbour, Joe, as she felt that being attacked and pinned to the wall on their first date might be a deal breaker for Marcus. Stevie stood in front of her full-length mirror, trying to tame her auburn tresses into a tidy chignon. Eventually, once every strand had co-operated, Stevie stepped into her little black dress and picked up her clutch and jacket. She slipped on her favourite purple stilettos and made her way downstairs to the lounge.

There was a knock on the door, right on time, and with more than a little trepidation, she opened it with a smile.

Marcus looked very handsome. He wore a black suit and oddly enough a purple tie that matched her shoes and accessories perfectly. *Okay...is this fate's way of telling me something?* He smiled and revealed a perfect set of white teeth. Not fake white. Just normal, clean, and fresh white. His hair was cropped short, styled neatly, and his eyes sparkled in the light coming from her hallway. There was no doubt about it. He was attractive in a clean cut, smoothly shaven kind of way. Different to Jason. But attractive all the same.

'Hi, Stevie. Are you ready to go?' His voice was deep and he was very well spoken.

'H-hi Marcus. Yes, I'm ready.'

'Great...shall we?' He gestured towards his car. His very nice...sporty...new...black Mercedes. *Gulp.* He waited for her to step out of her door and lock it before placing his hand at the small of her back and escorting her to the waiting vehicle. He was probably around the same height as Jason. Not quite as broad, but it was clear that he looked after himself simply from the hang of what she presumed was a tailor made suit.

He held the car door open for her to climb in. Once he was behind the driver's seat, she could rake her eyes over him whilst he watched the road. His seat was pushed back to accommodate his long, lean legs, and his wrist sported the very latest designer watch.

'So, how much hassle have you been getting from my kid sister about meeting me?' he asked after a few moments silence.

She felt the heat rise from her chest to her cheeks. 'Oh, quite a lot actually. Has she been the same with you?'

He cringed. 'I have a little, tiny, teeny confession to make.'

'Oh? Go on.' She was intrigued now.

He glanced at her briefly and then back to the road. He was biting his lip. 'I actually was the one who asked her to do the hassling.'

She pulled her brows in. 'Sorry? What do you mean?'

'I saw you when I was out with Mollie awhile after Sian and I had split, and you were out with another man. She pointed you out, and I asked if the man was your boyfriend. She told me he was Darren or...or Dean or something and that he was a friend of yours from work but that you weren't seeing anyone. To cut a long story short, I...oh God this makes me sound like such an idiot...I found you incredibly attractive and begged her to set me up with you.'

Stevie was stunned at hearing this confession but smiled nonetheless. 'Oh, that's really sweet.' She felt herself blush again and was thankful that the interior of the car was dark enough to hide her crimson hue from Marcus.

He glanced over at her again. 'So you don't want me to turn around and take you back home?'

'No, you're fine to take me to dinner. I should at least get a meal out of the situation.'

He laughed heartily, and she couldn't help joining in. She

liked him immediately. Mollie may have been right. Perhaps this *is* what she needed.

The restaurant was busy, but conversations were at a low hush. The intimate setting oozed romance, and the subdued lighting was the kind that made her feel sexy. Marcus pulled out her chair and sat opposite her where she could fully take in his features. His nose was aquiline, and his eyes were a deep, dark blue. She wasn't sure if it was the lighting or if they were naturally so dark.

'So Mollie tells me you're divorced.' As soon as the words had left his mouth, he clamped it shut and closed his eyes. 'Oh great. You can tell I haven't dated in a while. Next I'll be asking you when was the last time you had a root canal treatment.'

Stevie sniggered. 'It's fine. Please don't worry. And yes, I'm divorced. It's been around a year now. We stayed friends for a while, but it wasn't helping him move on.'

'I see. So it was *you* who ended things?'

Stevie nodded. 'If I'm completely honest, I should never have married him. I wasn't in love with him. I cared deeply for him, but...oh I won't bore you with the details.' She waved her hand in a dismissive gesture.

'I'm sure you're very much aware that my beloved wife couldn't keep her hands off our twenty-five-year old male nanny.'

Stevie cringed. 'Yes, Mollie did mention that. How awful.'

Marcus laughed dryly. 'I should've expected it. It wasn't the first time she'd been unfaithful. I forgave her the first time because we were young, but there's only so many times a man can be made to feel inadequate I guess. I ended things then and there. The stupid thing is she wasn't even upset. Jaiden, the manny, was only interested in her money and dumped her as soon as I did. She's alone now with our four-year-old son. If my job wasn't so hectic, I would sue for full custody but...'

Silence descended on the two new friends for a few moments, and Stevie began to feel uncomfortable. Suddenly, Marcus exhaled noisily and began to speak again.

'Okay, I've ruined this, haven't I? I'm so sorry. I think I'm still very bitter about the whole thing. I shouldn't be dragging you down with me.'

She felt sorry for him and reached for his arm. 'No...no it's understandable that you feel that way. Look, whilst we're being honest, I should show you the same courtesy. I'm kind of getting over someone. It's a very long story, and I won't bore you with the details but—'

'Would that be Jason?'

Stevie gawped at the man. *Okay, Mollie has really given him the low down.* 'Erm...yes, it would. How much do you know?' She narrowed her eyes.

'He was your first love, and I know what that's like. He left you...you accidentally found him again on a school trip. You had a brief relationship but neither of you wanted to relocate, and you don't like doing the long distance thing, so you ended it.' Marcus smiled. 'She pretty much told me the whole thing. I hope you're not upset with her. She wanted me to know what I was letting myself in for. I told her it was worth it.' His eyes locked on hers, and she gulped.

'Oookay then. Well, this is not awkward at all.' Her cheeks heated, and she felt sure she must be lit up like a Belisha beacon.

'No, Stevie, please don't feel awkward. I understand that your heart is currently stuck in limbo, but...and I don't want to come across all Miles when I say this but...I would like to see if things could be different for us. I find you incredibly attractive. I think maybe you find me attractive too.' He held his hands up. 'And I don't mean that to sound as arrogant as it no doubt does, but I could tell from your reaction when you opened the door. And I really do like you too. You seem warm and funny, and I'd love a chance to get to know you better.'

For some reason unbeknownst to herself, Stevie felt overcome with emotion and her eyes began to sting. *Don't cry you idiot. Don't you dare cry.* 'Gosh you know more about Miles than I thought too. I...I don't know what to say, Marcus.'

He leaned forward and took her hand across the table. 'Just give me a chance. I promise I won't expect things of you. We go at your pace. And if you don't fall for me, you get another male friend who secretly fancies the pants off you.' His smile widened, and she couldn't help smiling back.

Her thoughts flicked to Jason. He still held her heart, and that would take some getting over. But maybe...*just maybe* she could begin to let go of the hope that he would somehow turn up and tell her he had changed his mind about London. And perhaps the handsome, tall sweet man before her could be the one to help loosen Jason's hold over her.

Just maybe.

'I know this is only our first date, and maybe it's been a little unorthodox in the way we've talked about our baggage, but if I promise to leave my baggage in a dumpster somewhere and focus on us. Do you think you could give me a chance?' He gazed at her with pleading eyes and squeezed her hand.

'I...I can't make any promises to you, Marcus.'

'Hey, who can? When anyone starts a relationship, there's always the chance that it won't work out, but at least if you are willing to try...' His words trailed off as if he was feeling they were a waste of breath.

'I am. I'm willing to try.' She nodded as if to affirm her answer. Marcus smiled widely. His dark eyes lit up with an obvious happiness that surprised Stevie. *He must really like me. Like…really, really like me.*

The rest of their date was filled with chatter about their likes and dislikes. They had different tastes in music and film, but Stevie decided that would only give them more to talk about. At the end of the night, they pulled up outside Stevie's house, and for the first time in a long while, she was filled with something akin to hope.

'Would you like to come in for coffee?' she asked, hoping that it wasn't a mistake.

'Ah…no. As much as I want to, I won't this time. I think maybe you and I need to process everything that's happened tonight, and if I'm honest…if I come in…' He bit his lip and turned away.

She twisted towards him. 'What? If you come in what?'

He removed his seatbelt and turned to face her. His voice was low and incredibly sexy. 'I think what we've established tonight is that we're both a little broken. We need to take this slow for both our sakes, and if I come in with you, I'm going to want to kiss you. If I kiss you in the privacy of your home, I'm not going to want to stop.' He leaned forward and caressed her cheek, making her heart race. 'I'm going to want to undress you and touch you…and make love to you.' He closed his eyes for a moment and inhaled deeply. 'Okay, that may have been a little *too* honest.'

Stevie gulped as she felt desire pool deep in her belly. She cleared her throat, but her voice still came out as a whisper. 'Oh, I see. And no…no, it wasn't too honest. I think…I think it was the right amount of honest, and I think maybe if you did come in, I'd want those things too. So maybe tonight I just say *goodnight* and walk away.'

'But we'll see each other again?'

She smiled. 'Y-yes. I'd like that.'

He leaned towards her until his lips almost touched hers. She could feel his warm breath feathering over her mouth. 'May I kiss you goodnight?'

'I...I think that would be acceptable.'

She saw the smile play on his lips before they connected with hers in a slow, languorous kiss. His lips were soft but firm as his mouth glided over her tenderly. Thoughts of Jason clouded her mind and she suppressed a moan that was building within her and slipped her hand into his hair as her fantasy took her elsewhere. As she did so, his tongue sought entry to her mouth and she let him in, his hand still gently cupping her cheek.

When the kiss ended, she fluttered her eyes open and gazed, not into the eyes of Jason but into those of Marcus, which were now ablaze with lust. Her breathing was a little faster, and she was tingling in places that begged for his touch. Or was it Jason's touch? She pulled her bottom lip into her mouth suddenly overcome with a sense of grief at Jason's absence.

Marcus swallowed hard, his eyes now focused on her mouth. 'I think you'd better go now before I lose my resolve and change my mind.' His husky whisper made her stomach clench.

She nodded slowly. 'Goodnight, Marcus.'

'Goodnight, Stevie.'

She exited the car and walked on wobbly legs to the front door, turning to raise her hand in a wave as he watched her go inside. Only when she closed the door on the night did she hear him drive away. Leaning her back on the door, she allowed herself to slide to the floor. Her mind went immediately to the place she didn't want to venture. She suddenly felt guilty. As if she'd somehow been unfaithful to Jason. *It was a kiss for goodness sake, Stevie. Get a grip! That's all it was...just a kiss.* A hot, sensual kiss, fair enough, but it was Jason who had invaded her mind and he wasn't even here. And she didn't *belong* to him.

Feeling a little overheated after her passionate exchange with Marcus, she decided a soothing shower and bed would be the best thing. It was getting late, and she had preparations to make over the weekend for the Head of Science interviews taking place the following week.

Once showered and dried off, she slipped into a pair of old comfortable pyjamas and climbed into bed. She rested her head back, closed her eyes, and allowed her mind to wander back to her date with Marcus. More to the point, to the kiss they had shared. The man could certainly kiss. But his kisses took her mind somewhere she couldn't be. He had nice hands. But they weren't Jason's hands. His touch could bring her all manner of pleasures. *Stop it! God woman, you're so bloody sex starved you're getting obsessed!* She chastised herself. Taking a deep, calming breath, she did her best to relax and eventually sleep took her...

She looked around and realised she had somehow ended up back in the shower. A little confused, she fumbled around her brain trying to remember getting out and actually going to bed. She was sure she had, but maybe she'd been daydreaming. Could that be it?

Out of nowhere, warm hands slipped around her stomach from behind, making her gasp in surprise. She looked down at the hands but didn't recognise them. Long fingers caressed her skin, and a mouth began to kiss her neck. She arched, allowing whomever it was to continue their ministrations, seeing as it felt so damn good. A tongue joined in and licked a trail from her shoulder to just below her ear, and a shiver travelled the length of her relaxing spine. She turned around and found herself looking into hooded, deep blue eyes. Blue eyes? She opened her mouth to ask, 'What the hell are you doing in my shower?' but before she could utter a word, Marcus' mouth was on hers, drawing the breath from her body in a luscious, wet, deep kiss. His tongue laved at her mouth, and her hands involuntarily scratched at the smattering of hair on his toned chest, eliciting a deep groan from within him.

Suddenly, she was turned around again to face the tiles, and Marcus' hands were all over her body, slipping and sliding as the soapy water cascaded downwards. His fingers toyed with her breasts and tugged at her nipples until they stood to attention, aching for more. He released one breast in favour of sliding his hand down her body. His long fingers sliding into her dampness and massaging her most sensitive place. She moaned and writhed against him and was on the brink when he entered her, making her yelp with shock. This is a little strange and forward for our first time, her mind was telling her. But her body was too involved in the overwhelming sensations to react. She could feel the tension building and then a voice from behind her spoke... 'Stevie, I want to hear you call my name. You have all of me. Now give me something of you.'

Oh my God! Jason! It was Jason's voice. Filled with confusion, she turned her face and raked her eyes up a tattooed bicep and ended up locked onto a dark chocolate brown gaze. 'Come for me, Stevie...give in...give me this much.' Jason's voice was filled with desperation. She shuddered and called his name as her orgasm ripped through her body.

Woken by her own voice calling out, her eyes snapped open, and she looked around frantically, feeling completely disoriented. Her body thrummed, and her breathing was a set of erratic inhales and exhales punctuating the silence of the room. Realising she was in her own bed, tangled in her own sheets, completely alone, brought her back to earth with a mentally resounding thud. She rubbed her hands over her face as she tried to make sense of the highly erotic dream. She had begun by dreaming about the potentially *new* man in her life only to end it in the throes of a mind shattering orgasm at the hands and body of the man she gave up. It made sense when she thought about it.

Guilt was a *major* player here.

Glancing at the clock, she realised it was still very early morning. *Shit!* She rolled over once again and tried to clear her mind, but the fact was that it was buzzing in the wake of an incredible sex dream, and so she knew that her attempts at relaxation were futile. After around half an hour, she grabbed the novel from her nightstand and began reading. Ironically, the story was about a love triangle, and that fact didn't help matters, so she eventually gave up, deciding that she would go and make coffee instead.

As she stood in the kitchen waiting for the kettle to boil, she went over and over the dream. She was attracted to Marcus. There was no doubt about that. But Jason wasn't vacating her mind any time soon, so it would seem. But it wasn't her mind she was bothered about. It was the over-whelming sense of love that filled her heart when she had orgasmed that was most disconcerting.

CHAPTER SEVENTEEN

*I*t was a late September mid-morning, and Jason was sitting at the table with Dillon, eating bacon sandwiches. The executives from the week's corporate event had eaten breakfast earlier and left, and all the cleaning had been finished. The brothers were shortly heading out for a weekend trip to do a little brotherly male bonding. Dillon had made a big fuss about leaving Dorcas behind for a period of two whole nights, and Jason had wasted no time ribbing him about being pussy whipped.

Dorcas was very easy going and had encouraged the pair to go and make the most of the chilly but decent weather. Autumn was most definitely on its way, and the colours that were taking over the landscape were rich golden and red hues. The Highlands in autumn were just as stunning, if not more so, than summer.

They were heading up to Shieldaig. Jason had remembered the posh man—the one who had said *bloody* rather a lot at the old second hand book shop in London that he had visited with Stevie—saying that a former employee had moved up there to run a small camp site. He had located the place and called to make a booking. Their holdalls were packed and everything was set. Jason had even purchased a new helmet for Dillon, seeing as he had point blank refused to wear the one that had been bought for Stevie. Apparently, the teddy bear ears had put him off. *Go figure.*

Dillon clapped, then rubbed his hands together, and speaking through a mouthful of food he said, 'Right, bro. Ready when you are. Let's get this lads' weekend underway.'

'Sure thing. I'll grab my jacket and then we're away.'

Although the trip had been an almost last minute decision, Jason was keen to spend a little quality time with his brother. The events of the last couple of months had put a strain on their relationship, and this weekend would go some way to easing the tension and mending fences.

Once both men were clad in the appropriate safety gear for a two and a half hour bike ride, they mounted the hunk of metal and set out. The northbound A9 was fairly busy, and there were several traffic jams, but eventually they were off the main concrete motorway and riding through dramatic mountainous scenery. The smaller road took them through a changing colour palette of greens, browns, and purples. Majestic green pine trees swayed in the breeze, creating a heady fragrance even in the chilled September air. Every so often, they passed a little white crofters cottage or two at the side of the road, and Jason wondered what it would have been like before someone came and stuck a tarmac monstrosity right through the middle of this paradise.

Glancing up, he noted that darker clouds lay overhead, heavy with the threat of rain, and he said a little prayer that they would get the tent set up before the heavens opened. *Just a little further.* They passed several smaller lochs as they travelled through the Torridon area and eventually arrived in the pretty Wester Ross lochside village of Shieldaig. The site was set along Main Street behind a double fronted white cottage which overlooked the pretty loch. Just offshore there was a little island covered in trees. *What a stunning place. I can see why this Jim bloke was keen to stay here.*

Jason pulled the bike around the back of the house following a little sign that he spotted by a building to the other side of the lane. The sign on the building read *The Coffee Shack* and looked to be closed. Once the bike was parked, Jason made his way down to the back door of the cottage and knocked.

Within a few seconds, the door was pulled open and the brothers were greeted by a tall dark haired man in jeans and a Pearl Jam T-shirt—*bloody good taste*—and a very pretty blonde woman wearing loose fitting dungarees, who had what looked like paint on her face. Her wavy hair was in a scruffy knot on the top of her head.

'Hi there. You must be Mr. Reynolds.' The man spoke in a distinct Scottish accent and had a very welcoming smile.

'Yeah, I'm Jason. This is my little brother Dillon.' Both shook hands with the man.

'I keep telling him I'm not so little,' Dillon interjected.

The man chuckled. 'Great to meet you both. I'm Jim and this is my girlfriend, Flick.' He slipped his arm around the woman. Not in a *keep your hands off* kind of way. It was more of a *she's gorgeous and I'm besotted* kind of way. Jason smiled and shook hands with the woman. She seemed quite shy, and her cheeks turned pale crimson. *Sweet.*

'You can stick your tent wherever you like. It's a quiet weekend. There's a brick barbeque at your disposal, and the wash block is over here to my right. There's a nice pub just along the road if you fancy a beer and a good meal. Give me a shout if you need anything.'

'Great, thanks, Jim. Flick.' He nodded to the woman, who

waved and disappeared into the cottage. Jim followed her in and closed the door. Jason turned to walk with Dillon back towards the bike where the small tent and their bags were tethered.

They managed to erect the tent and make it to the pub just as the rain began to pitter-patter down. Once inside, they ordered beer and began to peruse the menu. Both settled on the homemade steak pie and took a seat at a small table with beers to wait.

'Thanks for bringing me, Jace. I know this last couple of months have been tough on you, but you still seem to be thinking about me in it all.'

'That's what brothers do. And you *are* my brother, after all.'

'I appreciate the fact that you keep saying that. It's hard for me to know how to act now. Since finding out I was adopted I've felt a little…I don't know…*lost* I suppose.'

Jason nodded. 'I know you have, but things haven't changed between you and me. I almost wish the letter had never been found. But at least it gave me answers.'

'Exactly. You can't regret finding out about Oliver and your half-brothers either, mate.'

Jason thought for a moment. 'No, you're right. I feel so…*guilty*…about so many things. I've fucked up *so* much, Dill.' He ran a hand back through his hair. 'At least with you I get to try and make amends.' He looked into the bottom of his glass.

'But you don't with Stevie? Is that what you're getting at?'

Jason sighed. 'Exactly. It's well and truly over. At some point I'll have to get my head around that.'

Dillon fidgeted restlessly for a few moments. Something was wrong. Jason watched him with his brow pulled into a frown, waiting for him to confess whatever the hell it was.

Eventually, Dillon said, 'She texted me yesterday.' *Ah.*

'She did?' Jason sat up a little straighter. His heart began to pound. 'Why?'

'Just asking if I was okay after...you know, everything that happened. And if I was enjoying Scotland.'

'Did she...did she mention me at all?' Jason couldn't make eye contact. Instead he twisted his glass between his palms. He already knew the answer.

'I'm sorry, Jace. She didn't. But I couldn't keep it from you. I hope you understand.'

'Yeah...yeah, course I do. It's fine. It's probably for the best anyway. No point dragging things out, eh?' His heart ached when he thought about her getting in touch and not even passing on a *hello.*

'I'm so sorry.'

'Hey, stop that. It's fine. Anyway...enough of me wallowing. Come on, tell me if you've come up with any plans for the future yet.'

'As a matter of fact, I think I have.' Dillon beamed.

Jason couldn't help returning the enthusiastic smile. 'Okay, out with it then.'

'I think...I think I want to stay. Up here I mean. With you, if you'll have me.'

Jason lifted his eyebrows, and a grin spread across his face. 'Really? Oh that's fantastic!' He slapped his brother's arm fondly.

'Yeah, I may apply for a few jobs...or better still.' He hesitated. 'You know how you talked about expanding?'

Jason frowned, wondering where this was leading. 'Yeah?'

'I want to be involved. I want to invest in the business. Help you open another camp.'

'Seriously?'

'Seriously. I've loved being here, Jace. The fresh air...the variety of working at the camp...everything. What do you think?'

'I think fuck yeah!' The brothers stood and embraced, slapping each other on the back. Jason ruffled his brother's hair. 'Welcome to the family business, Dillon.'

'Fan-fucking-tastic! I was terrified you'd say no. But me and Dee are getting on so well and I think...I think she may be the one.' His cheeks coloured as he spoke.

Jason's face softened at his brother's words. 'Aw, Dill, mate. I'm so glad things are working out for you and Dee. She's a sweet girl. You both deserve to be happy.'

'Thanks. I think...well...I know I've fallen hard. She's so... God, I can't even put it into words... I just fucking love her.' The wide chasm of a grin on Dillon's face said more than his simple words could express. Jason was happy for his brother, but the deep ache in his chest was slowly returning.

After a decent night's sleep, the brothers were up bright and early and set out for a walk. They called into The Coffee Shack, which was open as they passed this time. Jim was serving an elderly lady as they entered. She smiled fondly and bid him a good morning as she left.

Jim greeted them with a wide smile. 'Now then, gents. What can I do for you today?'

'Hi, Jim. We were thinking of heading out for a walk and thought we would pick up some water and some snacks.'

'Aye, grand idea. It's a nice bright day, and the forecast's good too. I've some lovely home baking in this morning, courtesy of one of the local ladies. I can highly recommend the flapjack.' He gestured to the fridge. The brothers collected bottles of water and some of the delicious looking cakes.

'So where are yous heading off to?' Jim enquired.

Jason shrugged. 'Not really sure. We thought we'd head out and see where we ended up.'

'Okay...if you like spectacular views, head along the road and turn up the track. Keep walking and you'll come to one of mine and Flick's favourite places in the world. The viewpoint looks down over a wee loch. We usually take a flask of coffee up there and just sit taking in the fresh air. Beautiful view from up there.'

Jason smiled. 'Great. Thanks Jim. See you later.'

'Bye, gents. Have a nice walk.'

Jason and Dillon headed in the direction of the lane Jim had talked about. Once on the lane, they headed up the track that led away from the main road. Eventually, a little out of breath they reached the place Jim had mentioned, and Dillon gasped.

'Fuck me, he wasn't wrong, bro. Look at that.'

Jason joined his brother, and looking out at the view, he felt an overwhelming urge to snap a photo and text it to Stevie. She would simply *love* this place. From their lofty viewpoint, they had the amazing panoramic vista. Before them, they looked down into a lush valley with a loch at the bottom, which was edged by trees.

'Yeah, it's stunning. Really, *really* beautiful.' Jason slumped to the ground and stared out at the view, awash with regret that he would never be able to bring Stevie here to show her this place.

Dillon sat down beside him. 'You can't stop thinking about her, can you?'

Jason glanced at his brother and smiled. 'That obvious, is it?'

Dillon snorted. 'Oh yeah. *That* obvious.'

'Ah...sorry, mate. I must be a bit of a drag right now.'

Dillon nudged him. 'Don't be daft. I do understand you know...and I'll be honest...I think you maybe should give things another try. Try to convince her that she should be *here* with *you*.'

'What's the point? I'd just be going over old ground again.'

'But you said yourself the other day you're miserable without her.'

'Yeah, but she doesn't feel the same. I mean...she didn't even ask about me when she contacted you.'

'I bet she wanted to.'

Jason shook his head. 'That's as maybe...but she didn't. It'll take me time, but I *will* move on. I have to.'

CHAPTER EIGHTEEN

A week had passed since Stevie's first date with Marcus. He had been in contact by text, there had been a couple of calls over the week, and they had arranged to see each other again. He very much enjoyed cooking and had invited her around to his home for dinner. His four-year-old son, Archie, was staying with his mother for the weekend, which Stevie was relieved about. It wasn't that she didn't like children. She worked with them after all. But meeting one that could potentially be involved in her personal life long term if her relationship with Marcus lasted was more than a little scary. She wasn't quite ready to play mummy yet.

The cab dropped her off at Marcus' rather beautiful Georgian town house at half past seven. She clutched the bottle of Pinot Noir as if doing so would afford her some protection for her weak will against this man and his Roman god good looks.

He opened the door before she had a chance to knock and stepped out onto the steps to greet her. 'Stevie...wow, you look gorgeous.' She glanced down at the blue floaty skirt and white fitted shirt she wore, needing to remind herself of what she had actually chosen to put on.

Her cheeks heated. 'Oh...thank you. So do you.' Her eyes took in the tall handsome man before her dressed in dark denim jeans and a fitted white T-shirt. His feet were bare. *Oh, goodness me.*

'Oy-oy Marcus! No prizes for guessing what you're up to tonight, old chap!' Came a voice from a little way down the road. Both Stevie and Marcus snapped their heads towards the interruption.

'Oh God, that's all I need.' Marcus rolled his eyes, grabbed the bottle of wine from her grasp, and tugged her through the door quickly. Once inside, he led her to the spacious lounge and placed the bottle down on his coffee table.

'Who was that?' Stevie asked as she straightened herself up again.

'My neighbour and colleague. Bit of an arse really. It was very bad karma buying a house so near to his. Had I realised who he was at the time I would've looked elsewhere, I can assure you.'

She was surprised at his strong reaction. 'So he's a lawyer too?'

'Yep. He is. Although I wouldn't let him get me out of a parking ticket, but don't tell anyone I said so.'

She giggled. 'I'll bear that in mind. Anyway, something smells good.'

'Why thank you...not as good as you though,' he said as he leaned in to kiss her cheek. She felt the heat return again and fiddled with her hair for a second, unsure of how to react to his outward display of affection. Realising she must seem like a lovesick teenager, she immediately pulled her hand back to her side.

Marcus cringed. 'Sorry was that cheesy?

'Not at all. I'm glad you like my perfume.'

He stepped towards her and slipped his hands around her

waist. Lowering his face, he rubbed his nose down hers. 'I really do. Can I kiss you?'

She nibbled her lower lip. *Will it be as heated as last time? Will I be able to stop myself from thinking about Jason? OhGod. OhGod. OhGod, what do I say?* 'Yes,' she whispered. *Shit where did that come from?* He smiled and lowered his mouth to hers, gently touching her lips with his. There was no tongue. No urgency. Just a sweet, heart-melting kiss.

She sighed. Thankfully there hadn't been enough time for Jason's 'ghost' to ruin the moment.

'Come on. Let's go eat.' He took her hand and pulled her towards the kitchen diner, collecting the wine from the coffee table as he walked. 'I was going to set up the dining room, but I thought it'd be too formal. I thought we could eat in here.'

'Sounds good to me.' She glanced around the sleek, modern units that skirted the walls and the glass table situated at one end. 'What are we having?'

'We're starting with goat's cheese and cranberry filo parcels, and for main I've made salmon en-croute. Then for dessert...chocolate dipped strawberries.'

'Mmmm. Sounds delicious. I'm starved'

On the same night, Dillon and Jason were sitting on a wooden bench on the campsite chatting to Jim about the area and the village.

Dillon stood. 'Well, I'm off to give my lovely girl a call. Speak to you soon.'

'See you soon, bro.' The other two men watched as Dillon walked off to find the best place to get a mobile signal.

'So, Jason, is there a woman in your life?' Jim asked as he took a pull from his beer bottle.

Jason laughed a little and shook his head. 'Now therein lays a very long, very confusing tale, my friend.'

Jim raised his eyebrows. 'Ah, complicated?'

'You wouldn't believe it. It's thanks to *her* that I'm here. She took me into a book shop in London—'

'Let me guess. It was the Book Depository.'

'It sure was.'

'What did you think of the place?'

Jason quirked his eyebrow. 'I thought it was bloody fabulous.' He replied with a chuckle.

Jim threw his head back and laughed loudly. 'I guess from that answer you met Charles too?'

'I bloody did old chap. He's a rather bloody spiffing old boy.'

'Aye, that he is, that he is. How many times did he say bloody in one sentence? Did you count?'

'I tried but I lost count after...ooh...about one hundred.' They both laughed.

'He's a top bloke though, Charles. Smashing guy. Did he tell you about me then?'

'Not in great detail. Just that you'd moved up here and your girlfriend had recently moved here to be with you.'

'Ha...you want complicated? Did he happen to tell you that Flick is actually my ex-wife?'

Jason raised his eyebrows. 'What? Seriously?'

Jim nodded and took another swig of his beer. 'Aye. Never a truer thing said, my friend. We went to hell and back. Another long story. Alls I will say is that no matter how complicated things get if you are meant to be together you will be. Nothing'll stop you. I thought Flick and I were done for. She left me. And then several years down the line, I'd moved up here to get away from the hell that is London—'

Jason laughed. 'So you feel that way too, eh?'

'Abso-fucking-lutely, Jason. Not my idea of a home, but each to their own, eh? Anyways, to cut a long story short, I decided that whatever happened I'd be with her. If it meant me moving back there then I'd do it. No matter how much I hated the place. Being with her was more important to me.'

Jason sat in silence as he pondered Jim's words. 'But you ended up *here* anyway.'

'Aye, there was an incident. I won't freak you out with the details, but Flick ended up in hospital. I nearly lost her.' His voice broke and his eyes misted over. The memory was clearly still painful.

Jason placed a hand on his shoulder. 'Shit, Jim, I'm sorry, mate.'

'Aye, thankfully she came out the other side and decided she wanted out of the rat race. And so, a few months on and here we are. I couldn't be happier.'

The cottage door opened, and Flick appeared in a pair of tattered old jeans and a long thick cardigan, which she had wrapped around herself apparently to guard against to chilled evening temperature. She cocked her head on one side. 'Jim, sweetie, I'm off to bed, and I was hoping I wouldn't be going alone.'

'Ah and there she is...my gorgeous girl. I'll bid you good-night, Jason.'

'G'night Jim. Night Flick.' He saluted her with his beer bottle, and she waved back briefly, clearly far more interested in her man. *Just as it should be.* Jim walked back towards the house, turning at the last minute to address Jason again. 'Oh, and Jason...I don't know your reasons for needing to get out of the big smoke, but if they can be resolved...if that girl is the one you love then...maybe you need to rethink your priorities, my friend.' And with that he entered the cottage and closed the door behind him, leaving Jason to ponder his words.

Dillon returned just then, and Jason watched as he walked towards him smiling. 'Ah here he is...love's young dream,' he teased.

The brothers walked together towards their tent. 'Awww, mate. She's missing me. The bed's apparently too cold without me to put her feet on.'

'Urgh! Get me a bucket! I'm gonna hurl,' Jason mocked again.

'Fuck off. You'd be the same if St—' He clamped his mouth shut.

Jason rolled his eyes. 'It's fine. You *are* allowed to say her name. And yes, if she were here it'd be *me* making *you* hurl. I know.'

'So, has Jim gone to bed?' Dillon asked quickly changing the subject.

Jason nodded. 'Yeah. We had a good chat when you'd gone. Fairly brief but good. He's a decent bloke. Gave me some things to think about.'

'Great. Well, I'm knackered, so I'm turning in.' Dillon yawned and rubbed his eyes.

Jason automatically yawned too, suddenly realising he was exhausted. 'Yep, me too.'

Dillon clasped Jason's shoulder. 'Night, bro. Sleep well, eh?'

Jason smirked. 'I will if you don't talk in your sleep.'

'Ah, get lost.' His retort was accompanied by a one-finger salute.

Shaking his head and grinning at his younger brother, Jason followed Dillon into the tent.

Thankfully, sleep took Jason easily and his dreams were a little more peaceful than he had become used to lately. The next morning, Jason made coffee as Dillon slept. He was formulating a plan in his head. What Jim had said had really affected him. Hearing the same things from his brother had not moved him for some reason, but the story Jim had told him about how he and Flick ended up together made him see things a little more clearly. If he could just give London a chance.

If he could just try.

'Morning, ugly spud.' Dillon yawned and stretched as he crawled out of the two-man tent in his pyjama bottoms and T-shirt.

Jason laughed. 'Have you looked in a mirror this morning?'

His younger brother scrunched his face. 'Fuck off.'

His eyebrows raised and he smirked. 'Oooh, mature.'

'I'm taking my cue from the best.' Dillon grabbed the mug of coffee from Jason's hand. 'You were restless last night, Jace. Is everything okay?'

Jason nodded. 'Yeah…fine…just been thinking. I may need your help.'

'Oh yeah? With what?'

'Look, don't be pissed off okay—'

'Ahhh, you see, whenever someone says that you automatically *know* that you're going to get pissed off. Because nine times out of ten, people only say that when what they're about to say is something bad. And that means that you saying, 'Don't be pissed off', is a bit of a waste of time because the fact that you had to say it means—'

'Dillon, for fuck's sake! Will you shut up and listen?' Jason knew he was scowling at his jesting brother but couldn't help it.

Dillon held his empty hand up. 'Oooh, sorry! What's eating you?'

'Okay, so I know you came up here to be with me. But after talking to Jim, I think maybe I need to think about giving things a go with Stevie. But that would mean—'

'You moving down south for a while? Yeah, I'm cool with that. I really think me, Dee, and Harry could manage running the place whilst you guys figure out your shit. I mean, if you *don't* go, you'll always wonder, won't you?'

Feeling rather shocked at the easy-going reply, Jason nodded fervently. 'Yeah. That's just it. I love her. I should try to make things work. Do you think I'm crazy?'

'Not in the slightest. I'd think you were crazy if you didn't.'

'Great. Don't mention a word, okay? I'm going to set off next Friday. When we get home later today, I'm going to arrange cover rotas for the camp and sort things out. I know that you'll all manage fine, and I'll be a phone call away. I need to do this. It feels like the right thing to do.'

Dillon put his arm around him and pulled him into a half hug. 'Yeah, you do.'

Later that day when the brothers arrived back, Jason called a meeting and explained to the staff that he would be going away again. He didn't go into great details as to the reason for his trip, but the crew gave each other knowing glances, making Jason aware that they knew far more than they were letting on.

Once everything was in place, he began to feel the butterflies spring to life in his stomach. The smile returned to his face, and he felt positive about the future.

'You should let her know you're coming down, you know,' Dillon said, breaking Jason from his daydream.

'Nope. I'm going to surprise her. I want to see the look on her face when she opens the door. That'll be the best bit. So, you, my dear brother, will keep schtum.' He wagged his finger in his face.

Dillon held his hands up in surrender. 'Have it your way. But if you turn up and she's not looking her best, you'll experience the wrath of a woman in the throes of unpreparedness. It's not a pretty sight, bro. Believe me. When Dee and I were first together, she made a thing about getting to the bathroom before I woke up so she could brush her teeth and do her hair.' He sniggered. 'I tried to tell her that morning hair and carpet tongue are some of the things I adore about her, but she still won't have it, even now. I'm telling you, if you turn up and she's wearing no make-up, scruffy yoga pants, and a T-shirt with something spilled down the front...' He made a whistling noise and shook his head.

'I don't care if she comes to the door wearing a bin liner and Wellington boots. She'll still be as hot as hell to me.'

'Well, don't say I didn't warn you.'

'Don't worry, I won't.' The warning fell on deaf ears. He was far too excited for that. As he walked back to his cabin, his phone rang. Recognising the number as that of his friend and former employer, Jack Hilton, he answered breezily, 'Now then, mate! Long-time, no speak. How's it going in the security world?'

'JR, buddy. It's going very well. Hence the reason for my call. I'm not sure if you're interested at all, but I've got a posting in Africa for a few months. I could really use you. What do you say?' the disembodied but familiar voice asked.

'Ah, no can do, my friend. Just about to make the craziest move of my life.'

'What? Crazier than leaving the army to come and work for me?'

'Oh, hell yeah. Much crazier than that.' Jason couldn't help the stationary grin on his face.

'Okay, JR, if you change your mind, you know where I am. The pay wasn't that great anyway. Just a charity job.'

The two old friends made small talk and caught up on each other's lives, but Jason didn't go into details about his plans. He had no reason to do so. They were all in his heart and head, ready to be put into motion…

CHAPTER NINETEEN

Stevie was feeling rather nervous yet again. After having such a lovely meal at Marcus' last weekend, she had rather foolishly invited him to her house for dinner the following Friday. He had been the perfect gent when they were at his house, and whilst they had got hot and heavy kissing on his couch, he hadn't pushed her too far. It almost seemed as if he was holding back on purpose to make her desire him more. The problem was, every time their kissing had become passionate it was Jason's mouth she was imagining. It had been Jason touching her breasts and kissing her neck.

At just gone midnight, they had been lying on his couch, his hot breath sending shivers down her spine as he tugged at her nipple through her satin bra. His firm arousal had pressed against her thigh, and she clung onto him, wondering how far things were going to go. His hand had trailed down her body until he found the hem of her skirt and slipped his hand up her thigh until he was cupping her bottom. His breathing was heavy, and her own heart had hammered against her chest.

Suddenly, he had pulled away and stood up, adjusting

himself in his trousers. 'Oh God, Stevie, I'm so sorry. You must think I'm some sex maniac with roaming hands.' He ran his hands through his hair.

Relief had washed over her. It would've been too soon. She pulled her own clothing down. 'No...not at all. It's fine.'

'I've had too much wine to drive you home, but let me get you a cab. I think I'm moving things along too fast, and I need to hit the brakes a little.

She nodded. 'Yes...yes, I think you're right. I'm sorry. I feel like such a tease.'

He sat beside her once again. 'Hey, no, it's my fault. Please don't feel that way. I would like nothing more than to take you to bed. But I don't want to mess this up, you know?'

She had nodded again and he had reached for the phone and called a cab to come and collect her. Once he had ended the call, he took her hands in his. 'Is this going at all well to you? I mean us...are we...can you see a future?' There was hope in his eyes, but she felt stumped as to what to say in response. Her head had buzzed with several possible answers, but none of them felt appropriate.

'To be honest...I...I—'

He had huffed the air from his lungs, puffing out his cheeks in the process. 'There I go again, eh? Putting you on the spot. I seem to keep doing that. Forgive me. I haven't done the whole dating thing in so long, and if I'm honest, I haven't got a clue what I'm doing.' He stood again and smiled down at her.

'Really, Marcus, it's fine. Stop putting yourself under so much pressure.' The cab had pulled up outside the front of the house and honked its horn. Stevie had grabbed her bag and jacket. 'Come to mine for dinner next Friday. Okay? Sevenish?'

A look of relief had washed over his features and he

stepped towards her. He cupped her face in his hands. 'That would be lovely. Thank you. I'll look forward to it.' He bent and kissed her softly.

Friday had come around very quickly, and she had racked her brains trying to come up with something she could cook that would be tasty but couldn't be easily ruined thanks to nerves. She had settled on lasagne. You couldn't go far wrong with Italian.

The food was in the oven, and she had taken the time to select her favourite black satin underwear and a black dress that was fitted to the waist and flared out from the hips. It was rather formal but she didn't mind. The dress made her feel sexy, and she *so* wanted to feel sexy. She was hoping that perhaps they could both put their demons to rest and take the next step. Maybe that way she would eradicate Jason from her thoughts and her heart. Maybe then she could start to think about a future with Jason... *Dammit, Marcus. With Marcus! Fuck, this is not going well, and he's not even here yet.*

She pinned her hair up and applied a little lip gloss, nervously assessing herself in the mirror for what felt like the hundredth time. At seven o'clock sharp, there was a knock on the door. She slipped on her black stilettos and carefully descended the staircase.

When she opened the door, a very handsome man in black slacks, suit jacket, and a white shirt greeted her. The wide smile on his face told her he appreciated what he saw.

'Wow, Stevie, look at you...just breath-taking.'

She felt her cheeks and was sure she was probably as red as the roses he had in his hand. 'You don't look half bad your-self, Mr. Sumner.'

He held the flowers out to her. 'Roses for an English rose.' She took them and inhaled their sweet scent, stepping back to allow Marcus into the house. Once inside, she walked to the kitchen and placed the flowers down on the counter top. His arms slipped around her waist, and he nuzzled her neck. 'Mmm, the food smells great. But as I always say...not as good as you.' He kissed her, sending shivers around her body. She closed her eyes, intending to relish the sensations, but once again guilt took over.

She moved away. 'Dinner is almost ready. Could you open the wine?' She turned to smile at him, hoping that doing so would reassure him. *Why the hell can't I enjoy one evening without Jason appearing in my bloody mind?* The anger she felt at herself caused her to slam a plate down with a little more force than intended.

'Stevie, are you okay? You seem tense.' He stepped behind her and massaged her shoulders.

'Yes, yes I'm fine. Just tired,' she lied. 'I've been doing some more preparation for the Head of Science interviews. They were delayed a little, which you would think would help, but it's quite exhausting.'

He kissed her hair. 'You should've called. We could've rearranged or...or I could've cooked. Or we could have eaten out...or had a takeaway maybe?'

'I'm fine,' she snapped.

He stiffened behind her and dropped his hands from her shoulders. 'Perhaps I should go. I...I get the feeling that you're not really in the mood for me being here tonight.'

He stepped away, and now the guilt that washed over her was there as a result of how mean she'd been to him. It wasn't *his* fault Jason infiltrated her every waking thought. Perhaps only waiting several weeks before dating had been a mistake. But Marcus was sweet and funny. Not to mention *very* attractive. He deserved better from her.

She turned and walked over to where he stood. Placing her hands on his hard chest, she gazed up into his eyes. 'I'm so sorry. Please don't go. I've been... It's tiredness but I *am* glad you're here.'

He slipped his arms around her waist and bent so that their noses were touching. 'It's good to know. Now dish up and then we can snuggle.'

She smiled at his words. He was very affectionate, even though they had technically only just met. He seemed to want to take things somewhere and to see a future. She wished she could say she felt the same. But she was confused. The silly thing was that the guilt she felt over Jason was completely unfounded. Their relationship had ended.

Her choice.

Over dinner they chatted about Archie and his likes and dislikes. Marcus beamed when he spoke of his little boy.

'He sounds like quite a character.'

'Oh, he really is. Some of the things he comes out with. I'd like you to meet him...if...if you felt the time was right. Maybe not right away.'

She gulped. Meeting another woman's child was not something she relished the thought of, nor was it something she had ever planned. Being the step-mum in the scenario was something she hadn't contemplated before. Archie was always with his mother when she met Marcus. It was easier that way. She could almost, cruelly, pretend he didn't exist. She hated herself for feeling that way, but being a stand-in mum of any kind terrified her. She imagined it would be different if the child were her own. But this situation didn't fill her with that kind of joy.

'Oh...I...it's not something I've...I'm not sure.' Her cheeks heated.

His smile dissolved. 'Oh, okay. Not to worry. I wasn't sure if it was maybe a little too early to mention it. I see that it was. I apologise.'

'No, don't be sorry. I'm sure he's a lovely little boy, but we're still in the early stages of our relationship, and I'm sorry but I don't think it's a good idea for Archie that I'm introduced to him, in case things don't work out.'

He nodded as he stood to clear the plates away. 'Yes, you're probably right.' He turned to face her. 'If I'm moving things too fast, you will tell me, won't you? I know this isn't easy for either of us, but it's important to me that you're comfortable.'

'I'm comfortable. I feel a little uneasy about jumping into a little boy's life at such an early stage. But please stop worrying so much.'

He kissed her forehead, and a sense of calm washed over her this time. They set about clearing the dinner plates. A domesticated silence ensued, and she couldn't help smiling at how natural it felt. But then another thought plagued her. *It feels natural to do all the things that friends would do, but when things get more serious I panic...*

'You're deep in thought again,' he said as he poured some more wine.

'Sorry? Oh...yes, sorry. I keep drifting off and thinking about lesson plans.' She was getting too good at lying.

Once the dishwasher was loaded, they retired to the lounge. Stevie put her iPod onto the random setting and hoped that she had managed to clear off all the songs that reminded her of Jason. Doing so had been hard but a necessary step if she wanted to be able to listen to music at all. Marcus sat on the sofa and held his arm out for her to snuggle next to him. She slipped off her shoes and got comfy resting her head on his shoulder.

He traced lazy circles on her bare arm as they sat in silence listening to the music for a while. She closed her eyes as 'Canonball' by Damien Rice floated across the room from the speakers. Even though it wasn't a song that usually evoked memories of Jason, as she listened to the words images of him flashed through her mind. In her mind's eye, she could see him laid across his bed. She would be resting her chin on his chest and gazing into his melted chocolate eyes as he told her stories about his travels.

Or he would be striding along the road in London when they spent the day shopping. Every so often, he would glance down at her and smile lovingly. He would clasp her hand in his and squeeze it tight.

Or they would be sitting on the riverbank in their special place. He'd have his guitar in his lap and would reach forward and tuck a strand of hair behind her ear before singing something meaningful that he'd learned especially for her. A smile played on her lips as she pictured him. She couldn't hear him. Damien Rice's song became the soundtrack for the images as they rolled around her mind.

Before she knew what was happening, her chin was tilted upward and lips were covering hers. A hand was in her hair. Tingles travelled from top to bottom, the full length of her spine, following the zipper on her dress as it slowly travelled the same route. The dress was slipped downwards, and an appreciative moan could be heard. She reached her hands up to unfasten the buttons on his shirt, smoothing her hands over his skin as they now lay on the sofa caressing each other. She let out a contented sigh as his lips found her neck.

CHAPTER TWENTY

*T*he Friday evening traffic had been a complete nightmare. It seemed that every bad driver had been given a pass out for the night and every road presented more than the normal amount of expected hazards for a proficient rider. Jason had lost count of the number of times he had cursed and honked at people who simply had no regard for other road users, let alone bikes. As if making this journey wasn't difficult enough.

He had gone over and over things a million times in his mind. What would he say? How would she react? Was this still what she wanted now that she'd had time to think? A combination of excitement and fear caused the adrenaline to course through his veins. Another idiot pulled out without looking, causing him to swerve and almost come off his bike. His fingers were on the horn and he gestured, but the driver was completely oblivious. *Fucking moron!*

Eventually, after what felt like the longest ride of his life, he pulled into the Sure Stay hotel. He removed his helmet before entering the reception and ran a hand through his shaggy hair. The blonde receptionist's eyes lit up when she saw him. She wasn't one he had encountered before. He walked over to the desk.

'Good evening, sir.'

He flashed his best smile. 'And a good evening to you.' He bent to read her name badge, and she thrust her breasts forward. 'Stacey. And how are you today?'

She blushed and fiddled with her hair. 'I'm fine, thank you. Are you checking in?'

'I certainly am. The name is Reynolds. Jason Reynolds.'

'Okay. You were in room fifty but...' She glanced around conspiratorially. 'I think I may upgrade you to room twenty five. It's one of the recently refurbished ones.'

'Why thank you, Stacey. How very kind of you.'

He signed all the necessary paperwork and handed over his credit card to be swiped. She ran through all the usual information about fire exits and breakfasts, and Jason was about to walk away.

'Erm...Mr. Reynolds...I finish at ten if you'd like a little company.' She fluttered her eyelashes at him and he smiled back.

With a wink he said, 'Thank you, Stacey. I'll bear that in mind.' He had absolutely no intentions of doing anything with the information, but he wouldn't complain about the room upgrade, that's for sure.

He located room twenty-five, and when he entered he was pleasantly surprised to see freshly painted walls, modern bedding, and aesthetically pleasing artwork adorning the walls. He was only planning on being here one...maybe two nights. If things went according to plan, he hoped Stevie would invite him to stay there whilst they worked out things like living arrangements. Would she want him to live with her? Would she prefer he rented somewhere whilst he was here? He had enough money to do so but not long term.

After a hot shower, he pulled out the ironing board and plugged in the iron. He was determined to look the part of the wooing lover tonight. He pulled out his white linen shirt and cargo pants. He had enough clothes for a couple of days in his bag, but they were crammed in so tight that if he didn't iron them he would look like he had been dragged backwards through a hedge.

Once dressed, he ran his fingers through his hair but left it shaggy, knowing how much Stevie loved to run her fingers through it. After checking his appearance and splashing on some cologne from the tiny bottle he had managed to squeeze into his bag, he grabbed his wallet and the letter he had written and set out to find a cab.

He stopped off at the supermarket and picked up the largest bouquet of flowers they had along with a nice bottle of Pinot Noir. Back in the cab, his palms were sweaty, and his heart was tripping the light fantastic in his chest. This was it. He was going to tell her what he'd decided. He'd rehearsed the speech over and over in his mind. He had gone over it on the phone with Oliver.

'To be honest, Jason, I would just go and be yourself, son. From what you've said, she doesn't strike me as the kind of girl who needs the pretence. In my opinion, flowers and an *I love you* will be sufficient.'

'But I want to make this work, Dad. I need her to see that I'm serious. If I go in there just as *me*, it'll all come out wrong.'

'Okay. I have a solution to that. You write it down. When she opens the door, don't speak, just hand her the letter and treat it like a gimmick. She's got a sense of humour. I think she'd go for that.'

'Do you know what, Olly, I think you may have a great idea there.'

'Yeah? Well, us old folks have our uses,' he had chuckled.

'Although...won't it seem a bit mushy?'

'You're a six foot two giant of a man. Anything you do where you place your heart on your sleeve will be wonderful to her. Just tell her how you've felt without her in your life. Tell her that you can't continue like that.'

He had nodded even though Oliver wasn't there to see the gesture. 'Okay...okay...I can do that.'

'Great. Now when you're all done, you'll let me know, yes? Then we can get our flights booked to come see you. It doesn't matter whether you're in London or Aviemore, son. We want to come visit.'

'Yeah. I'll let you know as soon as possible. I can't wait to see you all.'

'Great. So you go get your girl. And remember...heart on your sleeve, okay?'

'Heart on my sleeve. Got it.'

'Goodnight, son.'

'Bye, Dad.'

Sitting there in the back of the cab, he remembered the conversation fondly. His relationship with Oliver, Hannah, and his brothers had been taking off. It had been limited to telephone calls and emails, but they had chatted plenty. They had asked if he would mind if they visited, and he'd jumped at the chance.

The cab pulled up outside Stevie's house. The letter he had written was in his back pocket, and he clutched the flowers in one hand, the wine in the other. After fumbling around for his wallet and paying the driver, he climbed out of the open door.

Hesitantly and with his heart still pounding like a jack-hammer, he made his way to Stevie's front door. After several deep-cleansing breaths, he tucked the wine bottle under his arm and rapped on the door. He heard voices inside. *Oh shit...*

she's got a friend around. Bloody typical. He began to think maybe Dillon had been right. Maybe surprising her wasn't such a good idea. But then on second thought, he decided whatever he had to say could be said in front of the crazy Science teacher friends he had heard so much about.

The door flung open. A familiar but flushed face and wide eyes greeted him. Stevie was fiddling with the sleeve of her dress and a bare chested man appeared behind her looking puzzled.

Jason's mouth suddenly dried up. Peering over Stevie's shoulder he trailed his disbelieving gaze down the man's body and noticed his fly button was open. He was either dressing or undressing and neither were good conclusions to reach. Jason lost the ability to speak. Stevie's jaw dropped open and her hand covered her mouth. Shock registering in her clear blue eyes.

Jason's heart leapt and he stumbled to find words. 'Erm...erm...'

The man stepped forward and rested a hand possessively on Stevie's shoulder. 'Are you all right? Can we help you?'

Jason glanced between the man and Stevie as realisation sank in. The bottle of wine slipped out from under his arm, crashing to the ground and sending shards of broken glass and blood red liquid into the air.

Jason stared blankly down at the mess.

'Oh God...Jason!' Stevie called out, but he had dropped the flowers too and had turned to walk away. 'Jason! Please! Wait!'

He kept walking, but could clearly hear the raised voices behind him.

'Oh so that's *him*, is it? Why the fuck is he turning up here? Were you expecting him, Stevie? Is this why you were in a mood earlier? Because I turned up when you knew he was coming?' The man's voice boomed around the quiet street. 'You've nothing on your feet! You'll get hurt! Stevie!'

'Please...please, Jason! Slow down. I need to explain!'

He didn't stop, nor did he turn around.

He could hear her footsteps gaining on him, bare fleet slapped against the pavement. But he carried on straight ahead with determination. He needed to get away. The man's voice continued to shout, although Jason had blocked out his words. He didn't much care for what the man thought or said. Nor did he care what Stevie was trying to achieve by running after him.

Eventually, she reached him, grabbed his arm, and swung him around, bringing him to an abrupt halt. 'Jason, what the hell are you doing here?'

He clenched his jaw. 'I came to see *you*. Isn't that obvious?' His calm voice belied the turmoil beneath his skin. Absently, he wondered if the anguish he felt within was etched all over his face.

Her brow creased in confusion. 'But...*why*?'

'Because in my stupid fucking head I thought it was a good idea. I can see now that I was wrong. You've clearly moved on. Now, let go of my fucking arm, or I'll drag you along with me, because I'm leaving.'

Stevie closed her eyes for a second. Tears were rolling down her face. 'I don't understand. What's going on, Jason?'

'Nothing is going on. Now get the fuck off my arm. *Please.*' He could feel heat rising from his chest to his cheeks. His heart was thumping so hard it was almost painful.

'You...you dropped this envelope on my doorstep.' She held it out to him with a shaking hand but he stepped away.

Through gritted teeth he said, 'Burn it. And the damned flowers. Just burn them.' His voice cracked as the words tumbled from his mouth.

Tugging his arm from her grip, he walked away leaving her barefooted and sobbing in the street.

'Please, Jason. Please don't leave. Talk to me. It's not how it looks.'

He shook his head as he continued; again without looking back. How could it not be *exactly* how it looked? His chest ached. He was too late.

He'd lost out to another man.

CHAPTER TWENTY-ONE

*S*tevie turned and jogged back down the street, trying to see through the fog caused by her tears and ignoring the pain of the gravel digging into her bare feet. Back at her house she stepped over the broken glass and wine that stained her doorstep. Marcus was sitting, fully dressed again, on the sofa when she walked in. His elbows rested on his knees, and his head was in his hands. He didn't glance up when she entered, but sat there staring at the floor.

'Marcus, I'm sorry about all that. I honestly had no idea he was coming.' Her voice wavered as she sniffled a little.

He looked up, confusion etched on his face. 'Why was he here?' His voice was a hoarse, hurt-filled whisper.

'I...I actually don't know. I don't get it. We ended things. *I* ended things. I told him I couldn't do the long distance thing. So I have no clue what it was all about.'

He dragged his hands over his hair. 'The thing is, Stevie. The way you ran after him... You're still very much in love with him, aren't you?'

'I...I care for him deeply. It's not something that can just be switched off. There's so much history—'

His eyes were now filled with a resigned sadness. 'You never had any intention of giving you and me a fair go, did you?'

She stared into the deep blue of his irises. 'I wanted us to work. I *was* trying. I really was. There's nothing I want more than to move on.' As she spoke the words, she realised they were a lie. Moving on was the last thing she wanted.

He stood and stepped in front of her. 'But when *I* was kissing you...when *I* was touching you...were you thinking about him? Were you wishing it was him? That's why you couldn't go through with sex with me, isn't it? That's why you pulled away.' She wished his questions were rhetorical, as she couldn't find words that wouldn't hurt him further.

'I don't want to talk about this now. Please can we just—'

His nostrils flared and he rolled his head back. 'That means the answer's yes, then. Every time I caressed you. Earlier when we nearly ended up making love... The only reason that happened was because you were thinking of *him*.' He dropped his hands and stepped away. 'You know, I could handle you still having feelings for him to a point. I still have feelings for my wife. I get it. Like you said, there's history there that you can't just switch off, but this...your reaction when you saw him. I could've been on *fire*, and you'd have still run down the street after *him*.' He gestured towards the window. 'I need some time to think. And I think you do too. Decide what you want. If it's him then so be it. If it's me... well...we'll talk. But I have to know one hundred per cent that you're committed to giving *us* a try. I can't go through this when you get reminiscent, Stevie. It's not fair.'

'I'm sorry. I really am.'

He grabbed his jacket and walked to the door. He looked back with his jaw clenched and deep sadness emanating from his very being. 'I know we haven't been together long and I know that I have baggage, but I care for you, Stevie. It's happened fast for me, and I can't help that. But I don't want *half* of you. I want to know that you're *mine* completely. Otherwise, I'd rather be alone.' And with that he left.

She watched him walk down the street whilst talking on his phone, presumably calling for a cab to take him home. She looked down and realised she was still holding the envelope in her hands. Jason had told her to burn it. The front was blank, but she had a feeling something important was inside. She closed the door, then slumped onto the sofa, and ripped it open.

Hi Stevie, my beautiful soulmate ,
You're probably wondering why I'm standing before you like some kind of bad mime act whilst you read this. But I was advised to place my heart on my sleeve, and I was so terrified I would muck things up that I decided it was better to write down what I wanted to say to you. That way I wouldn't miss a single word. I know I'm probably grinning like a complete tool at the moment, and I can only apologise to you for this. But here goes...
When I left you ten years ago, I did so with such difficulty. My heart broke with each step I took away from you. Knowing that I was breaking your heart at the same time made that fact so much more painful. The physical pain I felt was sometimes unbearable. What you and I had wasn't just puppy love. It was deep and intense. I spent so much time sitting alone and listening to songs through my headphones that reminded me of you. I tortured myself over and over, but it felt like I deserved to feel that way.
When you turned up in Scotland, I was so horrible to you, and I can't express how bad I feel for that. Seeing you knocked me sideways. You were still as beautiful as I remembered. But you

*had blossomed into this stunning, sexy, curvy woman. I wanted
you from the second I realised that it really was you. But I was
afraid of letting you in. I didn't deserve you and I know I still
don't.*

*Making love to you was the most amazing experience I have
ever had. EVER. Seeing you fall apart in ecstasy was just the
most beautiful sight I've ever seen. I think I said that before.
But I'm being real and honest and that's how I feel. Watching
you leave me on that bus shattered me into a million pieces. I
could and should have done something about it. But I was a
coward.*

*Coming down to London and spending time with you there
made me see that the place has lost its fear factor for me. All the
bad things have gone now. And it's where* you *are. And* I *want
to be where you are.* I need *to be where you are.*

*Not so long ago Dillon and I visited that campsite up in Shiel-
daig that Charles at The Book Depository mentioned. I got to
chatting to the guy who owns it. Remember? Jim who used to
work for Charles? Well, he talked real sense to me. He made me
see that it shouldn't matter where we are. As long as we're
together. That's what counts. Being together. I can't be in a
place where you are not. I can't wake up every morning and
look at the same sky you're looking at but know that you're
hundreds of miles away.*

*I want to wake next to you and make love to you. To hold you
in my arms and watch you fall apart beneath me. I want to love
you and be loved by you. Someone I know once told me that I
was their puffin—because they mate for life. That's what I'm
offering you. My love, my heart, and my life. If you'll have me. I
will live wherever you want me to live so long as I'm with you.
It doesn't matter anymore.*

*Say you still love me and that we can start the rest of our lives
together today. Please.*

I think that's everything said. If you look up at me, I know I'll be chewing my nails. I've timed how long it should take you to read this, and I'm going to be standing anxiously waiting for some reaction. Take pity on me please! All I want is for you to throw your arms around me and kiss me! I'm waiting...

Tears cascaded down her already damp face as she came to the end of the letter. Now that she knew his real reasons for being here, she was inconsolable. She let out a guttural scream and slammed her fists into the sofa.

'No, no, no, no.' She wanted to go to him. To make him understand that *he* was all she wanted. That Marcus had been a distraction, but that all she'd thought about whilst Marcus was touching her was how much she'd wished it was Jason, that she had literally told Marcus she couldn't sleep with him only moments before he arrived at her door. But she couldn't. She felt humiliated and dirty, like she *had* cheated on Jason. Technically she hadn't because a) she hadn't actually gone through with it and b) she and Jason weren't even *together*. But the look on his face had made her feel that way. Seeing him like that tore at her heart.

She rocked back and forth hugging her arms around her body as if doing so would comfort her and take away the pain she felt. He had been willing to move *here* to be with her. She could have been with him *tonight*. She could have been with him *forever*. But she'd ruined it all. It hadn't been intentional. She was simply trying to get over him. But he didn't see it that way. Marcus had been standing behind her, shirtless, when she had opened the door to find Jason on her doorstep and it looked so, so bad. She knew that. And Jason clearly felt betrayed. There was no wonder.

~

Jason opened the door to his room. He had bypassed Stacey, the receptionist at the desk, even though for a split second he considered taking her up to his room to seek his own revenge on Stevie by sleeping with her. But after what had happened with Jenna, he was done with disrespecting women and using them for his own gratification. He wouldn't lower himself to that level again no matter how hurt he was. He closed the door behind him and slumped onto the bed. At least he truly knew where he stood now. She had well and truly moved on.

Straight into the arms of another man.

He could *almost* sympathise with her still besotted ex-husband, Miles. He snorted at his ridiculous train of thought.

After dragging his few belongings together and shoving them haphazardly into his bag, he decided he had to leave. And he had to do it *now*. He couldn't risk Stevie turning up at the hotel. His resolve wasn't in any way firm enough to turn her away if she showed up. Especially if she seemed as lost as she had when he had stormed away from her. No...he would leave now. And then when he arrived home, he would make a call to Jack Hilton that would help him put things behind him, for a while anyway.

Grabbing his bag, he made his way to the reception desk where Stacey sat talking on the telephone. Her eyes widened when he handed over his key card.

She hung up her call and pouted up at him. 'Leaving so soon?'

He didn't smile at her this time. 'Yeah, something came up. I have to head home.'

She cocked her head to one side. 'That's a shame.'

'Yeah, it really is.'

Once checked out, he made his way to his bike. Listening to music whilst riding was something he usually avoided. Knowing full well that being distracted and in control of a huge hunk of speeding metal was not the best idea. But tonight he didn't care. He slipped in his ear buds and filed through the songs on his player, looking for the soundtrack for his journey home. Locating 'Broken' by Seether and Amy Lee, he set it to repeat and hit play.

Stevie paced the room. She'd done nothing but sob, pace, and sob a little more since Jason had left her standing on the pavement. She had thrown around her decisions of what to do next like juggling balls in the air. Still no decision seemed to be the right one. If she went to him and he rejected her, it would break her heart all over again. But on the flipside of that, if she *didn't* he would never know that she hadn't slept with Marcus. But if she *did* tell him and he rejected her anyway... *Aarrgh!* She punched the couch in a fit of frustration and anger.

Realising that procrastination was getting her nowhere fast, she grabbed the phone and called a cab. The wine she had drunk had probably left her system by now but she wouldn't risk it. After checking her appearance in the mirror over the fireplace and staring with horror at the puffy, red eyes, and blotchy face that peered back at her, she decided that puffy face or not she *had* to take action. *Okay, so there's no way of improving on that in a hurry.* She dragged a brush through her long, wavy locks and scraped them back in a ponytail. She had to stop absentmindedly chewing on her thumbnail for about the hundredth time as she waited for the taxi to arrive.

A horn honked and she grabbed her bag. Pulling the door closed behind her, she made her way to the waiting transport, thankful that her wonderful neighbour had Rowdy for the night again. The poor dog had seen more of Joe than he had of her lately. But his possessive nature around the men she brought home...all two of them...had her fearing a blood bath every time she so much as looked at someone else.

She barked the hotel name and address at the poor unsuspecting cabbie and immediately felt guilty. He must have sensed her erratic state of mind, as he made no attempts at idle chitchat, which was a huge relief. She wasn't sure she could manage small talk right now. On reaching the hotel that Jason had stayed at recently, she hoped that her instincts to find him there were correct. She virtually ran to the reception desk. A rather flustered blonde was trying to appease a group of disgruntled revellers who had clearly arrived late after imbibing far too much alcohol. If she hadn't been in a rush, she'd have felt sorry for the girl, but her current state of mind left her tapping her foot and glaring at the group of drunken, bumbling fools as if her death stare would make them suddenly sober up and get the hell out of her way.

Eventually the group were ushered away by a woman in a suit, who had a distinct air of authority about her.

Stevie stepped forward to the desk.

'Hello, Madam. I'm so sorry about your wait,' the receptionist said as she smiled sweetly, despite her obvious tiredness.

Stevie softened a little. She glanced at the woman's name badge. 'That's okay, Stacey. It looked like you had your hands full a little there.'

The woman rolled her eyes and gave a little humourless laugh. 'You can say that again. I was supposed to finish at ten but the night receptionist called in sick and the manager hasn't been able to locate anyone to cover yet, so I'm still here. And I'm completely frazzled.'

Stevie cringed on realising it was now the early hours of the morning. 'Oh dear. I hope they find someone soon.'

'Oh gosh, listen to me. I'm so sorry. You've been waiting long enough. How can I help you? We don't have anyone due to check in. Are you joining someone? If you were hoping for a room, I'm afraid we have none available at the moment. We've had a guest check out, but the room hasn't been serviced as yet.'

Stevie began to feel her nerves jangling again. 'I'm here to visit Mr. Jason Reynolds. He didn't give me his room number, I'm afraid.'

Confusion washed over the woman's face, and a line appeared between her brows. 'Was he expecting you?' *Was?*

Stevie felt her cheeks heat up. 'Erm...no...it's a surprise visit.'

Stacey cringed. 'Oh dear. I'm so sorry, but *he* was the guest who checked out. He left about an hour ago.'

Stevie's heart plummeted as tears needled her eyes. *Too late.* 'Oh...I see. Thank you anyway.' She turned and left the hotel with heaviness in her chest, pulling her phone out to call the cab company once again.

CHAPTER TWENTY-TWO

*J*ason pulled into the camp and killed the engine. He yanked his helmet off and was greeted by the confused expression of his younger brother.

'What are you doing back?' Dillon asked.

Jason scowled wordlessly at him and his expression must have given Dillon the information he had needed as he simply formed his mouth into an O shape. Giving Jason a sad smile, he shook his head.

After a few moments of standing astride his bike staring at the gravel-covered ground, Jason took a deep breath and rubbed a hand over his stubbled chin. 'She's moved on, bro. I feel like such a fucking idiot.'

Dillon's brow crease deepened. 'Moved on? Seriously? But...but she loves—'

'She was with another man. A shirtless one at that. She was pulling her dress up. Well, straightening it out anyway.' He clenched his eyes at the painful memory as it assaulted his frontal lobe for the millionth time. 'I obviously interrupted something intimate. God, the look he gave me. Honestly, it's a wonder he didn't punch my lights out.'

Confusion was still evident in Dillon's features. 'I don't get it. I felt sure...'

Jason shrugged. 'Me too, but I guess love makes you naïve, eh? Anyway, I'm not staying. I've made plans for you and Dorcas to look after the place anyway, and I need to go clear my head. You'll be okay.'

It wasn't a question. They'd *have* to be okay. He was feeling the urge to run. He'd promised he'd never do that again, but he needed space and time. And at least this time he was explaining in a roundabout way. Distance would help, wouldn't it? He kicked the stand down and climbed off his bike.

Dillon's mouth curved down at the corners. 'So where are you going to go? America?'

'Nah, I've got a call to make, and then all being well, I'll be putting several thousand miles between me and Stevie and... my replacement.'

Jason began walking towards his cabin, unfastening his leather jacket as he tried to focus on putting one foot in front of the other. Dillon jogged behind. 'Are you sure running is a good idea? I mean, what if she comes looking for you?'

Jason snorted. 'Not going to happen. That guy she was with...he looked...' Jason's nostrils flared as he spoke, but he didn't stop. 'He looked fucking perfect for her.' He clenched his jaw as the words he had uttered sank into his own brain and took up residence in his heart. That man seemed so together, clean cut, decent, all the things Jason felt he wasn't. Okay, so you should never judge a book by its cover, but *this* man looked like he'd walked off the cover of some fucking romance novel. Unwanted images were suddenly created in his head once again of Stevie and the shirtless man making love. Of him kissing her and touching her, making her come. Anger and bile rose up within him, and he slammed the door to his cabin open, causing the glass panel to smash. 'Awww fuck!'

Dillon held his hands up in surrender, making Jason feel even worse. 'Go make your call. I'll sort the door. Just...just calm down, bro.'

Jason tried to calm his breathing and to eradicate the images from his mind. He nodded at Dillon and made his way to his room. After closing the door, he slumped onto the bed. His guitar stood in the corner of the room, and he suddenly felt the urge to smash it into a million tiny pieces so that it resembled his disintegrated heart.

After taking a few moments to calm down, he pulled out his phone and dialled. His call was picked up after three rings.

'JR, mate. How you doing with your crazy plans?'

'Yeah, it's me and don't ask. You know how you called and said you had a security detail that you needed me for? Well, I need a posting. What do you got for me?'

'I'm still a man short for the African assignment.'

'Okay, how soon do I need to be there?'

'Try yesterday. Things are starting pretty damn soon, and I'd been thinking about asking if you knew anyone who'd be good enough. Are you sure it's not too far for you at the moment?'

'No, I'm sure that's not too far. There's no such thing as too fucking far right now. I'll get the next available flight.'

Stevie gripped the phone in her hand and stared as if willing it to ring. Jason's mobile had been switched off last night *and* this morning. She had tried hard to sleep, but the harder she tried to sleep, the more images cavorted through her head, taunting her. How things must've looked.

Oh Jason's face.

The betrayal he must have felt had been clearly evident in his dark eyes. Her last hope was to call him at the camp. She'd been toying with the idea for hours now, but she was terrified he would actually answer and tell her to leave him alone. That was the worst-case scenario. She desperately needed to tell him that Marcus and she were over...not that they'd ever really started.

Strengthening her resolve, she dialled the camp's landline and waited. After several rings, a male voice answered.

She cleared her throat. 'Ahem...hello? It's...it's Stevie. Could I speak with Jason, please?'

A sigh was audible from the other end of the line. 'I was wondering how long it'd take for you to call, Stevie.'

Her heart skipped a beat. 'Jason?'

'No, it's Dillon. I'm so sorry, but you've missed him.'

Story of my life. 'Oh, okay. Would you please tell him that I called?'

'No, I mean you've *completely* missed him. He left about an hour ago. He had a flight to catch.'

Oh. Shit. 'Oh, has he gone to the US?'

Another sigh. 'No. He's gone to...erm...actually I'm not sure I'm supposed to say.'

'Just spit it out, Dillon. Where has he gone running off to this time?'

'Africa.'

'What?'

'He's gone to act as security detail for some aid workers. He's done this kind of thing before after the army. He needed some distance.'

She snorted as her heart plummeted. 'Yes, I knew he'd done that before. He mentioned it once. You can't get much more distant than bloody Africa.'

'I'm sorry, Stevie. I don't know what to say to you. I tried to convince him to talk to you.'

Her lip began to tremble, and her palms were clammy. She swallowed the lump lodged in her throat. 'Did he say anything before he left?' she whispered.

'Only that he'd found you with another man. That he'd interrupted something intimate. That you've moved on.'

'Gosh, he said quite a lot then.' She sighed a deep, pain filled sigh. 'It wasn't how it looked. I haven't moved on. I still love him. If he contacts you, will you tell him that please?'

'I would but he's not likely to call. Apparently, the work doesn't allow for a personal life, and to be honest I'm pretty fucking pissed off with him at the moment. I'm still going through therapy, and I need him. At least in London he would have been on the same continent.'

'Oh, Dillon, you're doing so well. Don't let this break you down again, okay?'

'I won't... Well, I'll try not to. If I hear anything, I'll let you know.'

'Thanks. I'd appreciate that. Before you hang up, do you know how long his assignment is for?'

'I think he said it's for three months initially. But it may be longer.'

'Gosh, that long? I suppose I've blown it now.'

'Look, Stevie, and I'm saying this because I care about you, move on. If this guy you've met is a decent man and he treats you well, then just let it be, eh? You and Jason have been through a lot, but there's only so much heartache a couple can go through before it's time to let it go.'

He was right. She knew it. And if she'd thought that the five hundred and odd miles between London and the Cairngorms was a lot, his latest relocation was certainly not do-able. Even if Jason had wanted to try, which he clearly didn't.

Move on.

She'd have to try.

The man in the black suit, Jack Hilton, former Special Forces, stood with a stern expression on his face as he addressed the small cluster of men. It was a face that Jason had known for many years but hadn't seen in several. A rumble of disgruntled acquiescence traversed the room. 'There will be no fraternising with the clients. You are here to ensure their safety and welfare. This does *not* mean tasting of the forbidden fruit. Understood?'

Jason was leaning against the wall, watching the man at work. He'd heard this lecture plenty of times before and knew the ropes well. His arms were folded across his chest, and he felt sweat trickle down his back and chest as he absently wondered why the air conditioning unit wasn't being used considering the sweltering heat.

'Now, there is a French interpreter working with the crew. She speaks excellent English and can translate for you when necessary. She'll be with you all of the time, but she is also going to be very active in assisting the doctors who will be carrying out the vaccination programme. The villagers around the area are very wary of newcomers, which is to be expected given the recent spate of violence and kidnappings. You must be vigilant at all times. These people are relying on you to protect them. Keep your eye on the ball, men. No slacking. Do I make myself clear?'

The rumble came again, and Jason witnessed a couple of eye rolls. He smirked to himself that they didn't know what they were letting themselves in for. This was no walk in the park.

Work like this seemed an easy way to make good money, but the reality of it was *not* the case. There was nothing easy about three months of little sleep, driving around the desert in a beat up old four wheel drive vehicle, wishing you were back eating home cooked food and sleeping next to a warm, sexy body. These guys were in line for a serious wake up call.

Jason ran his hand over the top if his damp hair and lifted his eyes to the door as it opened. A beautiful, tanned woman with long, blonde hair walked into the room. She was wearing khaki cargo pants and a beige shirt tied in a knot at her waist. She glanced around the room and settled her eyes on Jason's. He smiled but in return she cocked her head to one side and frowned. *Strange response.*

'Ah and here she is. Gentlemen allow me to introduce to you Mademoiselle Oriel Maçon.'

The blonde woman made her way over to Jack. 'Bonjour.'

Jack whispered something to her, and she glanced over at Jason again. Still frowning. Suddenly, she turned and faced the small cluster of ex-army operatives that sat spread legged, arms folded, each and every one of them no doubt undressing her with their eyes. Jason could see it in their expressions.

She cleared her throat. 'Bonjour, gentlemen. It's good to see such eager new recruits,' she said sarcastically with a glint in her eyes. *I wonder what colour they are.* 'My primary function during our time here will be to act as interpreter for the doctors and to reassure the villagers, many of whom are familiar with me. This is my third time working with these people, and I have seen them go through so much. Your respect and compassion should be evident at all times, but obviously the safety of our workers is paramount.'

Jason listened as she spoke eloquently in her second language. Her accent was incredibly sexy, and he found himself mesmerised by her mouth as it formed the words.

Stop it, Reynolds. No mixing business with pleasure. He chastised himself as he made eye contact with her once again. Although judging by the expression on her face, there wouldn't be much chance of mixing anything with her.

To his surprise, she was making her way over to him. He pushed off the wall and stood ready for whatever she was going to say. He took a deep, calming breath.

'Monsieur Reynolds. I'm Oriel. I understand you are to be the main one to guard me. I felt we should become acquainted.' She held out her hand, but he just stared. *Why the fuck has Jack assigned me to her?*

After a few moments, he shook his head and snapped himself back to reality. He briefly glanced over to his long-time friend and colleague who was smirking. He winked as Jason scowled back at him. Oriel cleared her throat and dragged his attention back to the matter in hand.

'Oh, Mademoiselle Maçon, forgive my rudeness. I was a little...erm...*surprised* to hear that I'm to be your bodyguard. Mister Hilton hadn't mentioned that to me as yet.'

'Yes, I can see that it came as a shock. My apologies, but I didn't ask for this.' She folded her arms defensively across her chest, which unfortunately pushed her breasts upwards and drew his attention away from her eyes again. He heard her heave an impatient sigh and lifted his face to focus on her eyes once more.

She was *not* amused.

'No...sorry...not a shock in the negative sense of the word. I was expecting to be part of the larger group, not assigned to an individual.'

'Monsieur Reynolds, if you are unhappy, I can ask—'

He held up his hands. 'No! No need. I'm sure we'll get along fine.'

She snorted derisively. 'We don't have to *like* each other,

Monsieur. Ensure that I don't get killed or kidnapped, and I'm sure all will be well.' She turned on her heels and stormed away.

A firm hand clapped him on the shoulder. 'I see that went well, JR.' Jason turned and was met with the green, sparkling, amused gaze of Jack Hilton.

'Oh yeah. She fucking loves me.' Jason shook his head, feeling rather exasperated at the encounter.

'Fancies you. That's the issue. Knew she would.'

'I sincerely doubt that, mate.'

'She does. I could tell as soon as I spotted the two of you making eye contact. Rule number one of working with people in situations such as this: Know your non-verbal signals.'

'Okay, so you're telling me that the fact she pursed her lips and looked like she was sucking lemons is a sure fire way to say she's into me?' Jason laughed.

'No, but the nipples poking through her top and the flush to her chest were a bit of a giveaway.'

Jason scrunched his brow. 'Eh? What are you talking about?'

'Ha, so you didn't notice the pink tint to her cheeks, and the way she thrust her breasts in your face? God, JR, you really are losing your touch.'

'I think it's you who's losing it, Jack. And anyway, why have you assigned *me* to her? This is not how things usually work.'

'No, you're right. But she needs the best. Without her, the whole operation goes down the pan. There aren't many inter-preters who are willing to step into a war zone to do this job. She's one of a kind. A feisty little stick of dynamite. You're the best here. That's it.'

'But she clearly doesn't like me, even if there is some phys-ical thing there that I'm missing.'

'She doesn't *have* to like you. She has to *trust* you.'

Jason shook his head. 'I'm guessing that'll take some serious work.'

'Better start ASAP then.'

'Don't count on it going well, mate.'

Jack patted his shoulder once again. 'We'll see, JR. We'll see.'

The room began to empty, and Jason made his way back to his room. This was the last night he would sleep in a decent bed for quite some time. The vaccination run would take a couple of months, and during the time he was out here, the team would be holed up in a kind of concrete bunker earmarked as their base. There would be very long days ahead, including the treacherous journeys from base to the villages and back to base again. It was a little different to the work he had done before. He was usually paid a hefty sum to carry out security detail, but this time he was doing it voluntarily. It was the perfect distraction, and to top that off, it was for a very good cause. He'd be giving something back.

As he stood waiting for the elevator, he felt a presence beside him. He turned and a smile spread across his face.

'Mademoiselle Oriel. We meet again.'

She rolled her eyes. 'Oh for goodness sake, Jason. My name is Oriel. Please use it.'

Her accent did strange things to his insides. *So sexy.* But he still had to bite back a smirk and nodded. 'Okay...*Oriel.*' He tested the name out on his lips and she looked up at him. She swallowed and her eyes travelled from his eyes down to his lips before she snapped her head back to face forward and pulled her lips in.

'What are your plans for dinner this evening?' he asked.

'I was going to get room service. Why do you ask?'

'I was thinking it'd be a good opportunity to get to know

one another. I think if I'm going to protect you, I could do with knowing a little more about you.'

She sighed and rubbed her eyes. 'Fine. I'm in room two-oh-five. Give me an hour to shower. The humidity is so draining. We'll order when you arrive.'

He raised his eyebrows. 'Oh, I was going to suggest the restaurant, but room service with you is fine too.'

Her cheeks flamed bright red. 'Oh...we...we can eat in the restaurant. I didn't mean...I mean...I—'

Fighting a chuckle, he turned to her. 'No. Room service is fine.' He leaned down so that his lips were an inch from her ear. 'I don't bite...not at first anyway.' He glanced down, and the indication that Jack had mentioned earlier was present again, pressing through her shirt.

She jerked her head around and glared at him. 'May I remind you that this is purely a professional arrangement, Monsieur Reynolds?' Her voice was getting louder. 'There will be no need for biting or...or anything other than professional conversation...between...between professionals!'

He laughed out loud now, and held up his hands in surrender. 'Calm down, Oriel. I was teasing you.'

They stepped into the elevator, and she stood as far away from him as she could. He chewed on his lip, trying to eradicate his smile.

She folded her arms and tapped her foot.

'I can see I'm going to have a lot of fun winding you up.'

She turned to scowl at him, her nostrils flaring. His smile was now very wide and he didn't much care that he was clearly making her feel uncomfortable. The elevator came to halt and the doors opened. She didn't move for a moment.

He pulled his brows into a frown, gestured to the opening, and cleared his throat. 'Ahem, this is our floor. You're in two-oh-five, and as luck would have it, I'm in two-oh-six...almost straight opposite.'

She huffed and stormed past him. He threw his hands up in exasperation and shook his head. *What the fuck?* Once he was back inside his room, he slumped onto the bed. This was not going well. She clearly had no sense of humour, regardless of the fact she *allegedly* found him attractive. Things would need to change or his time here would be no better than being miserable at home.

An hour later, he knocked on her door. She opened it and sighed when her eyes connected with his.

He was a little annoyed at her greeting. 'Well hello, Oriel. I'm happy to see you too.'

'Please, come in. I apologise for my attitude. I'm having a difficult time in my personal life, and I shouldn't take it out on you.'

He stepped into her room, feeling a little taken back by her admission. 'Is there anything you'd like to talk about?'

'No, thank you. I don't want to bore you with my troubles. Let's order food and a bottle of wine, I think. We won't get a chance for a while.' Her smile this time was warm, and he returned it with an equally friendly one.

They chatted easily whilst they ate, and once they had finished, they moved to the small sofa at the other side of the suite. He told her about his camp, and she told him about the university in Marseille where she worked teaching English. She had taken some time out as she usually did when these trips came about. Her employers were very understanding, it seemed.

'So they don't mind you taking off for months at a time?' Jason asked.

'Non, these trips only occur every other year usually, and I feel it is important to do my bit for the cause.'

'It's good that they are so supportive.'

'Oui...you are correct. So tell me Jason, are you married?' She peered at him quizzically over the rim of her glass. She had drunk two thirds of the wine whilst Jason paced himself. She had relaxed now and was becoming very chatty, and he was surprised at the sudden change in direction the conversation had taken.

He smiled and shook his head, glancing down at his glass. 'No, not even close.'

'You surprise me. Forgive me for saying so, but you are a very attractive man.'

He felt his cheeks heat, which surprised him, as he didn't embarrass easily. He put it down to the fact that Jack had been correct, and he was embarrassed at not seeing it himself.

'You're forgiven for saying so, thank you. It's kind of you to say.' He didn't know how else to respond.

'That was the problem when I first saw who you were. I'm usually landed with some ugly bald headed brute of a man. But you...you're different.'

He smirked. 'Different? In what way different? Am I not brutish enough?'

'Oh you are, but you're not bald.'

'And that's a problem because?' Jason was baffled by her openness once again.

She made a growling exasperation-filled noise and rolled her eyes. 'My partner is very possessive. Any hint of me being attracted to someone else and things get complicated.'

'But he's presumably back home in France, and you are here so he never has to know if you're attracted to someone else. And in any case, you don't have to act on it.'

She narrowed her eyes. 'My partner...is female.'

Jason's eyebrows shot up. 'Oh, I see.'

'Non...don't get me wrong. I'm not a lesbian. I'm bisexual.

Colette has been in my life for a long time, and she knows how my tastes go. And sadly, you are the epitome of everything I find sexual in a man.'

He swallowed hard and pulled his lips in to contemplate his next words carefully. 'But I would never overstep the line of professionalism, Oriel. Please don't worry about that.'

She pouted and stroked a finger down his arm. 'You are a spoilsport.'

He laughed. 'And *you* are a tease.'

She gasped, feigning offense. 'Moi? Je suis innocent.'

Hearing her speak in her mother tongue sent shivers down his spine and his blood rushing south. He had to remind himself that he was working. 'So do you think you and I could be friends?' he asked taking another small sip of his wine.

She glanced at the ceiling as if to contemplate his question. 'Hmmm...I've never been *friends* with my bodyguard before. Perhaps it is something I should try?'

'I think so. Otherwise it will make for a very difficult few months.'

'Oui...Je suis d'accord.'

'You do know that I don't speak a word of French, don't you?'

She winked. 'Oui...qui rend les choses plus amusant.'

'Ah, now I heard the word amusement or something there, so I know what you're up to.'

She bit her lip and giggled. 'Whatever do you mean, Monsieur Reynolds?'

He grinned. 'You're going to keep saying insulting things in French so I have no clue what you're saying.'

She paused, pursing her lips and eventually smiling widely. 'Oui, coupable...guilty.' They both laughed and Jason decided perhaps Oriel was going to be fun to work after all.

CHAPTER TWENTY-THREE

*T*he following day, the crew set out for the edge of the dessert where their work would begin. The doctors working on the project were mainly from America, the UK, and Germany, seven in total. All were there voluntarily, and Jason remained in awe of such people giving up their time to work in a dangerous area fraught with tumult and chaos. But the cause was a great one, and these people were clearly selfless, Oriel included. Regardless of the danger they would be facing day in and day out, they were determined to do their bit to help eradicate the threat of Cholera, a terrible disease that killed thousands of people every year.

The area they would be working in was one where the villagers were subjected to violence on a regular basis, and the fact the aid workers were there for the good of the people made them no less of a target. The drive out from the hotel to the base that would be their home for the duration of their time here was a tedious five hours long. The convoy of vehicles kept in touch via radio, and every so often there would be a conversation to check in between all the vehicles involved. The atmosphere was one of tense anticipation.

The heat was almost unbearable.

Jason absentmindedly stared out of the window at the harsh landscape that surrounded them. Nothing but vivid blue sky and sand. Every so often, they would pass through a kind of shantytown where people would stop what they were doing to stare at the passing chain of armoured vehicles. Such a far cry from the luxuries he was used to taking for granted back home. Seeing the poverty tugged at his heart, and he forced himself to think of something else, *anything* else other than what he was witnessing firsthand.

He wondered what Stevie was doing now. Was she with her new man? Were they in bed wrapped around each other, taking pleasure from one another's bodies? Was the man making her feel incredible things? Did she miss Jason in the slightest? Sure, she seemed upset when he walked away, but nostalgia will do funny things to your heart. It'll make you believe you feel things that you really don't. Realising this train of thought was futile, he switched to the memory of the conversation he'd had with Oliver when he was waiting to board his flight to Africa.

'Oh, son, I'm sorry it didn't work out for you. I expected things to end differently.'

'Yeah, me too, but end is what they did.'

'And she seemed to be *with* this man? I mean no disrespect to Stevie, but is there any chance this was just a... I don't know...' Oliver seemed hesitant to express his thoughts.

'A one night stand? No, Stevie doesn't do one-night stands. I think I know her well enough, and I'm pretty sure that if she's with someone she's *with* them.'

'I'm so darn disappointed for you. Will you be okay?'

Jason sighed. 'I'll have to be.'

There was a silent pause. 'I wish you'd come over here

instead of going to Africa. It would've been good to see you. You're always welcome you know.'

'Thanks...thanks...erm...Dad.' It still felt strange using such a familial word, but he liked the sound and feel of it. 'I appreciate that, but I need some time doing something completely differently. Something that's not a holiday. Holidays leave you with time to think. And I don't want to think. I don't want to feel. I just want to work. For now at least. It's only a few months, but I'm hoping it helps me get over her. I need to move the fuck on.'

'Well, if you decide you need more time, son, you know where we are, okay?'

'Thanks again. Anyway, they're calling my flight. Bye for now.'

'Bye, Jason. Take care out there.'

Stevie sat with a pile of papers strewn across the table in front of her. Planning for the Head of Science interview was taking over her life, and she was glad of it. The welcome distraction was helping her to dwell less and less on the fact that she had lost the love of her life...*again*. Marcus hadn't been in touch, and she had mixed emotions about that situation. She really liked him. She'd hoped that there could be something between them, but she knew that while there was still the chance of being with Jason, however remote, Marcus would only ever come a close second. And he had made it very clear that playing second fiddle was in no way good enough for him. And why should it be? He deserved so much more.

The phone rang as she sat staring at the pages until they had become a fuzzy mass of white before her tired eyes.

'Hello?'

'Stevie, it's Mollie.'

'Oh hi, Moll. How's it going?'

'Oh, fine. I saw Marcus last night. He's a mess.'

She sighed and rubbed her tired eyes. 'Please, Moll, don't do this. I know I hurt him. I feel terrible, I really do. But I didn't want to lead him on.'

'He knows that. He's been so lovely about you. Not a single bad word. He understands completely.'

Shit, that makes it worse. 'Awww, Mollie.' The stinging behind her eyes returned for what felt like the millionth time.

'He misses you.'

She snorted derisively. 'We only dated a couple of times. He can't miss me.'

'He does though. He thought he had a real future with you.'

'Mollie, I love you dearly, but I knew this was a bad idea. Me dating your brother was always a recipe for disaster. Look what it's doing to us.'

Mollie sighed. 'No, it's not doing anything to us, honestly. I just wish things could be different for both of you.'

'Me too.' Stevie really did wish that.

'I see what this situation has done to you. You've *never* loved anyone else. You never *will* love anyone else until you let him go.'

The stinging behind her eyes gave way to full blown tears. 'But that's just it, Moll. I can't let him go. I never could. I don't even know how to begin to try.'

'Well, maybe when you figure it out you could give Marcus a call?'

'*If* I ever figure it out, I will.'

After the call, Stevie sat with her head in her hands, wondering where Jason was right then. She wondered if he was okay. He'd been gone almost two weeks, and she had heard nothing from Dillon. Not that she expected to if she was totally honest with herself.

The ride back to the base was getting longer. Jason felt sure it was. The smell in the vehicle was becoming unbearable, and he was desperate to get back and shower. Oriel sat opposite him with a wide smile on her face. Her eyes sparkled with mirth.

'What's so funny?' he asked.

'You.'

'And why would that be?' He didn't remember saying anything humorous, yet there she was with a huge grin on her face.

'Oh, I was just thinking back to when that little boy vomited on you. Your face was hilarious.'

'Oh, gee thanks. I didn't find it funny I can assure you.' He scrunched his nose up at the smell sticking to his clothing.

'You were so sweet, though. You didn't yell. I think he was scared you'd be angry.'

He shook his head and smiled. 'Considering I have an inherent fear of needles, I could hardly be angry with the poor kid. You should see me when I get tattoos. *Not* pretty at all.'

'A big strapping man like you is scared of a little prick?'

Jason burst into laughter. 'I'm not scared of *pricks*, Ori. That's you!'

She swiped a playful hand at him. 'I'm *not* scared of pricks, and you know what I meant. Merde, you're such a boy.'

'You noticed then?'

She rolled her eyed with a giggle. He loved to tease her. Their friendship had blossomed over the short time they'd been working together. These past few weeks had flown thanks to Oriel. She was amazing. The way she dealt with people, he was in awe. She was so warm and caring. People instantly took to her.

During these last weeks, he had felt happy; tired but happy. And it wasn't that he wanted her. Their relationship had developed into a solid friendship, the kind that usually took years to establish. He had still been thinking of Stevie, but for some reason being around Oriel had helped him look back on the happy times they had shared. One day whilst they had been talking about their reasons for being in Africa, he had talked with Oriel about Stevie, and he had appreciated the way she had listened without judging him.

At the end of their conversation about his failed relation-ship, she had said, 'Jason, some things are meant to be...some are not. But those that are meant to be *will be* regardless of the odds stacked against them. If you are *meant* to be with Stevie, then this is not the end. It's merely a fork in the road...just not the right time. But if you are not meant to be, you *will* find a way to get over her.'

Listening to her words had made him think. He wondered if there was truth in them. Although even if there was, it made little difference. It meant that he would either be with her eventually or he would find someone else. Neither felt in the slightest bit possible.

A week later, Stevie sat nervously outside the school's meeting room with the external candidates. She glanced around and was thankful that each and every other applicant seemed as nervous as she felt. She was trying her best to keep her hands still, but the more she tried, the sweatier her palms became. She knew the Head Teacher well, had known him for several years now, but for some reason, being interviewed by Mr. Carmichael was a big deal. No, a *very* big deal. This job was the culmination of years of hard work. This job was what she had wanted since starting at Wilmserden High School all those years ago.

She had prepared very well. She'd gone over the top, if the truth were known. Her planned lesson and presentations had been done using the latest software, and her laptop and memory stick had been checked, rechecked, and checked some more. She was *not* going to mess this up. This job was going to be the *making* of her. Wasn't it? Because she desperately wanted it. Didn't she? Yes. She did. Absolutely. Noooo doubts at all there.

None.

Mr. Carmichael welcomed the group into the room and gave a brief introduction about the school, the facts and figures about grades, etc. Stevie fought an eye roll along with the urge to stand up and shout, 'Can we bloody get on with it?'

Once the introduction was over, the eight candidates were taken on a tour of the school. Having worked there for a few years now, Stevie was waved at and called to by over-eager learners, earning her disapproving looks from the other candidates. Her cheeks heated on several occasions and she resorted to standing at the back of the group.

That evening, Stevie arrived home in a bit of a daze. Rowdy did his best to get her attention, nuzzling her hand and following her around making snuffling noises as if sulking at her lack of fussing. But she was feeling rather shell shocked at how gruelling the day had been and decided to open up the bottle of Shiraz she had been saving for the weekend. Well, it *was* Friday evening, officially the start of the weekend. The exam papers awaiting grades could bloody well continue to wait. She gulped down the first glass in one go. The second wasn't drunk quite so speedily. And by the third she was numb enough not to give a crap. She kicked off her shoes and sat on the sofa.

Listlessly, she grabbed the remote control and barely had the energy to aim it at the TV. After flicking through the channels, something caught her eye on the news channel. She leaned forward and turned up the volume.

The vehicle convoy was ambushed at around noon, and several of the volunteers were shot dead at the scene. It is believed there are four people missing. One of whom is a French national by the name of Oriel Maçon. Ms. Maçon is an interpreter for the charitable organisation and works in a voluntary capacity. It is also said that her bodyguard, a Mr. Jason Reynolds, is also missing.

Her glass of wine slipped through her fingers and caught the edge of the coffee table, sending its liquid contents and shards of glass flying. Rowdy jumped and ran to the other side of the room.

She stared at the screen, unable to move. If she hadn't known better, she would have thought her heart had ceased to beat. The room seemed to disappear, and she suddenly felt very cold and numb.

CHAPTER TWENTY-FOUR

*J*ason groggily gained consciousness. He was surrounded by blackness, and the pain in his head throbbed to the beat of his racing heart. Realising he had something covering his head, he began to cough as he inhaled dust from whatever it was. His hands and feet were tethered, and he began to panic. *What the hell had happened? Where is Oriel? Is she alive?*

'Oriel?' he spoke just above a whisper. 'Oriel are you here?'

'Jason? Mon Dieu, Jason, are you okay?' Her voice trembled. She sounded terrified.

'My head hurts, but apart from that I think I'm okay. Are you all right?'

'Yes, but they are making threats. I'm scared, Jason. We have to get out of here.'

'Have I been unconscious a long time?' he whispered again. His throat felt dry and scratchy.

She sobbed. 'Yes, I think so. I kept trying to get your attention, but you wouldn't answer, and I thought you were dead.'

He pulled against his restraints but was unable to pull

free. 'Hey...hey, don't cry. We'll get out. We'll figure this out. Are you able to see?'

'Oui, they took my cover off, so they could talk to me.'

'Are there any of them in here?'

'Non, they left about half an hour ago. Jason, I'm so scared.'

'I know, but I won't let anything happen to you.'

'How can you say that? You've been knocked out. You could have...une commotion cérébrale. Sorry, I mean a... a concussion.'

'No, I think I'm fine. Sore, but okay. Where are we?'

'I don't know. It looks like a similar building to our base. But darker. The windows are boarded over, and there isn't much light. Only what is coming through the gaps in the wood.'

'Okay...okay. How long have we been here?'

'I'm not sure...a few hours. Jason, they killed some of the others.'

He dropped his head forward as the pain of her words sunk in. 'Oh fuck, no.'

'They say they will kill us next.'

'But what do they want? Have they told you why we're being held?'

'They want us to leave, but they want weapons in exchange for letting us go.'

'Shit, that won't happen. Shit.' He stamped his foot on the gritty floor beneath his boots and clenched his jaw. He had to get them out. He had to.

He rifled through his memory, trying to remember what had led to them being captured. He'd been so vigilant. They had been travelling along the road back to the base. He remembered that it was dusk and that he'd been thankful the temperature had cooled somewhat. Suddenly, there had been a commotion, and the car in front had swerved and skidded around. Their vehicle had collided with it. There were gunshots, and he had reached for his own piece, clambering out of the vehicle and ducking to dodge the flying bullets. There had been a lot of shouting as his colleagues tried to contain the attack. Something had grabbed his arm, and he'd swung around only to find a terrified looking French woman clinging to him.

'Get back in the truck, Ori,' he had instructed her gruffly. She had shaken her head, her eyes pleading with him. More bullets flew past them, and he reached the front vehicle to find the driver and passenger had been shot dead. He had muttered expletives under his breathe and turned to face Oriel only to receive a fast blow to his head. He heard a loud, blood-curdling scream before everything went black.

'I'm so fucking terrified, Stevie. What the fuck will I do if he… if anything—'

'No! We can't think that way, Dillon! We just can't.' Stevie's hands shook as she held the telephone in one hand and clutched the handkerchief that was scrunched up in her other hand. She'd had to take a leave of absence from work for a few days after finding out about Jason's kidnapping, and her life had gone into a kind of emotional meltdown.

She couldn't sleep or eat, and her mother had resorted to staying over on a regular basis. Stevie blamed herself entirely for what had happened. If only she hadn't been with Marcus when Jason arrived. If only she'd reacted quicker and gone after him. If only she'd called as soon as she knew he was on the way back to Scotland. All the *if onlys* in the world couldn't change the fact that Jason's life was now in danger, and she may never see him again.

Taking a shaking breath, she spoke again. 'Dillon, I'm so sorry. This is all my fault.' Her voice was a mere whisper.

'Hey, stop that right now! He chose to go out there. This is his doing. I'm so fucking angry with him. Terrified, but fucking angry. He could've gone to America. Hell, he could've bloody stayed here and faced up to life like an adult. But no. He had to fucking run! I'm sick of this. I know he's had shit to deal with, but so have I. So have we all.'

'I just feel so responsible.' Stevie sobbed as she felt her mother's hand squeeze her shoulder.

'Well, don't. I don't blame you. Oliver doesn't blame you either. So get that out of your head, okay?'

'Okay,' she lied. 'Please call me if you hear any news.'

'Of course I will. Take care, Stevie.'

'You too. Bye, Dillon.'

The following Wednesday was a big day for Stevie. With everything that was going on in her personal life, she almost handed in her resignation, but Mollie convinced her that she could get through it all. And so there she sat nervously waiting for Anthony Carmichael to call her in. Several minutes later and the moment arrived.

She walked nervously into his office.

'Ah, Mrs. Norton, good to see you. Please come in.'

Stevie couldn't be bothered anymore. All she wanted to do was hear what he had to say and to go back home again to drown her sorrows. 'Anthony, why the hell are you being so formal? I've known you for years and this,' she gestured between them, 'formality isn't necessary, is it?'

Anthony frowned and cleared his throat. 'Ahem...okay, Stevie, as you know there were many people interviewed for the post of Head of Science. The post will begin following the Christmas break, and so there will be a lot of preparation involved...'

After receiving the news she had been waiting for, Stevie left the office in a bit of a daze. Christmas. It was hard to think of such a happy time when she knew that Jason was sitting somewhere he didn't want to be with cruel people doing goodness knows what to him. She shuddered. Deep down she hoped that by Christmas Jason would be back in the UK and he would be fine, but realistically these situations rarely ended positively.

She had been watching the news avidly for some sign that he was still alive, but as yet the news had been focussing on other seemingly more important stories like the recession. Never mind that the love of her life was being held against his will in some shit hole being tortured or worse yet...he was dead. It was strange how the world carried on around her whilst her own was falling apart.

She walked back into the staff room where she knew Mollie was waiting.

Mollie stood up and rushed over as soon Stevie stepped in through the door. 'Well? How did it go?'

'I...I got the job.'

Mollie squealed and pulled her into a hug. She didn't reciprocate, but instead stood feeling completely numb. She knew she should be excited. This was a fantastic career move after all, an amazing opportunity. But the excitement she *should* be feeling had been quashed, stamped on by so many things it was hard to even decipher them all.

How the hell she was going to get things organised in her current state of mind was beyond her, but she knew she would do it. She *had* to. Mollie was still jabbering on, but all Stevie caught was, 'And the rest of your life starts now!'

The rest of my life? Oh.

A door opened and there was a lot of shouting in French. Jason heard Oriel's panicked voice. He could tell she was pleading with their captors as they shouted. The next noise he heard was a loud slap, and Oriel's pained voice crying out. A loud growl left his throat involuntarily. He too was hit with a force so great his head whipped back and struck the hard surface of the wall behind him. Determined not to show that he was hurt, Jason made no sound. A husky voice spoke venomously in his ear.

'Il ne parle pas francais!' He heard Oriel call through her tears. Her voice was laced with fear, and he was desperate to get to her. The husky voice spoke to Oriel in a demanding tone.

'Jason...he...he says you are a pussy, and he is going...to... cut your eyes out. I'm so sorry.'

'Oriel, it's okay. We'll be okay. Can you try to get them to let you sit beside me? Tell them I'm your lover or whatever and that you want to be beside me before we die or...just do what you can.'

'What? Why? I don't—'

'Please, just do it.'

'Okay. S'il vous plait, laissez moi m'asseoir avec lui.' Her voice wavered as she uttered the words that he didn't understand.

'Pourquoi?' the husky voice replied.

'Il...il est mon fiancé. Je l'aime. Et J'ai peur. S'il vous plait...s'il vous plait.'

There was some quiet chatter in French again, and Jason inwardly cursed himself for not paying more attention in school.

'I told them you are my fiancé and that I'm afraid and want to be near you. They are trying to decide if I can sit by you. But they are arguing.' Once again she sounded scared and the confident tone Jason was used to had gone.

He heard shuffling sounds and suddenly felt what he presumed was Oriel's body heat beside him.

The husky voiced man laughed eerily. 'Vous serez bientot mort.'

'What did he say?' Jason asked, turning his head towards where he believed Oriel was sitting.

'Ohhh...non...non...Je vous en supplie...non.' *Whack!* He felt the air shift as Oriel was struck again. Her body jerked towards him on impact and he heard the pain filled grunt rush from her body.

'Stop! Please stop! Arreter! S'il vous plait!' Jason shouted pleadingly, hoping that his words made sense to them and that they listened. They just laughed. The men seemed to quiet down, and they left the room, slamming the door behind them. The bottom of the door made an ear-piercing screech as it scraped along the floor. And once again they were left to the silence and stench of damp and urine.

'Oh God, Oriel, are you okay?' He wanted to put his arms around her but couldn't move.

'Yes...yes. Don't worry. I'm okay.' Her voice was still shaky and filled with emotion.

'What was it they said that scared you so much? I heard mort which I'm pretty sure is something to do with death.'

'They said that we will be dead soon.' There was a distinct note of desolation to her voice.

His mind began to spin as he tried desperately to formulate a plan.

'Okay, I think I have a way to try to get us out of here. But we'll need to work together. For the next couple of days or whatever it takes, we need to figure out and memorise their routine, okay? What time of day is it now?'

'I...I—'

'When the door opened, did you see any light coming through? Or did it seem dark?'

'It was not quite dark yet.'

'Okay, let's see if they come in again tonight. I think I have an idea, but if it doesn't work we'll either still be in this situation...or worse.'

A couple of weeks later and there had still been no news. Stevie had reluctantly returned to work in a bit of a daze. The kids knew that something was amiss and were behaving very well. She managed to get through her days without knowing how to function. She had lost weight and stopped caring about her appearance. People at work behaved like they were walking on glass around her. Like she was made of glass in fact and would break at any moment.

'I know this is a silly question, but have you heard anything?' Mollie asked tentatively at lunch.

'Erm, no, nothing. I don't know what's going on. Dillon and Oliver have been speaking with the British Consulate.

But I don't think they've made much progress yet. It's a very sensitive situation.'

'They will, hon. Don't give up hope, eh? Jason's as strong as an ox, and he won't let them get the better of him. Trust in that.'

'I'm trying, Moll. But the thought of them hurting him. Of them...of...' Nausea washed over her at the thought and she began to shake.

Mollie stroked her arm soothingly. 'Hey, come on. We're stopping this right now. Me and my big mouth. I should've kept it shut. You're doing so well. I'm so sorry I brought it up.'

Stevie shook her head. 'It's okay...honestly. Not talking about it doesn't make it go away.'

'I know. But I think we need a distraction.'

She turned to face Mollie. Her interest only slightly piqued. 'Like what?'

'Like I come to yours tonight. I bring a Johnny Depp movie...or...or a Channing Tatum flick...or better still, both! And we get drunk, eat crap, and drool over hunky men.'

Stevie forced a smile. 'Sounds like a plan.'

Deep down, however, she knew that no distraction was going to work. No amount of hunky men ogling was going to take her mind away from the only man she gave a tiny rat's ass about. He was off in some foreign country being tortured, kept against his will, and goodness knows what else. Her heart ached at her apparent ineffectuality in the whole situation.

Mollie arrived at Stevie's door with her arms full of bags. It was seven in the evening, and Rowdy was skipping around, clearly excited to see one of his favourite humans.

'What the heck have you got there?' Stevie reached to take

a bag from Mollie's hand. Mollie immediately used the free hand to scratch behind Rowdy's ear.

'Chinese food. Three bottles of red wine. *Magic Mike* and *Chocolat* on DVD. Two huge bars of dark chocolate with mint —your fave—two big bags of sweet and salty popcorn—my fave and my jammies. Figure I'd stay over if that's okay.

Stevie's eyes began to water yet again.

Mollie's face crumpled. 'Oh no, no, no. What did I say?' She stepped inside and placed the other bag down, removed the one Stevie had taken, and placed that down too. Pulling her into a hug, Mollie stroked her hair.

Stevie sniffed and wiped her eyes. 'Oh God, just ignore me. I'm a mess. Any time anyone is the slightest bit nice to me, I break down.' She tried to smile.

'There she is. There's that smile. Now come on. Let's pig out and watch hunky naked men cavort.' Her eyes sparkled and Stevie began to relax.

Jason heard the door scrape open, and he cringed as Oriel flinched beside him. The men this time sounded different. One spoke to Ori in a softer voice, and she responded the same.

'Jason, this man is going to remove your head covering. He's brought some bread and water for us. He's untying me so I can feed you.' This was strange. Up to now food, which had tasted like dry grain of some sort, had been shoved into his mouth by one of the captors, who thrust it up under the sacking. The temptation to bite the hand that fed him was at times overwhelming. Water had been poured into his face, literally through the holes in the sack, and as a result had tasted dirty and gritty.

But as Oriel had indicated, the cover was suddenly removed, and Jason gasped at the air around him as if coming to the surface of a deep lake. Whilst it wasn't exactly clean air, it was better than the dusty stuff that filtered through the sack over his head. He blinked his eyes open as they adjusted to the new level of light. Again, still not bright sunlight, but enough to make it sting as his pupils contracted. Once he was adjusted sufficiently, Oriel lifted the water bottle to his lips and tipped it slowly. He gulped down the lukewarm liquid as if it was nectar from the gods, breathing a sigh of relief and resting his head back to look at Oriel and the men. Her face was bruised, and her lip was healing from what had apparently been a blow to her mouth. Anger bubbled inside him, and his jaw clenched.

She touched his face and stared deep into his eyes. He felt sure she was willing him to stay calm and swore he saw the slightest shake of her head. He glanced around the room they were being held in. It was some kind of concrete bunker, similar to the one that had been their base. Dust motes danced in the beams of light shining in through cracks in the wood covering the windows. The room was empty and the floor covered in dirt.

Peering up at the men, he saw that they were armed, wore masks, and were kitted out in army style uniforms. One was very tall and the other of average height. He could tell nothing else about them other than they both seemed relaxed considering the situation. One handed a chunk of bread to Oriel, and she brought it to Jason's lips.

He kept his mouth closed and spoke through clenched teeth. 'Why are they feeding us if they plan on killing us?'

'I don't know, Jason. But please eat. It's been such a long time since you have eaten and drunk properly.'

'I'm suspicious. What are they playing at?'

'Qu'at-il dit?' one of the men directed what sounded like a question at Oriel.

She spoke with a wavering voice. 'Pourquoi etes-vous nous nourrir?'

The men looked at each other but didn't answer. One of them simply gestured without words that Jason should eat. So he did.

Once the men had re-tied Oriel's hands behind her back and gone again, Jason turned to her. 'They didn't cover my head, Ori. I'm not happy. This feels strange. Something's not right.' His breathing was rapid, and his heart pumped quickly in his chest.

Oriel's eyes filled with fear. 'What should we do?'

Jason took a deep breath as the plan formulated in his mind. 'Okay, they took my gun when they captured us, but I usually have a knife in my boot. I have no idea if they took it. Can you wiggle down to my feet and see if you can find it?'

Oriel dragged herself towards his feet as quickly as she could and positioned herself with her back facing his right boot. Awkwardly, she reached and slipped a finger inside. She gasped.

Her eyes were wide. 'How the hell did they not find this?'

'We were armed with guns. They probably didn't think we'd carry knives too. Not all of us do. Can you grab it?'

She delved into his boot to where the knife had slipped down and struggled. The door began to open, and she threw herself into his lap, head first. Jason bent forward to kiss her head. His back straining as he did so.

There was a hoarse laugh. 'Awww. C'est l'amour.' Came the husky, mocking voice Jason had grown to hate.

The door closed again, and Oriel pushed herself up, glanced at Jason, and apologised.

'Hey, don't worry. I don't care how we get out and what

we have to do to make that happen. We'll do whatever it takes, Oriel. You *will* be safe.' She smiled as tears made her eyes glassy. 'Come on, try for the knife again.'

She scrambled back to his boot and after some contorting managed to grip the knife and bring it out. The sheath still stuck in his boot, and she nicked his ankle with the blade as she withdrew it.

'Oh, Jason, I'm so sorry. Are you all right?'

He gritted his teeth and smiled. 'I've had worse from shaving. Don't worry. Now scoot yourself back up here.'

Once again, Oriel dragged herself back beside Jason and leaned against the wall.

He nudged her shoulder. 'You did good. Now, when we can be sure it's night, we're getting out. We're not staying here any longer than absolutely necessary. Not if they're planning on chopping things off...or worse.'

As the room became darker with only a tiny amount of moonlight filtering into the room, Jason glanced down to Oriel. She had dozed off leaning on his shoulder. He nudged her.

'Ori...Ori, wake up.' She sat bolt upright and squinted at him in the lessening light. 'Right, now you're going to have to swivel around and try to cut the rope that's binding my hands. I'd rather you do this first as I don't want you getting cut if I try to do yours first.'

She looked panicked. 'But...but what if I cut you again? I can't...I—'

'Ori, you *can* do this. If you cut me, I'll bleed, yes, but I *will heal* too. So please do as I ask. *Please.*' He pleaded with her, trying to convey his belief in her with his eyes. She nodded, and the pair moved so their backs were together. They heard a noise outside and froze.

Then, it went silent again.

Oriel began fumbling with the knife. Jason could tell she was being cautious and doing her best not to cut his flesh. But at one point he winced and drew a sharp breath. She gasped and stopped. Evidently she too had felt the warm liquid trickle over her fingers.

'Ori, it's okay,' he said as soothingly as he could. 'Carry on. Please don't worry. Just do it.' She continued and after what felt like an eternity, his hands were free. He moved them around to assess the damage and Oriel sobbed. He pulled her into a hug and kissed the side of her head.

He ducked down to meet her eyes. 'Hey, stop. I'm fine.' He smiled. 'You missed all the essential veins, so you can stop crying now.' He hoped his smile was encouraging. 'Let me cut your ties.'

He dragged the bloody blade through the ropes binding Oriel's wrists, working quickly. And then he cut the ties around their feet. He pulled her to standing and quickly embraced her as she cried again, clinging to him. The feisty, flirty girl he had grown fond of was gone. The one before him looked terrified and so very fragile. Her shiny blonde hair was matted with blood and dirt, and her eyes had lost their sparkle. His heart ached for her. He was angry with himself. He should have protected her from this.

Speaking calmly in the hope he would instil some peace into her, he said, 'Okay, we're going to check what's going on out there. If the coast is clear, we're making a run for it. I don't have a clue where we are or who we can trust out there if we make it, but this is a chance we'll have to take. You need to keep up. If I have to drag you or carry you, I will. I'm *not* leaving you. We're going home, Oriel. Do you hear me?'

She nodded as her widened, fear-filled eyes stayed focused on his.

Jason did his best to tug the door open quietly, but the scraping sound couldn't be avoided. He did it incrementally in a bid to cause less attention to be drawn to them. Once he had managed to open the door wide enough for them to squeeze out, he peeped out to see who was around. Two guards were standing off to the left, smoking and talking. They seemed engrossed in their conversation, and so silently Jason pulled at Oriel's hand and dragged her behind him. They rounded the corner of the building and stopped in their tracks.

Oriel gasped and her hand flew to her mouth. The masked man before them was the very tall one who had fed them bread and water before. He stood there. His eyes glinting in the darkness. Jason swallowed thickly. *Fuck.*

'If you are going, you had better run very fast. It won't take long before they realise you are missing. You must go *now*. And don't look back.' The man's heavily accented words were just above a whisper.

Jason was dumbstruck and frozen to the spot for a few moments. He scrambled around his head for something to say. 'B...but are you...are you going to shoot us as we run?'

The man shook his head slowly. 'Non. Just go. Head in a straight line up there.' He gestured off to a right hand diagonal. 'But run like the wind, my friends. Or you will be dead very soon.'

Jason scrunched his face. 'But why are you doing this? Why are you letting us escape?'

The man dropped his gaze to the floor. 'I hate war. I hate fighting. I hate to see people I love dying for no reason. This has happened many times now. You came here to help. You don't deserve to die for this. This is not your fight. Now go.'

He jerked his head in the direction he had told them to run. Jason turned to Oriel as his lip quivered. He forced a smile but fear gripped his heart. He didn't want to die here, and he couldn't help mistrusting this man.

He expected them to be shot as they ran like deer on a hunt, their escape turning this whole sick situation into a game, a sport that their captors would get some macabre enjoyment from. But he would rather die that way than watch as they did their worst, and so he gripped her hand.

'Come on. Let's go home, Ori.'

Her eyes widened, and she whispered, 'Non! Jason, it's a trap. It has to be a trap.'

He took her face in his hands and spoke with all the conviction he could muster. 'Oriel, do you trust me?' She nodded. 'Then we *have* to do this. We're running out of time. Please, take my hand and let's go. I can't stay here and wait for them to start hurting you. I couldn't bear it. *Please.*'

With a quivering lip, she nodded. So with firm resolve, he grasped her hand in his and took off running as fast as his legs and Oriel's would take them. Off into the night, praying a gunshot wasn't the last thing he would ever hear.

CHAPTER TWENTY-FIVE

*S*tevie was still feeling the after-effects of her drunken Friday night with Mollie on Sunday morning when she awoke. Instead of helping her to think positively and feel better, the night had ended with Stevie looking through old photographs, sobbing her heart out. Mollie had called her mum, and she had come over on Saturday and ended up staying over to look after her. Stevie had stayed in bed all of Saturday, seeing as she had the hangover from hell. Mollie, on the other hand, had woken bright and breezy and called a cab to take her back home, leaving her best friend in the capable hands of Dana, who fussed over her like a mother hen. It wasn't fair that Mollie wasn't suffering as badly.

Not fair at all.

Stevie lay in bed staring at the ceiling, thinking about Jason and how it felt to be held by him. She closed her eyes and remembered the many delicious times they had made love. Like a movie montage, the images rolled around her mind, taunting her with what could have been.

She thought about his lips against hers and his tongue sliding into her mouth. How he had made her feel incredible, so loved and adored. His hands and fingers stroking every sensitive inch of her body, heightening her senses, and making her tingle with pleasure. The way he caressed her breasts so reverently, pulling her nipples into his mouth, one, then the other, and then back again, as he watched her fall apart with an awe filled expression.

The look of utter adoration in his eyes as he moved inside her and kissed her forehead, cheeks, neck, and stroked her hair. The way he looked so blissful, floating in ecstasy as he came, his eyes locked on hers at the height of his own pleasure. She longed for him, ached for his touch. But knew he was so very far away, and as time went on, the prospect of seeing him again grew slimmer.

And slimmer.

The phone rang, but she couldn't even be bothered to get up. She knew it'd be Dillon with his weekly call to report no news was good news or some other crap. He was a swinging pendulum of emotion. One day he'd call and be so positive and upbeat she felt filled with hope, and others he'd be sobbing, telling her that he was terrified they'd already killed his brother and how he wished he'd not been so stupid when he tried to kill himself.

'How could I do that to him, Stevie? I love him. He's my brother.'

She had lost count of the number of times she had tried to convince him everything would be okay, even though she wasn't actually convinced herself. But today she wouldn't be doing that. Today wasn't a good day. The last thing she needed was to be second-guessing Dillon's fragile frame of mind when her own was so negative and equally as breakable.

Dana opened her bedroom door. 'It's Dillon, sweetie. You need to speak to him.'

Stevie rolled over. 'Tell him I'm asleep.'

'He sounds a little manic. I think you need to take the call.'

She sat up reluctantly and swung her feet over the side of the bed. 'I'll come downstairs.' She followed Dana and grabbed the phone from the windowsill, scowling. *It's a wireless phone for goodness sake. Why didn't she bring the fucking thing upstairs?* She slumped onto the sofa.

She rubbed her free hand over her face. 'Hi, Dillon. What's up?'

'They escaped, Stevie! They got away! They're being checked over by medics at the moment, but they are being flown back to Heathrow on Wednesday!' Dillon's voice was filled with excitement and relief washed over her. Tears began to fall relentlessly from her already sore eyes. 'We got a call from the Consulate this morning,' he continued. When she didn't speak he carried on again. 'Stevie are you...are you there? Are you okay?'

Her heart pounded, trying to escape her body. Her eyes grew wide as his words sunk in. She peered up at Dana, who had covered her mouth with one hand. The other reached out for Stevie. Hot tears were sliding down her face as she realised Dillon was asking if she was okay.

She laughed through her tears. 'Oh yes, Dillon. I'm...I'm shocked, but I'm so, so happy. So relieved. I can't tell you how amazing this is. I thought he was gone. That...that we'd lost him. I can't quite believe it. I'm scared I'll wake up and find it's all been a dream.'

'Believe it, Stevie. *It's real*. It's happening! He's coming home!' His voice was high pitched and wavering, his emotions evident.

'Oh thank God...thank goodness.' She sobbed as she leaned on her mother, who was squeezing her free hand so tight it was going numb. She stood beside her daughter with a hand still over her mouth and tears streaming down her face.

'Are you coming down to meet him?' she managed to ask.

'No...no. I was thinking...I was thinking maybe *you* could be there. He'd love that. He'd love for yours to be the first familiar face he sees. It'd be good for him to know you still love him, Stevie.'

She hesitated before answering. 'Oh, I'm not sure, Dillon.'

'Honestly. You should be there. Regardless of how things were left between you, he'll want to see you. He'll have had time to think...to get over that. Please, for both of your sakes. I haven't spoken to him, so he won't be expecting me anyway. Just think about it. He's only stopping in London briefly for a press conference, and then he's getting a connecting flight up to Inverness. You could come too. Even if it's for a few days. Or you could tell him you still want him. Then he can decide if he wants to come back here or not.'

The thought excited her more than words could express. Knowing she could be seeing him again so soon was the best feeling. The butterflies took flight and her heart began to beat again. 'Okay. I'll do it. I'll be there. If he calls, don't tell him, okay? I'll surprise him.'

'Fantastic! Oh, Stevie, you'll make him so very happy. I know you will. He thought you'd moved on, and he'll be so glad to hear that you hadn't.'

They finished chatting as Dillon told her he had to make a call to the US. So that was it. She would sweet-talk her boss, and then hopefully on Wednesday she would go to Heathrow Airport and see if she could sneak into the press conference. Then she would tell him how she felt and ask for another chance at a future with him. The scenario played out in her mind like one of those romantic movies where the person barges into the press conference and declares their love for the unsuspecting panellist. Goosebumps covered her skin as her mother pulled her into a wordless embrace and they both sobbed with relief.

Wednesday couldn't come around soon enough. Once she had explained the situation to the Head Teacher, Mr. Carmichael had agreed to let her take the day off. She'd wanted to kiss him but had managed to show massive restraint. However, several pupils, who sniggered as she walked by, witnessed the happy dance she did outside his office. She knew full well that her cheeks were glowing cerise, simply by the heat she could feel in them. She wouldn't live *that* whole debacle down in a hurry. Good thing she didn't care.

Once at home, she'd checked the flight arrival times, and she had figured out which flight would be Jason's. There was only one flight in from that destination, and unless they had chartered a private jet, he'd have to be on that one.

She stood before her closet with the door wide open, tapping her foot and chewing her thumb.

Dana sat on the bed behind her, waiting patiently.

'I think the navy dress that hugs your curves would be the biggest impact. Put your nude heels on and maybe a little scarf and you'll look stunning.'

Stevie nodded. 'I was thinking the navy dress too. I love that dress. I always feel special in it.'

'That's settled then. What about your hair?'

She turned to face her mother. 'Hmm...not sure. I can't think straight, Mum. My hands are so shaky and I'm so nervous.'

Dana's smile was wide and encouraging. 'Of course you are, honey. This is the beginning of the rest of your life.'

Stevie smiled too, but then the smile faded as quickly as it had arrived. 'Oh, Mum, what if he doesn't want me anymore? What if being over there has given him time to think and...and—'

Dana stood and embraced her daughter. 'Hey, stop it. He adores you. He came all the way to London to tell you so. That silly misunderstanding could've been resolved if he'd listened to you. But he's a stubborn man. You turn up looking gorgeous like you always do, and he'll remember exactly why he made that journey before all this horrible stuff happened. You mark my words, sweetie.'

'I hope you're right.'

'I *know* I'm right.' Dana cupped her face in her hands and planted a kiss on her nose. 'Now get ready. I'll come in the taxi with you to the airport, and I'll wait in the coffee lounge for you. Moral support and all that.'

Stevie nodded. 'What would I do without you, Mum?'

Dana winked. 'We'll never know.'

Smiling warmly, Stevie turned to pull her favourite fitted navy dress from its hanger. Dana made her way downstairs, telling Stevie she would call a cab. Once dressed, she pulled her hair into a chignon at the nape of her neck, applied a little lip gloss, and slipped into her nude heels.

Dana smiled when Stevie entered the lounge. 'Perfect, honey. Absolutely perfect. That dress brings out the blue of your eyes too. How could he *not* love you?'

'I think we'll soon find out,' she said, glancing out of the window. 'The cab has just pulled up.' She inhaled deeply, feeling her nerves jangling once again.

'Come on. Let's go get your man.' Dana clapped her hands like a giddy teenager, making Stevie giggle.

The cab ride seemed to take forever as they dodged in and out of cars, lorries, and bikes. Stevie tapped her fingers on her knees and looked out of the window at the people rushing around the London streets. It was bizarre how *their* lives were going on as normal when Stevie's future with the man she loved—the man she had *always* loved—was hanging in the balance. She glanced upward and noticed the sky had clouded over, and it looked like rain. *Typical.*

Once they had paid the cabbie, they tramped towards the arrivals entrance in a hurry, managing to avoid the rain as it began to pitter-patter down behind them. Stevie's heels click-clacked on the floor like a ticking clock. The seconds were counting down. She knew the flight was due to arrive in twenty minutes, and she checked the arrivals board to confirm that this was the case. The flight was on time.

After making their way over to a Customer Services desk, they waited in line as yet another flustered receptionist—*are all receptionists flustered?*—was trying to calm down a family, who from what she could gather, had missed their connecting flight by sitting in the arrivals area rather than departures. Flustered receptionists were seemingly becoming a regular occurrence in Stevie's life. *At this precise moment I could do without it!* She tapped her foot and chewed on her nail yet again. Her mother slapped her hand away from her mouth, giving her a frown. Stevie fought the urge to stick her tongue out like an errant child.

Eventually the family was ushered away by a Customer Service Manager, and Stevie stepped forward. 'Hello. I understand the press conference for the African hostages is being held here in the airport. I'm a close friend of one of them, and I'd like to get in there to see him. Can you tell me where that might be?'

The red-haired woman's face was almost the same colour

as her hair. *Poor woman*. She sighed heavily. 'I'm sorry but it's press only. I can't let you in without a press permit.' She looked apologetic, but it didn't help Stevie's plight.

'I *really* need to see him. *Please*. He's only at Heathrow for a limited time, and I have no other way of contacting him.' Stevie suddenly felt distraught at the thought of not being able to get through.

The woman shook her head. 'I'm so sorry. There's nothing I can do. I suggest you wait here and hope that you catch sight of him when he arrives before he's ushered away. Security for these things is usually very tight. Special companies are hired in and everything.' Stevie nodded slowly, tears welling in her eyes once again. They walked away from the desk, and she did her best not to let the tears escape.

Dana tugged on her arm. 'If I'm not mistaken that guy over there looks remarkably like a reporter.'

She glanced over in the direction of her mum's gaze. 'How can you tell?'

'Dunno...instinct probably...that and he's wearing an ID lanyard. Come on. I want to go have a little chat with him.'

As they approached the man, Stevie looked him up and down. He appeared to be about Dana's age. He was tall and nicely built with salt and pepper hair. He was concentrating on the notepad in his hand, presumably running through his questions. As Dana tapped his shoulder, he lifted his head and did a double take.

He frowned and then his eyes widened as Dana's mouth dropped open. 'Dana? Dana Watts?'

'Tom Grainger? Good grief! I haven't seen you in...ooh...it must be twenty-nine years!' The two old friends hugged. *Mum knows this guy?* Stevie gaped at the pair as they greeted each other. From the brief conversation, she gleaned that they had been at school together, and Tom had been one of Jed's—her father's—best friends.

'Wow, Dana...you look...*stunning,*' Tom said as he shook his head. It was clear that he had, at some point, had a bit of a crush on Dana—and maybe those feelings were still there.

'Oh, gosh how rude of me. Tom, this is Stevie, my daughter.' A look of pride appeared on Dana's face.

'Your daughter? Oh wow, Stevie, what a pleasure to meet you.' He pulled her into a hug that nearly took her off her feet.

She laughed nervously. 'Erm, nice to meet you too, Tom.'

'Gosh, Dana, I can't believe this. So are you still with Jed?'

Dana blushed. 'Oh, no. He and I split after Stevie was born. He wasn't really into the whole being a dad thing. And he got an offer he couldn't refuse with some big hot shot band, and so off he went.'

Tom frowned. 'No? Oh shit, that's awful and with a little baby to come home to. Stevie, I'm so sorry to hear that, love.'

'Oh, no. It's fine. Can't miss what you never had,' Stevie stated plainly and shrugged. Tom gave her a sad, knowing look before turning back to Dana.

'So are you married now? Family?' Dana asked.

'Divorced. No kids, sadly, although I would've loved them. It just never happened.' Sadness washed over his features for a moment but he shrugged it off. 'So what are you doing here? Going somewhere warm and sunny?'

'I was going to ask you the same thing. You're wearing a reporter's ID badge. Are you here on business?'

'Sure am. I'm off to a press conference. You know the hostages that escaped over in Africa? They're coming home in about...ooh ten minutes,' he said, glancing at his watch.

Dana bit her lip. Stevie watched a range of emotions flash over her mum's face. She was clearly uncomfortable asking this man for a favour now that it turned out she knew him.

'About that, Tom. The man who's coming home...Jason Reynolds. He's a good friend of Stevie's. I know this is very forward and I feel a bit bad asking but—'

'No, Mum. It's fine. You can't do this now. It's fine, Tom. Don't worry.'

Tom glanced between them. 'No, come on. What is it? What do you need?'

'Is there any chance you can get Stevie into the press conference with you? It's a lot to ask, and I don't mean to put you on the spot.'

He nodded. 'I'll get her in.' Stevie and Dana gasped in unison. 'On one condition.'

Dana narrowed her eyes. 'And what would that be?'

He took Dana's hand. 'That you'll have dinner with me tonight.'

Dana's face lit up with a beautiful, wide, beaming smile. 'Deal,' she answered without hesitation.

Tom's answering grin made Stevie's heart melt. He looked like he'd just won the lottery. The pair exchanged phone numbers and shared adoring glances. When he broke his gaze away from Dana and glanced over at Stevie, his cheeks were flushed.

He cringed. 'Oh heck, Stevie, I'm sorry about that. I must seem like a real sleazebag.'

Stevie couldn't help the smile on her face now. 'Not at all. I think it's sweet. And in case you're wondering, you both have my blessing.' She winked, feeling rather like the parent in the situation.

'Right, come on, ladies. We've a press conference to get to.'

'Oh no, I'm staying here. Just take Stevie.'

Tom beckoned for Stevie to follow him, which she did gratefully and willingly. They walked towards the security barriers, and Tom flashed his ID badge at the specially-hired-in-guard.

The huge brick wall of a man glanced at Stevie and shook his head. 'I'm sorry but you can't take the lady with you. No ID, no entry.'

'Oh, it's okay. She's my trainee. I called ahead and okayed it. Don't you have notification?' He shook his head. 'Does no one communicate properly anymore? If you need to go and check that's fine. We'll wait here. But can you hurry up? I need to do my job, mate.' He seemed very confident in his untruth and folded his arms as more journalists arrived.

'If you could step to one side please, sir. I'll get this lot through and then I'll radio management.

A glut of journalists trailed through flashing their badges as they passed, and Stevie felt sure she'd been scuppered again. One of the journalists was carrying video camera equipment, and from what the security guy was explaining to him, filming wasn't allowed, only still shots. The man protested vehemently, saying he'd had clearance to film. Stevie wondered if that was an untruth too. The guard was having none of it. Whilst the man was embroiled in a heated argument, Tom grabbed her arm and pulled her through past the barrier as another round of journalists did the same, all flashing their badges. He confidently walked down the corridor without looking back and Stevie followed suit. The guard was apparently clueless to what they had done.

CHAPTER TWENTY-SIX

S tevie continued to follow Tom down the long corridor and eventually they pushed through double doors that led into a large room. There was row upon row of journalists sitting and chatting whilst they waited. This was such a big story that it was now standing room only, and they took their places at the back. Suddenly, from the door at the other end of the room, there was a lot of shuffling and commotion. A police officer walked in, closely followed by a petite blonde woman, and then he was there. *Jason.*

He looked beautiful. Tired and bruised. But just beautiful. Stevie's heart skipped and then hammered in her chest as she fought the urge to scream his name and clamber through the throngs of people. But she stood stock-still. Frozen to the spot. Just staring as if seeing him was all a cruel dream.

His beard had grown in, and his hair was hanging shaggily down. *Wow.* His eyes darted nervously around the room as camera flashes went off. He blinked and jerked, covering his eyes. Her heart ached for him. *Poor Jason. My poor, poor Jason.* She clenched and unclenched her hands by her sides. She wanted to shout at the idiots to stop taking photographs.

Can't you see that he doesn't want this? Can't you see that he's been damaged?

A man in a suit told the gathered people that they could ask one question each but that if it got too much he would call an end to the conference and everyone would be asked to leave. That the pair had been through a major trauma and had agreed to do the conference under the proviso that they could stop at any time they felt it necessary. *What on earth did they put you through? How could they do this to you?* Her eyes began to sting and her lip trembled. Tom gave her a worried glance.

She watched as Jason ducked his head to the blonde woman and whispered in her ear. She felt a stab of jealousy but tried her best to quell it. Jason and the woman had been through this terrible ordeal *together* after all. She could see under the table that the pair was holding hands tightly. Another stab of jealousy. *Stop it, Stevie. Just stop it.* The suited man called for the first question.

'Roger Martin, Daily Post. Mr. Reynolds, Miss Maçon, you were held for several weeks against your will. The ordeal must have been horrifying. But the million dollar question is hanging on all of our lips...can you tell us please how you managed to escape?'

Jason cleared his throat. 'Erm...sure. We'd been kept in the same room but at opposite sides. It was a very lonely feeling. My head was covered and they'd beaten us both. Then they threatened to kill us both. We needed to comfort each other, and I wanted to formulate a plan. I couldn't bear to know that Oriel...erm...Miss Maçon was being harmed.' Jason closed his eyes and swallowed hard, the memory of the situation still evidently raw.

The blonde woman squeezed his arm with her free hand and glanced at the man who had posed the question.

With a shaking voice, she began to speak. 'We'd been kept in a concrete bunker. We were both on the floor. My head was not covered, but Jason's was...I explained that Jason and I were...I...I begged to be placed beside him. I told them he is my fiancé and I couldn't bear to be apart from him. And then —' The room erupted with questions and camera flashes as soon as the words had left her lips.

Stevie's ears began to buzz. The camera flashes around her made her eyes hurt, and her stomach plummeted as if she was on the steep descent of a huge rollercoaster. Her chest tightened, and she was overcome by dizziness. She could no longer hear what was being said. Turning around, she glanced at Tom whose gaze was filled with pity or compassion but she was too shocked to tell. She shook her head as she turned, pushed the door open, staggering through it, and began to run. Her heels pounded the tiled floor as she made her way back to the main area where she knew her mother was waiting. Thankfully the guard was no longer posted at the barrier, and she was able to run straight through.

Dana stood as Stevie approached. Her smile faded as realisation appeared to dawn on her face.

'Stevie? What happened?' She pulled her into a strong embrace and then released her to look into her eyes. 'Stevie?'

Her lip quivered as the tears spilled over. 'He's...he's engaged, Mum.'

Dana's brow furrowed. 'Sorry, what? How? Who?'

'The woman he's been held captive with. She announced it to the press. Please...please take me home.'

Jason glanced around the room full of journalists. They'd all gone crazy when Oriel began to tell the story of how they had escaped. The trouble was they had fixated on the part where she was explaining that she had told their captors he was her fiancé. She had tried to carry on, but they wouldn't let her. They kept barking questions about wedding dates and whether it was love at first sight.

Their lawyer stood and called for silence, and eventually the shouting had stopped.

'We are drawing an end to this press conference, ladies and gentlemen. My clients are feeling distressed, and I'm afraid their welfare is my priority, not what will be lining tomorrow's waste paper bins. If you would exit in an orderly manner, that would be much appreciated.' Some security guards entered and began to direct the disgruntled journalists out of the room. Questions continued to fly around. People pleading for exclusive interviews. Business cards being thrust through the arms of the security team and waved in their faces. Some resorted to throwing their cards straight at Jason and Oriel. One caught his forehead and stung, making him flinch. The man was wrestled to the ground and arrested. The whole situation was terrifying.

They were ushered out of the room quickly and escorted to the VIP lounge where they would wait for their flights home in relative peace.

Oriel hung her head. 'Oh Jason, I'm so sorry. I can't believe I was so stupid. And now Colette and Stevie will see the headlines and feel betrayed. I'm such a fool.'

He pulled her into his arms. 'Hey, don't worry. It was a total misunderstanding, and by the time the papers are out, you'll be home and able to explain. And so will I. It's not a big deal. Really it's not.'

A female police officer entered the VIP lounge and came to speak to Oriel. 'Miss Maçon, if you would like to come with me, your flight is boarding in thirty minutes. You will have a security escort, and you need to meet him.'

Oriel's eyes widened and glistened with tears. 'Jason, I'm going to miss you so much.' She flung her arms around him, and he lifted her petite frame from the ground, burying his face in her neck. His own eyes were damp, and his throat constricted.

He swallowed hard, keeping his emotions in check as best he could. 'We'll keep in touch. And don't forget you and Colette are welcome to come and stay at the camp any time you fancy an adventure that doesn't involve being kidnapped.'

She laughed and kissed him. 'Thank you. For keeping me sane. For looking after me, and most of all for saving my life. I owe you so much.'

'You owe me nothing. It was my job to keep you alive, remember.'

She pouted. 'Is that all I was to you? Just a job?'

He smirked. 'Are you kidding me? If I didn't like you, I'd have done a runner by myself.' They both laughed.

Jason became serious again. 'Seriously though, Oriel, we got through this ordeal *together*. We survived because of each other. And I'll love you forever simply for the fact that you saved me too.' His voice broke and he chewed on his quivering lip.

She clung to him once again as the female police officer placed a hand on her shoulder. 'I'm sorry, Miss Maçon, but it's time to go.'

Reluctantly, Jason released his friend and watched as she was led away. His lip began to quiver, and he ran a shaking hand through his long, shaggy hair. After everything they had been through, it would be tough not seeing her for a long while.

He had been hoping that Stevie might show up at the

airport. She must have heard on the news about his ordeal. And surely she'd been in touch with Dillon? He knew it was a long shot, but he'd hoped she come. His flight to Inverness was boarding in an hour, and there was no sign of her. He contemplated calling his brother but decided to wait until he saw him in person. The British Consulate had contacted Dillon to inform him of flight times, and so Jason knew there would be someone to welcome him home.

Home.

He. Couldn't. Wait.

The flight was uneventful much to Jason's relief, and the police escort he had was a nice guy. They chatted about everything except his ordeal, and Jason wondered if the officer had been given strict instructions to avoid the topic. If this was the case, he was very grateful. He wanted a break from thinking about what he'd been through. It haunted his dreams as it was.

After saying thank you and goodbye to his police escort, Jason walked through the security barriers at Inverness airport and spotted his welcoming committee. Dillon and Dorcas held up a sign with the words *Hero Jason Reynolds* painted in fancy lettering. Next he spotted Oliver, Hannah, and his younger half-brothers, Josh and Elliot. He almost took off at a sprint. Once he reached the group, he was enveloped in a group hug that took his breath away, and for the first time since he and Oriel had escaped, he let his emotions run free. His body was racked with violent sobs, and he let the tears flow unabashedly. His legs weakened, and his father held him up even though he was crying too.

'Oh, son, I thought I'd lost you. I thought I'd lost you.'

Oliver stroked his hair and held him tight as Jason leaned on him for support.

Next it was Dillon's turn. He clung to his brother and continued sobbing as Dillon did the same. No words were exchanged, but the tears of relief said everything that needed to be expressed.

Once Jason had calmed down, he was led to the car parking area and helped into the awaiting chauffeur driven, plush, ten-seated vehicle that had been sent by the British Consulate to ensure Jason and his family arrived home safely and in comfort.

Just over an hour later, they pulled through the gates of *Wild Front Here*, and Jason breathed a heavy sigh of relief. Home again, where he belonged. Without a doubt, he wouldn't be leaving again.

Oliver and the rest of his USA family bid him goodnight and said they'd see him the following day. They climbed into their rental car and drove away. They were staying at a nearby hotel. Dorcas and Dillon, however, had decided to stay on site in one of the cabins for a few days, seeing as there were no corporate events or schools booked for a while.

It was late and Jason was emotionally and physically exhausted.

Dorcas hugged him when they arrived inside his cabin. 'Can I get you some food, Jason? Or a drink maybe?' she asked stroking up and down his arms affectionately.

'To be honest, Dee, all I want is my bed. I just need to sleep.'

Her smile was warm. 'Of course you do. You have fresh bed linens and towels in your room. I've got the things to make you a nice Scottish breakfast in the morning. But don't rush to get up, eh? Nothing's spoiling.' She kissed his cheek and told Dillon she'd see him over at the cabin.

Once she'd gone, Dillon asked, 'Did Stevie show up at the airport?'

Jason pulled his brows into a frown and hung his head. 'Nah, bro. I honestly thought she'd be there. But I looked out for her and she wasn't.'

Dillon shook his head. 'I don't get it. She's been distraught. You should've heard her. She was blaming herself for the whole thing. She told me she would be there to meet you, today. I just...I don't get it. Why didn't she show?' Jason could see the question was rhetorical by the way Dillon looked at the floor. He lifted his head again. 'I have something to tell you, but I'll wait until you're ready.'

'Is it about Stevie?'

Dillon nodded.

'Tell me now.'

Dillon huffed out a long breath. 'She...she still loves you, Jace.'

'Yeah. And I still love her.' Jason shrugged as if this was old news.

'No, you don't get it. That guy she was with when you turned up...things...things weren't how they looked.'

Jason laughed bitterly. 'Yeah and that's why he was half naked when I got there, is it? Because I really need some sleep, bro.'

'Look, from what she told me...and I believe her...she had no reason to lie to me whilst you were...erm...*away*... Anyway, she said that just before you arrived that night, she'd told him she couldn't go through with it. She said she couldn't sleep with him. And she didn't. All she could think about was you, but she was trying to get over you, Jace. But your timing was crappy. The guy, he knows that she's still crazy about you. The letter you sent her broke her heart. She came to your hotel, but you'd already set off back here.'

Jason stared at Dillon for a few moments, trying to process it all. 'Okay. That's...' He rubbed his hands over his face. 'I don't know what to do with that information, Dill.'

'You don't have to do anything. I just thought you should know.'

Jason sighed heavily. 'One thing I learned whilst I was being held in that hell hole is that *this* is where I belong. I'm not leaving again. I can't. All that stuff about moving to London for her...I would've done it back then. But now...*now* I can't. Things have changed so much in such a short space of time. *This* is my home. You're here. My business is here. I *belong* here. And I think that changes everything where she's concerned.'

Dillon nodded his agreement. 'I'm kind of glad. I'd have missed seeing your ugly, hairy mug around the place.'

Jason laughed quietly, shaking his head. 'Yeah? Now you've seen me, you can fuck off as I clearly need my beauty sleep.'

The brothers hugged and Dillon left.

CHAPTER TWENTY-SEVEN

*J*ason awoke to the delectable smell of bacon and haggis. The sound of someone caterwauling somewhat ruined the effect of the mouth-watering aroma, and he was a little baffled as to why he could hear no accompanying music. After pulling on his sweats and a T-shirt, he made his way into the kitchen, where he stood, arms folded across his chest, chuckling to himself at the sight before him.

Dorcas was standing over the stove, blonde hair in bunches and ear buds in. Amazingly, her voice sounded nothing like the sweet one he was used to at campfire sing-alongs. Instead it was a kind of incoherent rambling, and she was clearly unaware of her audience of one. He tapped her shoulder, and she jumped so violently she almost fell over. The spatula she had been using flew out of her hand and narrowly missed Jason's head. He picked it up off the floor, shaking his head, and tossed it in the sink.

She pulled out her ear buds. 'Shit! You scared the bloody life out of me, Jason!' She placed her hand over her heart as if to emphasise the fact.

Jason couldn't help laughing. 'Yeah, well it's hard to sleep with that noise going on. I thought the purpose of headphones was so that the enjoyment of music was a private affair.'

She cringed. 'Oh hell, sorry. I tend to forget I've got them on. Are you hungry?'

'Bloody starving.'

'Great! Dill has gone to Aviemore to grab some fruit juice. He's been gone a while, so he won't be long. Your dad is coming around later.'

'Thanks for doing this for me, Dee. I really appreciate it.'

She blushed and dropped her gaze to wash the spatula. 'Oh, it's no bother. We want to make sure you're back to normal as soon as possible, eh?'

He grinned. 'Normal? I'm not sure I was *ever* normal to begin with.'

Dillon breezed through the cabin door. 'Hey, bro, you're up. Did you sleep okay?'

Jason nodded. 'Mostly. In between dreaming about being in that fucking bunker and trying to escape.'

'Shit. Have you checked your phone? I'll bet there are messages from Stevie.'

Jason shook his head. 'Just old ones. Nothing recent.'

Dillon seemed surprised. 'I don't get it. I'll give her a call later, maybe—'

'No!' Jason held up his hands. 'No, don't do that, mate. Just leave it, yeah? If she wanted me, she would've been there. Or she would've called. She must've thought better of it...so... just leave it.'

'Jason, she still wants you. I know—'

'I said leave it!' Jason's angry voice boomed around the cabin, and Dorcas dropped her spatula again.

He ran his hands through his hair. 'Look, I'm sorry, okay? I just...I can't think about Stevie right now. Every time I do, I'm reminded of how I fucked up so many times.' His voice wavered and he swallowed to try and dislodge the knot of emotion lodged in his throat. 'I clearly fucked up in a massive way if she didn't come to the airport when she said she would. I'm going to move on. I'm putting her behind me now. I *have* to for my own sanity. It's no use all this hanging around waiting for her to change her mind about us. She got my letter. I laid my heart out raw for her. And regardless of what you say, she clearly doesn't want me anymore. Until she turns up here to tell me otherwise, then it's...it's over.' He pushed past Dillon and walked out the door.

Jason found himself gravitating towards the riverbank where he had spent time with Stevie. When he closed his eyes, he could imagine her laid out before him on the ground as he kissed and caressed her body. And what a body. Gone was the teenage frame he'd been familiar with when he left her without warning. Instead she was the epitome of woman-hood. Soft feminine curves and rounded breasts that became heavy and full when she was aroused. God, what he wouldn't give for her to still want him. To still *need* him the way he needed her.

He thought back to the day they had almost made love out on the riverbank. He had teased her about outdoor sex. The memory made him smile...

Jason slipped his hand into her hair and pulled her closer. 'Come on...let's go back. I really want to make love to you again and I'm not sure it'd be a good thing to let that happen out here.'

'But it's so lovely out here,' she almost whined.

He feigned shock and gasped. 'Since when did you become an exhibitionist, Miss Wat...Mrs. Norton?'

Stevie giggled. 'I'm not an exhibitionist. I didn't mean I wanted to have outdoor sex. I just meant it's so beautiful here. It's a shame to go in.'

He folded his arms and pursed his lips playfully. 'Well okay. Let me give you a choice then. You either come back with me now or you become very much accustomed to outdoor sex and exhibitionism because I'm making love to you regardless, although I'm guessing the kids will be back soon, and I'm not sure that being found in flagrante delicto is such a good career move for such a talented Science teacher.' He winked. 'So what'll it be?'

'But the picnic—'

'We'll leave it for the ants. Come on.' He grabbed her hand and pulled her to stand in front of him. He tucked a stray strand of hair behind her ear. 'I want you, Stevie. I have no idea how many more times I'll have this opportunity to be with you so...please?'

How right he had been about the lack of time they had. There had been several occasions where they had made love knowing very well that it was temporary between them. But it didn't stop him allowing it to happen again and again and damn his heart.

On that particular occasion after the riverbank picnic, he had made love to her standing up whist she was perched on the kitchen counter top. It had been slow, languorous and deep. He had relished her curves. Trying to make her believe him when he told her how much he adored her womanly form with its softness and smoothness. She had been embarrassed about her body. Claiming that now she was no longer eighteen, her body wasn't all that great. But he knew different. He covered every inch of her in wet kisses to prove his point. And when they had both come undone together... Wow! Her face was the epitome of sheer beauty. He had once told her that the most beautiful sight he had ever seen was when she came for him. He still held to that belief.

No other woman would ever compare.

He slumped down in the spot he loved even more since sharing it with Stevie and glanced around him. Closing his eyes again, he could hear her laughter echoing through the trees as she lay on the blanket with her long, dark hair spread around her like a fan. She was almost like a ghost to him now, a memory that he would treasure but could never have for real.

The silly thing in all of it was that he really didn't understand why he couldn't have it, why he couldn't have *her*. There were so many reasons why they wouldn't work. Clearly there were trust issues, thanks to his ability to run at the drop of a hat. But overall, he was willing to give things a try when he went down to London. And from what Dillon had said, she had felt the same. Like he'd said to Dillon, he could only assume that she had changed her mind.

Tired of his melancholic state of mind, he stood and made his way back to the cabin.

Stevie stared at the newspaper headline as if doing so would help the reality of the situation sink in. She hadn't read the article itself. The headline was *very* self-explanatory,

HOSTAGES FIND LOVE IN A WAR ZONE AND GET ENGAGED

The photo that accompanied the article had been captured when Jason had leaned to whisper in the blonde woman's ear. But in the photo it looked distinctly like he was kissing her. Perhaps that's what he had been doing, and she had been in some kind of denial at the time.

Dana handed her a cup of coffee. 'Stevie, sweetheart, throw it away. Please. It's doing you no good staring at it.'

Stevie laughed bitterly. 'He really moved fast. He thought I'd moved on and so he did the same.'

'Love, they were in such an intense situation together. These things apparently happen in times like that. Don't be angry with him. Maybe now you can move on.'

'I don't have a lot of choice, do I?' She walked over to the window and looked out over the rear garden. 'I should let Dillon know what happened. He must think I'm terrible for not speaking to Jason when I said I'd be there to meet him.'

'I hardly think he'll blame you, darling. My guess is he's probably feeling terrible for putting you in that position. He can't have known. Dillon's not malicious. He wouldn't have asked you to be there if he'd known about the engagement.'

'No...no I guess not.'

CHAPTER TWENTY-EIGHT

*T*he weeks passed slowly for Stevie. Her spare time was taken up preparing for her new job. She had to make it her own. Put her stamp on it. This was to be her main focus now. It was all she had. She had to shake off a wave of depression before it gripped her in its claws and clung on. She was determined to make a go of things. This was what she'd been working towards.

This was meant to be.

She took a group of learners to the local community centre to watch a *Scientist Stu* show at the end of the week. She applauded in all the right places and laughed along with the kids, even though she wasn't really listening. This was usually one of her favourite parts of the curriculum. The sad thing was, as Head of Science she wouldn't get to do this anymore. No, there were to be far more important demands on her time than watching someone turn water into what looked like red wine or making *elephant's toothpaste* and *screaming jelly babies*. There would be facts and figures to sort through, grades and exams to think about, timetabling and staff appraisals.

She stepped out to get some fresh air, suddenly feeling a little overwhelmed by her impending responsibility. She noticed a leaflet rack of course information for the local community college. *Perhaps I need a hobby? Yeah, something to help me de-stress.* She thumbed through the leaflets. Karate, netball, metal work...*ooh metal work would be good*...archery... She grabbed a few of the brochures and shoved them into her handbag.

The end of the day was a welcome occurrence, and Stevie arrived home in a bit of a daze. Her phone rang and with a long sigh she answered the call.

'Hi, Mum.'

'How was your day, honey bun?' Dana asked.

'Oh, good actually. Saw Scientist Stu. He's really funny. The kids love him.'

'That's good then. Bit of a change.'

'Yeah, it was. Mum?'

'Yes, love?'

'What do you think about me getting a hobby?'

'I think it's a great idea. What were you thinking?'

'Oh, I don't know yet. I got some leaflets from the community centre. There are all sorts going on at the community college.'

'Sounds good. You'll need something to help you de-stress when you start your new job.'

'That's exactly what I thought.'

A few moments of silence followed, which was rare for Dana, and Stevie could tell her mother had something to say. 'Come on, Mum, out with it. I know you're hiding something.'

Dana sighed. 'Tom told me he loves me. So...I... I told him about my condition. I felt it was only fair that he knew what he was letting himself in for. I mean...things can change with Myasthenia and...you just never know...'

'Oh, Mum. You must really care for him. And it's not as if you're *ill* ill. You cope so well with things. What...what did he say?' *Please let him still be around...please...she needs this.*

'He said that nothing could change the way he feels about me,' Dana said dreamily. 'He says he always had strong feelings for me and he's grateful to have been given a chance to be with me.'

Tears of happiness and relief stung at Stevie's eyes. Dana deserved someone wonderful. It was about time. 'Oh, Mum, I knew he'd be the one for you. I just knew it.'

'He's just so...there aren't enough lovely words, darling. Anyway, sweetie. I'll have to go. He's picking me up soon. He's taking me to the cinema to see the new Gerard Butler film. And you know how much I adore him.' Her voice was chirpy and excited.

Stevie giggled. 'Who? Tom or Gerard?'

'Hmmm...both!' Dana squeaked.

'Okay, have fun, Mum. Say *hi* to Tom for me.'

The call ended and Stevie reached down to scratch behind Rowdy's ears. 'It's bloody typical, Rowds. My mum has a better love life than I do.'

The dog whined as if agreeing sympathetically with her. She was so very happy for her mum. After all these years of steering clear of men and the complications they brought, Dana had finally found love with someone she had known when Jed was still around. The familiarity of that seemed to comfort Dana. And Tom was great. A really nice, down to earth kind of guy. He treated her well and clearly adored her.

He was a handsome man, and Stevie could definitely see the attraction. Since Dana had been with Tom, she had relaxed a little and smiled a hell of a lot more.

Stevie wondered if this might mean she could worry less and concentrate on her own life more. If things continued the way they were going, Tom would clearly take care of her mum. The thought warmed her heart and for the first time in a long while she felt a weight lift from her shoulders. She noticed the leaflets she had picked up from the community centre laying on the coffee table. She was on the verge of looking through them when her phone rang again.

'Stevie?'

She sat upright. 'Dillon? Is everything okay?'

'Fine...fine yes. I had to call you. Something's been bugging me for a while, but I promised I wouldn't interfere. But...well...sod it, I'm interfering anyway.'

Stevie scrunched her brow. 'What are you talking about?'

'Okay...here goes...' He inhaled deeply. 'Why didn't you meet Jason at the airport like you said you would?'

Stevie snorted. 'You've waited all this time to call and ask me that?'

'Yeah. Like I said, I was *asked* to leave it, but some questions need answers.'

She remained silent.

'You said you'd be there, Stevie. You said you'd go. What changed?'

She took her own deep breath before speaking firmly. 'For your information, Dillon, I did go. I turned up like the dutiful friend. I even managed to get someone to help me into the press only conference.'

'Oh...oh right.' He sounded surprised. 'But Jason looked for you. You didn't approach him. You didn't go to him. You haven't been in touch since.'

'No. I haven't and there is good reason for that, don't you think?'

'How should I know?'

She laughed bitterly. 'Oh come off it, Dillon. He announces his engagement to the paparazzi and therefore the whole world, and I'm supposed to play nice, hug him, and tell him how happy I am that he's home. Actually I *was* happy he was home, but I couldn't speak to him. My heart kind of shattered into a million pieces when I saw them looking at each other.'

'You've got it all wrong.'

She was getting annoyed. 'What? What do you mean?' She tapped her foot and flared her nostrils.

'He *didn't* get engaged.'

'No? Whatever, Dillon, he moved on. I need to do the same, so please let me do it, okay?' She hit *end call* and slammed the phone onto the sofa.

'Who was it, bro?' Jason asked as he walked in and found Dillon hanging up the phone. He rubbed the towel over his head as he waited for an answer.

'What? Oh, no one. Nothing.'

Jason scrunched his brow. 'It doesn't look like it was nothing. You don't look too impressed.'

'No...no it's something and nothing. Nothing for you to worry about.

'Okay. If you say so. Are you still up for going to that La Fontaines gig at the Ironworks over in Inverness tonight?'

'Yeah, sounds good.'

'Great. I'll go get dressed and we'll leave now. We can get a pizza on the way, eh?'

'Yeah. Sounds good.' Dillon still looked distracted.

Jason went back into his room and pulled on his T-shirt. His iPod was on random and as he sat on the bed he was greeted with Aerosmith's 'What it Takes'. He smirked and shook his head. *Great fucking timing, Mr. Tyler*. He glanced over at his dresser at the photo of Stevie standing against the wall in her climbing gear. She may not have realised it at the time, but she had a glow about her that day, and seeing her in the harness had done strange things to his imagination. Images of her in *just* the harness...no clothes...danced through his head like they had done on the day itself. He adjusted his jeans and rolled his eyes.

He growled at his reflection in the mirror. 'I've got to stop fucking thinking like this.'

Friday night was yet another night of wine with Mollie, only this time they ventured out of the house. They ended up at a club not too far from Stevie's house and things were going well. They danced and drank...drank a little more and then danced more as a result of the drink. Stevie was feeling relaxed and quite giggly. That was until a guy approached her, asking for her number and if he could buy her drink. He was tall with mousey hair, fairly good-looking, and nicely built. Mollie was doing her best to encourage Stevie to chat to him, but she wasn't interested.

'What's your name?' Mollie asked him, her words a little slurry.

'I'm Jaz...Jaz Malone.'

Stevie was intrigued by his accent. 'You're not from here,' she informed him, pointing a drunken finger in his face.'

'That would be correct. I'm from a little place called the USA,' he told her with a smile.

Stevie scrunched her face at him. 'Why are you here then?' Her tone wasn't exactly friendly she realised, but it didn't put him off.

'Ah, long story. Came here with my girlfriend. Things didn't exactly work out. She met someone new and moved on. So here I am.'

Stevie huffed. 'Huh, I know all about being dumped for someone else, Jaz Malone.' She slurred his name into one word and he chuckled. 'Wanna get pissed with us?'

He glanced around as if looking for someone. 'Uh, yeah, why the hell not?'

'Oooh I like your accent...it's kind of sexy...schmexy.' *Oh god, what am I talking about? I really am fissed as a part, and should, therefore, go home. Go home, Stevie. Hang on though... I'm talking to myself in my head, so I can't be quite as think as I drunk I am...huh? I'm actually, quite most absolutely fine... ish. Another few shots won't hurt.*

Realising she had been standing having a conversation with herself whilst staring at the handsome American set her off giggling.

And so the night went on in a drunken blur.

The following morning, Stevie awoke with a throbbing head and a mouth as dry as the Sahara. She tried to recall the events of the previous evening and could remember being helped into a cab by...someone...a man...*Jazz hands? Jazzy Jeff? Jaz Malone! That's it! Jaz Malone.* She climbed out of bed, and when the room had stopped spinning, she made her way downstairs. Rowdy was giddy and excited, jumping around, and giving a high-pitched yip that felt like a drill at her skull. She opened the back door and evicted him into the garden.

Mollie appeared in the doorway, looking as fresh as a daisy. Stevie opened her mouth to speak and closed it again. She did this several more times until Mollie spoke.

'Okay, so either you're doing a very good impression of a fish out of water or you're trying to communicate with either me...or the mother ship. What's up?'

'How do you end up looking so fucking fresh? It's not fucking fair.'

'And how come every time you're hung over you swear like a boat builder?'

'That could be very insulting to boat builders, you know.'

Mollie glanced around her and spoke in a hushed tone. 'When they wake up, we'll apologise.'

Horror suddenly washed over Stevie. 'Was he a boat builder? And is he here?' Her own voice was a loud whisper.

Mollie burst out laughing hysterically. 'Who the hell are you talking about?'

'That...that Jaz bloke, obviously!'

'Oh *him*! Oh no, he saw us into a cab, and we went our separate ways. And he was a newly qualified teacher. He was only in London for the weekend. He lived up in the Scottish Borders.'

'Oh. Thank goodness.' Stevie leaned against the counter top as she breathed a sigh of relief. 'What is it about bloody Scotland and good looking men?'

'Hmmm. Dunno. He was really nice. Young too. Yeah it was quite sweet. I left the two of you alone to sit and wallow in self-pity about being dumped by the love of your lives whilst I went off and pulled a hunky guy called Todd. When I came back, you'd got your arms around each other's shoulders and were singing a delightful rendition of 'What Becomes of the Broken Hearted'. He was actually quite good. But then again, he teaches music. You on the other hand...' She sucked air in through her teeth and shook her head.

The phone began ringing, and the sound of that had the same effect as Rowdy's bark. Rubbing at her temples, she shouted, 'Chuck it in the garden and ignore it. That's what I did with Rowdy.' But the ringing stopped. *Ah shit. Too late.*

Mollie had already answered the call. 'Yeah, Dillon. She's just here. Hang on. Oh, be gentle though, eh? Yeah, bad hangover.' She laughed.

Stevie snatched the phone. 'Dillon.' She was very much aware that her monotone greeting was anything but cordial.

'Stevie, right, you need to listen. You need to stop jumping to conclusions and you need to listen. Can you do that?'

'Why are you whispering?'

'Because Jason is still in bed, and he'll kill me if he knows I'm calling you.'

She huffed out a frustrated sigh. 'Why? What's going on?'

'Right...for starters, he is *not* and I repeat *not* engaged.'

'No I—'

'Bah! List-ennnn.' He drew the word out patronisingly, and Stevie had the urge to hang up. 'Not only is he *not* engaged. But he is *not* in a relationship with Oriel Maçon.'

'Who's Oriel Maçon?'

'For fuck's sake, Stevie! You're supposed to be listening! I don't have much time!'

'Okay, keep your knickers on!'

'Oriel is the woman he was captured with. But she is in a relationship with someone else. A woman. Okay?' *Oh...right.*

'The way they were able to escape is that Oriel told them she wanted to sit by her fiancé, Jason, because she was afraid. They let her. Jason had a knife hidden in his boot. They used the knife to cut the ropes so they could escape. Now do you get it?'

The information overload made Stevie's head pound in her skull. She didn't know what to do with it.

'Stevie? You can speak now.'

'Yes, sorry. I just... I don't know what to say.'

'He was *looking* for you. He *wanted* you to be there at the airport. He *hoped* you'd be there. Do you understand?'

Stevie stumbled over to the kitchen table and sat down. 'Yeah...yes...I get it. But why didn't he contact me?'

'Because he still thinks *you*'ve moved on. I told him about Marcus and that you're not in a relationship with him. But he says he needs to hear that from you, but he won't contact you about it. Honestly, I could bang your heads together!'

'So he'd come to London again?' Something akin to hope swelled inside her, and her sluggish heart rate began to increase.

Dillon, however, sighed. 'That's just it. He says that being away and going through what he went through has made him feel that he... He says he won't be leaving here. That *this* is his home. So I'm guessing that, no, he won't come to London, Stevie.'

'Therein lies the issue, Dillon. I just got the Head of Science job, and so my life is here.' Her heart plummeted.

Dillon sighed. 'Really? No chance you'll change your mind on this?'

Stevie's eyes began to sting as all hope ebbed away as quickly as it had arrived. 'I'm sorry, Dillon.' The waver in her voice told of her anguish.

'Okay, in that case, this conversation never happened.' His voice was tinged with sadness and disappointment. 'Take care of yourself, Stevie. Be happy.'

The line went dead.

A little like Stevie's hopes of a future with Jason.

CHAPTER TWENTY-NINE

*S*ince her call with Dillon, Stevie had made a few
decisions about her life. It was time to start living it.
That was the first decision. In fact...it was the only one that
needed any consideration. Life would start right *now*.

Her resolve was set firm.

Saturday night had rolled around, and Mollie was out
with Todd whom she'd met on their girl's night. Stevie had
opened a bottle of wine and had been contemplating what
movie to watch when the leaflets from the Community
College caught her eye from under a pile of magazines.

There were several courses being run at the College that
she decided she'd like to try. The trouble was she didn't have
time for *several*. One maybe, but no more than that. And luck-
ily, one in particular had sparked her interest.

Without thinking it through, she picked up her phone and
dialled. Considering it was a Saturday evening, she didn't
anticipate anyone answering. She presumed it'd be a voicemail. But when a man answered, she was a little taken back.
Hoping she didn't sound too slurry, she spoke as politely as
she could.

'Hello, yes. I picked up your leaflet from Wilmersden Community Centre, and I'd like to sign up for lessons please.'

The call went on for several minutes as the man took down many details. Stevie wasn't sure which interrogation had been more intense, this one or the all-day interview she had undergone for the Head of Science job. At least with this particular one, she was told she could start on Monday, unlike the job, which she wouldn't be starting until after Christmas. Although considering the amount of new work that had surreptitiously landed on her desk, it appeared that the Head Teacher had forgotten *that* minor fact.

Monday at school was a mixture of annoying kids with no homework and looking out for the Head Teacher, who kept on sneaking those extra documents onto her already stacked in-tray. She had decided to subtly remind him that her post wasn't beginning until the New Year. But she kept missing him. By the time she was home, she felt incredibly frustrated and was ready to punch something...or preferably some*one*. She wasn't sure *whom* she wanted to punch. Once ready to go on her new adventure, she walked around to her neighbour, Joe's house with Rowdy in tow, knocked on the door, and waited.

'Hi, Stevie, are you coming in for a coffee?' Joe asked as he crouched down to pay attention to his canine friend.

'No, thanks, Joe. I need to get going, seeing as I'm running late. Are you sure this arrangement will work for you? He loves his long walks with you, but I don't want you to feel pressured.' Rowdy hated most men, but for some unknown reason he *adored* Joe. It worked out well, seeing as Joe loved to walk and enjoyed the company of the huge dog.

'Nah, not at all love. Don't worry. Me and Rowds have a great time, don't we boy? But are you sure you want to do this? It's a bit drastic don't you think? Just don't get hurt, okay?'

She was touched by his apparent level of concern for her welfare. 'Oh, I'll be fine, Joe. They know what they're doing. I'll be in the hands of experts.'

He nodded but his lips were pulled into a hard line. 'All right then... Did you manage to get the equipment you needed?'

She rolled her eyes. 'I did. Bloody expensive though.'

'No wonder. Only *you* could choose the most expensive new hobby going. Couldn't you have gone for...I don't know...crochet, needlework maybe? Even street dance would have been more preferable.'

Stevie laughed. His reaction when he had been asked to keep her new hobby a secret had been pretty much the same. 'You have obviously never seen me dancing. Anyway, I'm not sixty, you know. And I think it will be fun.'

Joe didn't appear convinced. 'Hmmm. I hope you're right. Take care, okay?'

'Will do, see you later. Bye Rowdy.' She nuzzled the fluffy animal's fur and then left. She had to be there for six. It was twenty to, and she was leaving home a little later than she had anticipated.

Walking into the community college, she felt like a child on her first day of school. This was a new challenge she had set herself, and in spite of her excitement, she was pretty terrified to say the least. A tall, muscular man with greying hair and tattoos walked towards her.

He smiled warmly. 'I'm guessing by the terror in your eyes you're Stevie?'

Stevie grimaced. 'Oh heck...can you smell fear or something?'

'Ahhh, you'll be fine. Don't worry about a thing. Come on over and join the group. We're having a safety briefing, and then we'll get cracking...not literally though.' He chuckled. *Oh shitty, shitty, shit. I think I'm having some kind of early mid-life crisis.* She glanced around the group and realised, with some dismay, that she was the only woman there. *Gulp...come on Stevie...suck it up...it'll be good for you.*

Her first session had been great fun and later that night, she sat reading through the literature she had been handed. Her muscles ached in places she didn't realise she actually *had* any. But overall, it had been a fantastic experience. The other guys had been very encouraging and in the end the fact that she was the only woman hadn't mattered at all. This was the start of a new, independent, fly by the seat of her pants Stevie. A new *Do what the hell I want to do and not just what I should do* Stevie. So what if people thought she was losing her marbles. She didn't much care anymore. This was a fresh start. One she desperately needed to make.

The following weekend, Stevie insisted on going shopping with Mollie. She was on a mission. She had no clue why but she knew it was another thing she had to do. *A whole new wardrobe. They do call it retail therapy after all!*

'What are we looking for exactly?' Mollie sighed outside the fitting rooms of yet another shop. 'It's not exactly the type of shop you normally frequent, Stevie. I'm beginning to think you've lost your marbles.

'You've noticed then? As for what I'm looking for, I think it's a case of I'll know it when I see it,' she shouted through the curtain

'Can we go for a coffee next? I need a caffeine fix...ooh and a chocolate muffin.'

The two friends left the shop ten minutes later. Stevie was loaded down with several bags. Stevie's phone rang, and she fumbled and juggled her bags trying to locate it. Eventually Mollie huffed and grabbed her handbag from her, pulled out the errant phone, and handed it to Stevie.

'Hello?'

'Oh hello there. May I speak with Stevie Watts please?'

'Speaking.'

'Oh hello there. This is Martha Graham. We were wondering if you could come and meet with us on December fifteenth?'

'Yes, yes that would be fine. What time?'

'Shall we say one o'clock?'

'Sounds good. I'll see you then.'

Stevie hung up the phone, glanced back up at Mollie, who stood with a questioning expression.

Stevie's cheeks heated. 'Oh...it was just...it was about getting my name changed back to my maiden name,' she lied.

Mollie's eyes narrowed suspiciously. 'Whatever you say. I know there's something going on, Stevie. You forget how crap at lying you are.'

With a deep sigh Stevie considered her words carefully. 'I've applied for another job. And that's all I'm saying for now.'

Mollie's eyes widened. 'What? Why? You've been desperate to get the Head of Science job. Why could you possibly want to leave now?'

'Because the more I've thought about it the more I've decided it's just not me. It's not what I want. I love *teaching*. It's what I do best, but from what I can see, the Head of Department role is mainly paperwork, statistics and targets.'

'You haven't even given it a go yet though, Stevie.'

'I know. I know, but I need a fresh start. I can't explain it all, Moll, but I just know it's what I need.'

Mollie pouted. 'You'll still keep in touch though?'

Stevie nudged her. 'You can't get rid of me that easily, you daft bat.'

Stevie could almost see the questions whirring in her best friend's mind and was relieved when she heard someone call her name. She looked in the direction of the voice and her jaw dropped.

The person before her smiled widely. 'Hi Stevie, how've you been?'

'Hi, Carrie. I've been...fine. You?'

Stevie had lost touch with her very best friend after school and following the disappearance of Jason ten years before. She hadn't coped well with what had happened and had ended up cutting ties with all of her school friends. It made things easier at the time, but she had missed them terribly.

Especially Carrie.

Carrie nervously tucked her hair behind her ear. 'Oh, I'm fine. Married now. Got a little boy called Alfie. He's at nursery.'

Stevie suddenly felt like the universe was conspiring against her, forcing her to face the past at every turn. 'Oh wow, that's wonderful. Congratulations. Who did you marry? Anyone I knew?'

'Yeah actually. Callum and I married. Childhood sweethearts and all that.' The woman's face dropped in horror, and her eyes widened as soon as the words had left her lips. 'Oh gosh, Stevie, I'm so sorry I didn't mean...oh gosh—'

Stevie held up her hands. 'Hey, it's fine. And that's really lovely. I'm sorry about what happened...you know when we left school. I didn't cope well with Jason's disappearance. I hope you can forgive me for breaking contact.'

Carrie's smile was warm. 'There's nothing to forgive. We all got it. We just...we wished you'd have let us be there for you. Did you ever find out what happened to Jason?'

'As a matter of fact, yes. I found him by accident.'

Carrie's eyes widened. 'Oh, my gosh! Is he okay? What the hell happened to him?'

'He's fine. It's a long story, and I don't feel it's my place to go into it, but let's say he had good reason to leave. And I've forgiven him.'

'Are you...you know...back together? Or did you marry someone else?'

'I did marry, but I'm divorced now. And no, sadly he and I are not back together.' She dropped her gaze to the floor as she spoke the words. Her heart squeezing in her chest as images of the two of them together flashed cruelly through her mind.

'Oh, I'm sorry to hear that...all of it. Look, here's my card.' She fumbled in her handbag and handed one to Stevie. 'I'd love to catch up some time. If you'd like to, that is.'

Stevie glanced at the card. 'So you're a physiotherapist, eh? Fantastic.' She smiled at her old friend, feeling a little sad for the years they had lost. 'Maybe I'll give you a call and we'll catch up.'

'Okay, great. You look really well, Stevie. It's been good to see you.'

'You too. Bye Carrie.' The two women hugged and went their separate ways. Seeing her old best friend from school only brought more painful memories of Jason flooding to her mind. Why did these things happen at the worst possible times? Her desire to curl up in a ball and cry was almost over-whelming.

As if sensing her distress, Mollie slipped an arm around her shoulder. 'I think that coffee and cake is called for now. Don't you?'

Stevie nodded and let her friend lead her towards Starbucks.

CHAPTER THIRTY

*T*he start of December was incredibly chilly. Jason knew that things were about to calm down at the camp as they always did in the winter season. The schools wouldn't put their students through the Scottish sub-zero temperatures, and corporate event attendees preferred the warmer weather too. Wintertime was when he and his staff would make the most of helping out at the local ski resort if the snowfall was sufficient—and it usually was.

Scotland had some of the best slopes in Europe when the snow hit, and the scenery in winter was a stunning sight to behold. The undulating mountains covered in their insulating blanket of white were one of Jason's favourite vistas. He worked at the ski resort for fun, but the others needed it to top up their income. Plus it meant they could all carry on working together as they dearly loved to do.

He had watched as the relationship between his brother and Dorcas had blossomed into something serious and committed. He was delighted for them. After his advice, Dillon had been very open with Dorcas about the suicide attempt and the fact that he was adopted. Dillon later informed Jason that she had vowed to help him find his birth family, stating that she would love him no matter what. She was so good for him. Jason had thanked her on the sly and told her she'd been the best thing that could've happened to Dillon.

He knew that eventually Dillon would announce that he and Dorcas would be moving in together, and it finally happened during the first bitterly cold December week. Jason was very happy for his little brother after all he'd been through. The counselling he'd undergone following what happened had been a great success. He wasn't seen as a threat to himself from very early on in the process, much to Jason's relief. He was very fortunate that the assessment had been thorough, and it had been decided that the undue stress of finding out he was adopted had been the reason for his breakdown. Seeing him now in a stable and loving relationship warmed Jason's heart. But it made him realise what he was missing too.

The staff rallied around the camp, clearing it ready for the annual winter freshen-up. Every cabin would be getting a fresh lick of paint. Even Jason's cabin was in need of it. But as he stood looking around the place, all he could think about was Stevie. They had made love on the couch, the dining table, the kitchen counter tops, and the floor. Everywhere he looked, he could picture her feminine curves and the red tint to her hair when the sunlight caught it.

I've waited for this for ten years, Stevie. I just didn't realise I was waiting. Ten years I've been lost. But now I know where my place is. I know where I belong and that's inside you. His words echoed around his head as images of her played like a movie on repeat.

Perhaps redecorating and moving things around would help rid him of the memories. Although it was crazy, he felt sure he could smell her perfume in the cabin when he'd returned from Africa. He'd even asked Dorcas if she had changed her perfume, but she hadn't. The memories were clearly very strong for him.

For the most part, he had been occupied with the last few school parties to visit, and after that, the final corporate event of the year. But whenever he found himself alone in his cabin, especially after Dillon had moved out, he would spend far too much time reminiscing. Music accompanied his melancholy mood swings. The sadder the song, the better. Soon he had the perfect soundtrack to his heartbreak, and torturing himself with it and the images in his mind of *his* soulmate , Stevie became the double-edged sword of his existence.

After everything he had been through, he still felt there was a huge gaping hole in his soul. The nightmares of being captured and beaten had gone, thankfully. Instead they were replaced with a particular recurring dream.

He opened his eyes to bright light. He was sitting on a blanket at the top of a hill overlooking a loch. Stevie sat before him with tears in her eyes and a smile on her face. He glanced around and saw two glasses and a small Champagne bottle. His guitar was in his lap, and he was playing but there was no sound. He stopped playing and looked up to Stevie. He couldn't see her face as the sun was shining in his eyes, but he knew he was waiting for her to speak. He knew he had asked her a question but couldn't remember what it was. And every time, right before she answered, he woke up clutching a pillow to his chest.

Sitting on the step to his cabin in the cold December evening air and clutching his hot mug of coffee, he surveyed his land, absorbing all that he had chosen over Stevie. Sarah McLachlan's 'I Will Remember You' drifted through the chilled night and enveloped him in sorrow as the bitter sting of tears became evident to him once again. He closed his eyes and rested his head back. Could he honestly say he had made the right choice? It was doubtful.

Stevie stood at the counter in the motorway service station. She desperately needed the bottle of water that she held in her hand, but the queue was massive and time was a-ticking. She had finally managed to finish the last little notifications of her change of name back to Watts before she set off on her journey. Miles, her ex-husband, had not been pleased about this at all.

'I don't see why you would *need* to change your name back though. You and I are still friends, aren't we?' he had asked when he had finally been to collect the last few items that Stevie had been storing for him and he had spotted the Deed Poll application.

'That's just it though, Miles. Friendship is all we are ever going to have from now on. And so I want my identity back. It feels right. It's time to start over. For both of us.'

Miles had sulked and walked out of the house with his box and large bag in a huff. She had simply smiled sweetly and closed the door, happy in the knowledge that she was moving on. All forward motion was good and her life was almost back on track.

Almost.

Tom being in her mum's life was a huge deal too. Stevie was beginning to realise that all the worry about her mother coping alone with Myasthenia Gravis had been a waste of time. Dana was more than capable of looking after herself, lifelong condition or not. Medication was working well for her, meaning that she was leading a full and almost normal life. And Stevie had watched the relationship between her mum and Tom blossoming with a deep-seated happiness and warmth. She could move on. She should've listened to her mum about the whole thing in the first place. Dana had never wanted to be treated differently—hence keeping her condition a secret—but in refusing to leave her, Stevie had been doing just that. She had been unintentionally wrapping her in cotton wool.

Well, no more.

Back in the present, and finally the cashier smiled and scanned the water bottle through the cash register.

'You look like you need this,' the cashier said, as she looked Stevie up and down with a grin on her face.

Stevie was aware that her hair was plastered to her head and she maybe didn't look her best. She would have to stop off and freshen up at some point. She paid as quickly as she could and dashed back out of the shop to continue on her way.

'Hi, big bro. How you doing?' Dillon asked as he sauntered into Jason's cabin.

'I don't know. I'm a bit down to be honest. I don't know why it's getting to me more today.' He sighed and rubbed his hands over his face. 'But everywhere I look I see *her*. And I know it's been ages, but I honestly thought she'd have met me at the airport when I got back, seeing as we landed at Heathrow. I thought maybe what happened to me might have made her change her mind. And the trouble is, I still can't get her out of my head. Being back home is somehow harder. Not that I want to still be a hostage, don't get me wrong. It's just that I missed her like crazy when I was away, and from what you said, she was worried and missing me too. I don't get it.'

Dillon looked sheepish for a second, and Jason frowned wondering why until Dillon finally spoke. 'Aw Jace, mate. I wish there was something I could do. I don't get it either. She was frantic with worry. She knew you were flying into Heathrow, I made sure of it. I don't know what to think other than now she knows you're safe she's letting you go. Getting over her was always going to take time, I guess. But have you thought about calling her?'

'No point. She'll have had the interview for Head of Science at some point during the time I was being held, and I reckon she'll have a lot of work on getting ready for her new role. She may have even started it. I don't know. Plus I can't do with the heartache. She chose London and her job last time. I chose Scotland and my business. Then I tried to choose London and Stevie and look where that got me. I'm done. Enough said. I think I can safely say it's over.'

Silence fell between the brothers for a few minutes until Dillon finally broke it. 'Oh hey, guess what?'

'I hope it's good news whatever you're going to tell me. I could do with some.'

'I think it is. I had a call from the estate agents earlier. The offer we made on the other site is being seriously considered again. The other buyers couldn't get funding through in time so we're almost good to go for *Wild Front Here Too!*' Dillon had been giddy for ages about his idea for the name for the possible second camp. 'This means I can invest my inheritance in something I actually want and go into partnership with you like we talked about. You were hoping to get the ball rolling on the second camp and now we can.'

'Awww, Dill, that's brilliant!' Jason stood and grappled his brother into a bear hug.

It was getting late, and Dillon and Dorcas were due to set back off to their flat, but Dorcas had insisted on doing a last minute check around the other cabins as she always did. Jason had always joked that she had the classic symptoms of OCD, but whenever he mentioned it he usually received some rude gesture or other.

She appeared at the door. 'Jason, you need to come quick. It's...it's really weird. Like really weird.' She was out of breath and sounded panicked, her panted words making little sense.

Jason stood quickly. 'Shit, Dee, what is it, what's happened?'

'Just come quick please!' Gesturing for him to follow her, she ran off. Jason and Dillon exchanged worried glances and followed close behind.

Out in the open parking area, glinting under the light of the bright full moon, was a dark menacing figure. Jason stopped in his tracks. *Who the hell?* The figure that straddled a black and silver motorbike was clad from head to toe in black leather and wearing a black crash helmet.

Shivers travelled Jason's spine, and he swallowed thickly as a sense of unease settled in his stomach. 'Can I help you, mate? You looking for someone?' He made his way a little closer to the silent figure but got no response. Panic that this was somehow connected to the kidnapping washed over him, and he suddenly wished he was armed. Straightening his shoulders in the hope of appearing tougher and more confident than he actually felt, he spoke again. 'I said can I help you?' The figure still remained silent. 'I'm sorry but we're not actually a campsite as such. I think you must be looking for the site down the road. He glanced behind him to where Dorcas and Dillon were watching. They both shrugged, and Dillon pulled Dorcas into his side protectively.

Feeling increasingly nervous, Jason tentatively walked nearer to the figure. On closer inspection, it appeared the black clad figure was smaller than he first thought. *I could take him...unless he's armed.* Jason inhaled and ran his hand through his hair.

The mystery person reached up, removed the black helmet, and partially unzipped the leather jacket.

He gasped. 'Stevie?' As the words fell from his lips in an exhaled whisper, her auburn hair cascaded around her shoulders. He felt as if the air in his lungs had been knocked from him. 'What the hell?'

Cocking her head to one side she smiled. 'You know ages ago when you were in London and you took me for a bike ride? Do you remember how I said I'd found the ride quite exhilarating?'

Jason scrunched his brow. 'No, no. I think what you actually said was that you were scared shitless.'

She laughed. 'Yeah whatever...anyway...I had some kind of pre-midlife crisis and learned how to ride.'

'You're joking?' He laughed in disbelief as his heart hammered at his ribs.

She raised her eyebrows. 'The local community centre was doing beginner's lessons in the car park and then out on the roads. It was great fun. So...does it *look* like I'm joking? '

'Well...no... Where are your teddy bear ears?'

She smirked. 'Oh, yes about that...I decided to get a *grown up* helmet to go with the *grown up* bike I bought.'

He nodded, still not quite believing his eyes. 'I see...I see... Oh, by the way, how did the Head of Science interview go?'

'I got the job.'

Jason's heart sank. 'Oh, that's great. Well done.' He looked her up and down. Now that the rush of adrenaline had calmed, he could take in the sight of her completely. The black leather clung deliciously to her curves, and he swallowed hard. *My God, she looks amazing.* 'So...erm...what are you doing here? I thought we weren't going to do the visiting thing.'

She bit her lip, looking nervous. 'Oh, I'm not visiting.'

He was baffled. 'Sorry? I don't get you.'

'Yes, you do.'

He folded his arms. 'I feel like you're talking in riddles here.'

Her mouth quirked up in a sexy half smile. 'Like I said I'm not visiting, and you *do* get me. *All* of me.'

The jackhammer in his chest stuttered a little. He scrunched his brow, reluctant to grip onto the hope that was rising within him in case he was misunderstanding. 'I'm sorry, *what?*'

'I turned the job down, put my house on the market, and bought a sodding motorbike, so how about you let that sink in and tell me if you still want me because I can't tell if you do, and it's kind of killing me here.' Her chest heaved as her words rushed out of her mouth like a deluge.

He took a tentative step towards her. 'Are you...are you telling me you want to *stay*? *Here*? With...with *me*?' His eyes began to sting. 'Is that what you're saying, or am I getting this whole situation wrong? Because if I am, I think my heart will rupture, and I'll die on the spot. Tell me, Stevie, are you here to stay?'

She swung a shapely leather clad leg over and climbed off her motorbike. After setting her helmet on the seat, she stepped towards him. 'I'm here to stay...if you'll have me,' she whispered.

On hearing her words, a guttural incoherent noise erupted from his body, and he quickly closed the remaining gap between them, grabbed her and pulled her into his arms, crashing his mouth into hers. Holding her was like coming home again. *She* was where he belonged.

He broke away and looked her in the eyes again. 'Oh God, Stevie I've missed you so, so much. Are you sure about this? Are you sure being here is what you want?'

'Absolutely.'

'But the job. Head of Science was important to you.'

'Not as important as being with you. And I've actually got an interview at Aviemore High School on Wednesday. They called me a couple of weeks ago whilst I was with Mollie. She's my best friend. She knew something was going on but I couldn't tell her everything. It was very awkward. Oh shit, I'm rambling. Anyway, they knew I was moving into the area, and they seem very keen to see me.'

He pulled her into his arms again, slipping his hands into her hair. 'Stevie, I know I said this to you before, but I don't think you ever really believed me. I think you were scared... and I get that...but...I love you. I've always loved you. And I want to carry on loving you for the rest of my life, if you'll let me.'

Her eyes were glistening in the moonlight that was now lighting up the camp. Reaching up she cupped his cheek. 'I think I can handle that. And I love you too.'

He glanced over his shoulder where Dillon and Dorcas waved as they climbed into their car and drove away, both smiling widely.

Turning his attention back to Stevie he rested his forehead on hers. 'Right now, I want to take you to bed and make love to you all night. I've a lot of time to make up for.' He stroked her cheek. 'And I was so *fucking* right.'

'About what?'

He looked straight down into her cleavage and smiled. 'You do look fucking hot in leathers.

Six Months Later…

'So why can't I go on my own bike?' Stevie asked with a pout. Jason had been acting strange all morning, and she was beginning to think he was scheming. Dillon and Dorcas had been sneaking in and out of the cabin, whispering to him too, which made her suspicions spark even more.

'Because for once I want you on the back of my bike, okay? I miss it, so shut up moaning and get your helmet on.' Jason laughed and flicked her nose with his fingertip.

She frowned at him as she fastened the chinstrap in place. Riding together and touring the area had become a favourite weekend pastime, and he had showed her some wonderful places, the likes of which she had fallen in love with immediately.

She clung onto to Jason as he rode through the Cairngorms and into the oncoming wind. Eventually, once he pulled into a little lane off the main road, he helped her off the bike and gestured that she take off her helmet.

'Okay, now I want you to close your eyes and keep them closed. You've never been here before, and I want it to have the right impact. I want this to be a fresh start. A new beginning and a new special place for us.'

She narrowed her eyes suspiciously. 'Oookay. But what's so secretive about today? You've been doing the whole cloak and dagger thing all morning.' She closed her eyes, clung on to his hand, and stumbled over her own feet.

Jason chuckled. 'Hey, trust me, okay? I promise you'll love this.' He led her along as they zigzagged through the trees that had stood before them when they arrived. After a few minutes of walking, he eventually came to a standstill, and a breeze hit her face as she sensed a more open space. 'Okay, you can open your eyes now.'

She did as instructed and gasped. Her eyes welled with tears as she looked out at the stunning view before her. Dramatic landscapes were all around them in their little pocket of paradise in the Highlands, but *this* view outshone them all. They stood at the top of a hill, looking down into a stunning, tree-lined loch. At the bottom, in the middle of the clear water, standing proudly was an old ancient ruined castle, its walls crumbling against a backdrop of lush green and heather covered mountains and set against an azure blue sky. The cotton candy clouds moved rapidly forward as if greeting them, and the rippling loch beneath mirrored the sky's vivid colour, making it look almost unreal like an enhanced photograph.

Jason slipped his arms around her waist as she looked out shaking her head. 'Wow, you've certainly surpassed yourself this time, Reynolds,' she whispered.

'You're looking down at Loch an Eilein. It means Loch of the Island. Do you like it?' he asked as he kissed her head and held her tight to his body.

'It's...it's beyond words.'

'I'm so glad. Listen...I had Dill and Dee come and bring some bits and pieces so we could have a little celebration.'

She frowned and turned her face towards him over her shoulder. 'What are we celebrating?'

He turned her around to face him fully. 'Well...in case you hadn't been counting like I have, you've been living here with me for six months now. And I think that's a big deal worth celebrating.' He kissed her forehead.

She had been taking each day as it came and hadn't really been counting, but now that she thought about it he was right. 'Gosh...yes. Six months. It's flown, hasn't it?'

'Hmmm. You know what they say about time flying when you're having fun, eh?'

She giggled. 'Very true. And it really has been fun. I still can't believe that Rowdy is getting to like you.'

He pursed his lips. 'I'd say *like* is a strong word. I think he tolerates me now he's moved up here too. Although he does come back when we're out walking and I call him now, which I suppose is his way of compromising.'

Stevie smiled. 'You see I told you he'd come around when he realised that I love you. Joking aside though, I can't express how much being here has meant to me. Having this chance with you...' She touched his cheek, feeling the stubble at his jaw.

He rested his forehead on hers. 'I know, sweetheart. Believe me, I couldn't be happier. Come on, let's see what they brought.'

Off to the side was a large wicker picnic basket under a bush that she hadn't spotted until now. He had obviously arranged every detail meticulously. He lifted the lid and pulled out a couple of blankets. Laying one of them down on the mossy ground, he gestured for her to sit. Once she was comfortable, he sat too and pulled out a pair of mini speakers.

'We're having music too, eh?'

He winked. 'Absolutely. I've made sure they remembered everything.'

She watched as he removed a mini bottle of champagne and two flutes. She shook her head with a smile. 'No tin cups this time?'

'No way. These are crystal, Miss Watts. You can't drink Champagne from tin cups. And it felt like a champagne occasion, but seeing as I'm driving, I figured we'd have a bigger bottle back at the cabin tonight. There's one chilling, ready for when we get back.' He leaned in towards her and she saw his pupils dilate. 'Then I can lay you out in front of the log burner and make love to you.'

Her heart fluttered at his words as she breathed in his scent. 'I like your thinking, Mr. Reynolds.'

Fumbling to remove his iPod from his pocket, he connected the speakers and filed through the songs, his brow furrowed in deep concentration.

Eventually, he smiled up at her and reached to touch her face. 'I was going to bring my guitar to do this, but I'm already quaking in my boots, and so I'd probably muck it up. So I figured I'd let someone else do the singing for me.'

She smiled lovingly at him. 'Oh Jason, you haven't played for a while. And I do love to hear you play.'

'I know, but I don't think my nerves are up to it today.'

She rolled her eyes. 'What is there to be nervous about? It's only me.'

'I know, but there are things I want to say, and I'm running the risk of breaking down as it is.'

She giggled. 'What's going on, Jason?'

'It's been six months since you came to stay with me. They've been the best six months of my life. I hope you're as happy as you make me. And I think we need a new song to celebrate everything we've come through. I think this song says everything I want to say, but it does a much better job than me blurting things out in my own ridiculous way.'

He hit play and grabbed her hand, squeezing it as the opening chords began. Her free hand covered her heart as she realised that what she was listening to was one of her favourite songs. Nickelback's 'Never Gonna Be Alone'.

He pulled her into his arms and held her close. She listened intently as the song played. He was right, it was a perfect fit for them. It made her think of the tattoo she had discovered on his back. It translated to *Never Alone With You In My Heart*, and he'd had it done to remind him of her after he had disappeared ten years ago. Every single sentiment behind the words to this song was meant to communicate his undying love, commitment, and deep devotion to her and to *them*. No more running. He would be there for her regardless of what life threw at them.

Once the song ended, Stevie sat gazing at him with glassy eyes. He restarted the song but turned the volume down so that it created a background for his words.

Moving to sit opposite her on the blanket, he took both of her hands in his, and with a racing heart he began to speak. 'Stevie for ten very long years I was...I was lost. I had no real life. I didn't belong anywhere. And then purely by some divine intervention, you arrived on my doorstep and I was *found* again. You rekindled emotions in me that had lain dormant for all that time. I'd been incapable of giving my heart away because you still held it in your hands. When I lost you again, I lost another piece of the heart that you had helped to mend, and I thought I was done for... but then...'

He swallowed the lump in his throat and bit down on his lip to abate the threatening tears as his own emotions began to get the better of him, and he closed his eyes briefly. 'But then you came back to me. I'm not prepared to lose you again. I never want to be lost again. I need to stay found, but that will only happen if you stay with me...so...' Releasing one of her hands, he reached back into the basket and pulled out a little tin, and Stevie's face lit up.

She covered her mouth with her free hand, and a little squeak of excitement escaped. 'It's a puffin tin,' she said as the tears over-spilled from her bright blue eyes. 'It's beautiful. What a thoughtful gift.'

He took a deep breath. 'Someone I love very much told

me that puffins mate for life, and so, Stevie, *my* beautiful soul-mate ...' He released her other hand and offered her the tin and pointed to the lid. Understanding his silent plea, she removed the lid and gasped. The diamond solitaire glinted in the June sunlight. He took a deep calming breath. 'I'm offering you my heart for the rest of my life. Will you marry me?'

A sob escaped as she nodded fervently. 'Oh yes! Absolutely yes! One hundred percent yes!' She flung her arms around him, and they sealed their engagement with a long, deep kiss. Jason pulled her onto his lap, and as he lowered them to the ground, he pulled the spare blanket over them. He kissed her eyes, cheeks, and lips as the salt water in his own eyes made its escape and mingled with hers. Slowly and languorously, he made love to her there in their new special place under the azure blue sky overlooking Loch an Eilein.

Being with Stevie there in that beautiful place made Jason realise that everything in his life had led him to that very moment. Every pain he had felt and every tear he had shed over losing her had been worth it. As they lay in each other's arms, holding one another close, he thought through the journey he had made over the last ten years.

'I never thought we'd get here, Jason,' she told him as he leaned over her body drawing circles on her bare skin. 'I can't quite believe we're getting married.' Her beautiful smile lit up her face and warmed his heart.

He tangled her fingers in his and looked deep into her beautiful, bright blue eyes that sparkled with love. 'You know...I think it's because we sometimes get lost along the path of life. We set off thinking that we know exactly what we want and where we want to be, but we end up making bad decisions even though they seem right at the time. I think it's those bad decisions that lead us astray so we end up making a detour. Take you and me for example. God, Stevie, I made so many mistakes.' He placed a gentle kiss on her lips. 'But I think it's what we do once we realise we've made those mistakes that counts.' He kissed her forehead and ran his nose down the length of hers as she gazed up at him. 'And now I know one very important thing...regardless of my reasons to leave all those years ago...when you've been lost for so long like I was...it's the reasons to stay that really matter.'

He covered her mouth with his for what felt like the first time. And it was the first kiss of the rest of their lives.

EPILOGUE

'*O*h darling look at you. You look so...grown up.' Stevie's mum clasped her hands in front of her face, her eyes welling with tears.

Stevie rolled her eyes. 'Um...Mum I hate to break it to you, but I've gone twenty-nine, which legally means I *am* grown up and have been for quite a few years now.'

The make-up artist and hair stylist who had been busy completing Stevie's look had packed away their things and had come to join the *let's-stare-at-Stevie* party. She was beginning to feel a little like a museum exhibit in a wedding dress and a feeling of déjà vu descended on her.

'Jason will probably damn well *faint* when he sees how stunning you look, sweetie. Don't you think?' Her mum dabbed at her eyes.

Feeling a distinct attack of déjà vu that took her back to prom night, Stevie stared at herself in the mirror. The bodice of her wedding dress was fitted to her waist and scattered with pearls and crystals. The skirt was full but not over the top. It had been the first dress she had tried and she had known immediately.

She smirked at her mum's overzealous reaction. 'I certainly hope not. It'd be rather tricky for him to say *I do* if he's sprawled out on the floor.'

As always Dana had been emailing and trying her best to cajole her daughter into being more organised, but since moving to Scotland to be with the love of her life, Stevie's priority was simply spending as much time with him as possible. They had a lot of time to make up for after all.

They had managed pretty well in the little cabin and had been putting off plans to find somewhere else. But eventually Jason had decided that his new wife and any family they may have would be more comfortable in a house made of brick or stone or something a little more stable and permanent.

Dorcas and Dillon were engaged to be married and were enjoying running the second camp. And after the wedding, Jason and Stevie would finally move into a *proper* house in Aviemore.

Stevie had become quite accustomed to, and fond of, the stunning Scottish landscape that surrounded their every journey. Her job at Aviemore High School had been the best career decision she had ever made. She had taken the Lead Science Teacher post there with a little trepidation but had settled right in and had made lots of new friends.

Jason took a deep, calming breath and sipped on the amber liquid in his glass, his single malt Dutch courage. The camp had been decorated with flowers, ribbons, and fairy lights and no longer resembled the rugged outdoorsy place that he was used to. The place that usually catered for muddy, noisy teenagers and loud corporate groups was now decked out like the garden of some stately home. Dorcas had told him she was doing something special at the gateway, and Jason laughed out loud when he saw what she had done. The *Wild Front Here* sign at the end of the lane had been draped partially with a banner that simply replaced the words *Wild Front* with the word *Wedding* in fancy scrolled lettering. Bless her. She really was sweet.

The clearing where the campfire sing along usually took place had been swept and the surrounding trees strung with more fairy lights and heart shaped bunting. A red carpet had been laid and rustic wooden chairs had been placed for the guests on either side. Even Matt from the Rothiemurchus Rough Trax had played a part. He turned out to be quite the craftsman and had constructed a driftwood and willow arched arbour, which would be where they would stand and take their vows. It too had been adorned with wild flowers from Jason's garden and looked absolutely stunning. Stevie had seen none of this. He hoped she liked what he had done.

It had surprised him that she had agreed so readily to get married at the camp. He had expected some protest about it being the least romantic place she could think of, but instead when he had suggested it, she had simply spoken his thought out loud. 'It's the place that brought us back together, so it seems very fitting to be married there.' His heart had swelled with love for her one again.

Later in the evening after the ceremony, he planned to take his bride and a picnic basket to their special place over-looking Loch an Eilein. It was all arranged. There would be Champagne and soft music. Dillon would play chauffeur for the night, leaving them to enjoy a few hours together. There Jason would make love to his new wife and tell her all over again how much he loved her and how he would never run again. The viewpoint was private and felt like it almost belonged to them. It was where Jason had proposed to Stevie six months after she had moved over five hundred miles to be with him in Scotland. Thinking back to that special day made his eyes sting. He wanted to make her happy like that for the rest of his life. And he would certainly try his very best.

Dillon would later collect them and take them to their plush hotel suite, where they would spend the night in each other's arms.

Looking over the camp at the wondrous sight before him, his heart thundered in his chest at the anticipation of what was to come in just a few short hours.

The guests began to arrive and Jason was overwhelmed by the amount of love that their friends, old and new, and their family were showing them. Some of their old school friends had made the journey along with others who had known their story from the beginning.

The Halfords had flown in especially for the big day, and Oliver had been emotional since the moment he grasped his son in a bear hug at the airport. He had told Jason over and over again how grateful he was that he'd been given the opportunity to be here for the special occasion and how very proud he was of him. He had even agreed to step in and give Stevie away when Dana had admitted she would be far too nervous to handle the role. Jason was so very touched by the gesture that he had struggled to speak the words when it came time to tell Stevie about Oliver's suggestion.

Once the guests were all seated and Jason and Dillon stood at the driftwood arbour with the Registrar, the nerves kicked in. Jason took deep breaths under the instruction of his brother.

'You've gone pale, Jace. Just breathe. In through the nose

and out through the mouth, yeah? We don't want you faint-
ing... I...I want to tell you something before Stevie gets here.'

Jason frowned, suddenly worried. 'Of course, Dill.
What's up?'

'Don't look so terrified. All I wanted to say is...you and
Stevie are to me how couples *should* be. You've spent so many
years apart, and you've pretty much been to hell and back, but
you still found each other again. That's real love, bro. It's
meant to be. You're an inspiration and...' He cleared his throat
as his emotions began to surface. 'In spite of the truth about
us...not being blood related...you've been such a great brother.
I wish we hadn't lost ten years, but the last year or whatever
it's been...maybe not that long...but however long it's been has
been amazing. I love you brother. Always have and always
will. Being your best man is the greatest honour.' His voice
broke and his lip quivered as he spoke. Jason, who was bereft
of words at that point, pulled Dillon into a strong embrace
and did his best to keep his composure.

Stevie's white, vintage Rolls Royce pulled up to the gates of
Wild Front Here and her heart leapt. She glanced up and saw
the *Wedding Here* sign and felt her smile grow. As they travelled on under the sign, her mother clung to her hand but
looked preoccupied. Stevie glanced out of the window and
suddenly felt overcome with emotion. She chewed on the
inside of her cheek in a desperate bid to fend off the threatening tears.

Dana squeezed her hand. 'Stevie...I need to say
something.'

She turned to face her mum as worry washed over her.
'Of course, Mum. What is it?'

'Look, sweetie, I know that you didn't have the best upbringing. Your dad...well, as they say any man can father a child, but it takes a special kind of person to actually *be* a dad. And I worry that you've missed out. Jed was less than useless, and so you haven't had a father figure in your life. Days like today are when a girl needs her daddy. He should be here to give you away. And then you've felt you had to look after me after my diagnosis when really you didn't. And I'm a coward because I daren't walk you down the aisle. I feel so bad for—'

'Mum! How can you even *think* that I'm lacking at all? Least of all through not having *him* here. You've been more than enough for me. Do you hear what I'm saying? *More* than enough. You're the strongest woman I know and what better role model could I have had? You've been a mum *and* a dad. And I can't miss something I never had. When I look at what Jason and Dillon went through with the man they both called *Dad*, I think I've been so very lucky. You've loved me...you've looked out for me and you've protected me. I didn't miss him then and I don't today. Because I have *you*.'

Dana wiped an escaped tear away from her eye and cupped Stevie's cheek tenderly. 'We've done okay, haven't we, Stevie? Me and you? We've been okay, haven't we? I haven't made any huge mistakes, have I?'

Stevie squeezed her mum's hand fondly as her eyes became glassy. 'Far from it, Mum. You've been *wonderful*. I count myself as one very fortunate girl. And I hope my children love me as much as I love you.'

'Children? But you always said you didn't want children. What's changed?'

'I'm marrying the only man that I would want to have children with. That's the difference. I can imagine being a mother if I have Jason by my side.'

Stevie clung to her mum as she dabbed at her eyes and

tried not to ruin her makeup. Dana's partner Tom came into view and was standing alongside Jason's dad, Oliver, chatting and waiting for them to arrive. When the car came to a halt, Oliver opened the door and helped Stevie to step out. Tom kissed Dana, and Stevie and smiled at how the pair gazed at each other, their eyes filled with adoration.

Oliver held Stevie at arms-length, and she met his eyes with her own. Knowing he was an emotional man, she braced herself for his reaction. 'Oh my word, Stevie, you look stunning, my darling girl.' He hugged her tightly and then stepped away to greet Dana, hugging her and telling her what a wonderful daughter she had whilst Stevie looked on, her emotions teetering on the edge once again. *Don't cry. You can do this, Stevie. Think of your makeup.*

They began to walk towards the clearing when Dana stopped Stevie in her tracks, grabbing her arm. 'Stevie, I've changed my mind.'

'What? What do you mean, Mum?'

'I mean...*I* want to give you away. You're *my* daughter. I've been there for *every* big event in your life up to now, and I have no intention of letting you down today.'

Stevie's battle with her fragile emotions was finally lost as the tears began to flow and she grasped her mum in the tightest hug.

'Thank you...thank you so much, Mum. I love you.'

'And I love you, darling. Now let's go get you married.'

Jason stood with his eyes closed, breathing slowly and deeply. He inhaled the sweet scent of the flowers around the arbour and tried to calm his shaking hands.

'She's here, bro,' came Dillon's whispered words, making Jason turn around.

His breath caught in his throat at the sight of his beautiful bride standing there waiting at the end of the red carpet in her white dress as the crystals glinted in the sunlight. The smile on her face as she locked her eyes on him was filled with love. Her beautiful auburn waves, scattered with white flowers and pearls, fell naturally around her shoulders. She truly was the most beautiful sight he had ever seen.

He glanced at the woman accompanying her and knew instantly that Stevie's dream had come true. With a wide smile, he turned and raised his eyebrows in a signal to his younger brother Josh, who waited in front of the sound system. The younger man nodded and hit play.

Jason mouthed the words, 'I love you,' to Stevie as she began to make her way towards him, and the sound of 'Never Gonna Be Alone' by Nickelback filled the air.

The End

ABOUT THE AUTHOR

Lisa is happily married to her soulmate and they have a daughter and two crazy dogs. She especially enjoys being creative and now writes almost full time.

In 2012 Lisa and her family relocated from England to their beloved Scotland; a place of happy holidays and memories for them. Her new location now features in all of her books. Writing has always been something Lisa has enjoyed, although in the past it has centered on poetry and song lyrics. Some of which appear in her stories.

Since she started writing in 2012 she has loved every minute of becoming a published author.

ACKNOWLEDGMENTS

I'm going to keep this brief as I know you don't want to read reams and reams of waffle from me!

I just want to say a simple thank you to every single reader, blogger and reviewer I have come across in my writing journey. As always your support means the world to me.

And a special thank you to Tammy from The Graphics Shed who designed the stunning covers and who continually comes to my rescue. You're an absolute star.

Lightning Source UK Ltd.
Milton Keynes UK
UKHW010031091021
391891UK00003B/1026

9 780995 665859